Unshackled
Courage

Pam Kumpe

Pam Kumpe

ISBN – 978-0-692-11938-9

DEDICATION

To Autumn
Thank you for being you. For waving at me.
For shining like a beacon of hope!

To Cindy Ross
You will never read this book.
But you had everything to do with my writing it!

To Charles B Pierce, Jr.
May your purpose on earth be found in God!

To Manuela Witthuhn,
Your life was cut short in 1981 by a serial killer.
The Golden State Killer was arrested in April, 2018,
the same month I completed this book.

To the *real* people who were attacked or
murdered by the Phantom Killer in Texarkana in 1946.
May you be remembered!

Pam Kumpe

DISCLAIMER

This is a work of fiction. Names, characters, businesses, places, events and incidents are either the products of the author's imagination or used in a fictitious manner. Any resemblance to actual persons, living or dead, or actual events is purely coincidental. Although, there are many historical events that ring of truth in these pages.

Pam Kumpe

Texarkana, Arkansas / Texas

The Tree of My Past

There was no way of taking a walk this morning; I had to sit in my tree—had to get out of bed. Out of the house. And into the daylight. My bad nights are leaking into my day, and by placing another photograph on a branch, I'll forget about the eyes in last night's nightmare. I need to remember though, so I can solve the cold case. But right now, I ache from a lack of sleep—and can't think. So I'll just swing my feet in this tree—to keep from thinking at all.

With the movie crew in Texarkana filming the story of the Phantom Killer, I'm resting less and suffering more—thanks to the hollow eyes piercing my soul. To think it's 1976, and I can't shake the shackles from my childhood—or the idea of knowing I hold the key to the lockbox of my memories.

"Stupid paper!" I tossed the newspaper article to the ground, wishing I'd not read the front page. Ernie wrote the story, recapping the attacks and murders with facts and half-truths, but the layers of a killer's actions are tortuous to those who get left behind—who struggle to forget, who live with wounded hearts. The story lacks hope, leaving me with tainted streaks of murky memories.

His article will never speak of the ache inside the heart of someone who said goodbye to a loved one by way of a killer. And yet, my own heaviness comes to me each night because I hold unanswered questions from the past. I saw the killer's face! And I can't remember enough details to give those eyes a name!

I've bragged on how I planned to solve this case since I was ten. And so far, I've become the person the people in Texarkana mock—but they don't know what I know. Even I don't know what I know—but inside me, I have the answer.

So yes, the nightmares have consumed me. They are more vivid and stronger since everyone's talking about the movie. I need a breakthrough before I have another breakdown. I long for the truth to come into the light before I drive my husband away. Or before I drive any more of my neighbors indoors with my presence.

The higher I climb in my oak tree, the thinner the branches become; a symbol of how fragile a tree appears to those who only look at those limbs. But the tree's real strength surges from deep beneath the ground at the roots.

I'm a lot like a tree—but I tend to break and bend and wobble more than this oak. But I also pray I'm growing into the person God called me to become. However, the process is taking way too long—by my timetable.

As the cars below crept, the drivers gawked at me as I've persisted in sitting in this tree. And I've waved at the families headed to church, smiling a crooked grin—to give them something to talk about later today. One small girl smiled from her seat —like she understood me.

Not many grown women sit in the top of a tree downtown. But I do. I sit here to escape the fog of conversations from folks who judge me. And this helps me escape my own fog when the day burns and singes—when it tries to snuff out hope and leaves behind ashes.

This outing may translate as one more crazy stunt from the woman who once rode the rail as a girl, but this is my secret spot. That's not so secret to anyone but me. But I can disappear up here. Like a breath going out. Like an exhale to freedom.

I stroked the tree's bark, the tree of my youth, a tree which held dozens of dangling photographs. I've created paper wind chimes from the dancing photos on my grandma's old tree at the corner of Beech and 4th Street on the Arkansas side of Texarkana.

This massive oak hovers taller than most trees after surviving a lifetime of storms and hot summers. And yet, the trunk rises higher each year, in spite of the winds of change. The rustle of sorrow does crackle like dead leaves, but the tree won't fall—as long as the winds aren't too intense.

The heat of summer is about to steam up for me because my husband stands firm on his decision to cut down my tree. He's tired of my tree climbing and escapades.

But maybe I'll reach heaven from this place and run from the nightmares I endure. The ones with my pulling the mask from the face of the Phantom Killer. I sense a change with unknown consequences, as the winds hiss, as the whispers intensify inside my head—as the voices become a roar like a tornado. I can only pray to stand tall, to weather the debris left behind, to unearth the answers of the unknown.

I swung my legs, remembering my grandma Elsie's manor which sat on this corner. I cherished the winter when I lived with her, when I was ten. Having her love me was magical, but those months were also laced with horror. Even with the tangled limbs of despair, the beauty of my grandma's acceptance will forever remain wrapped around my heart.

I treasure and despise my past though—but the love of my grandma made it worth coming to Texarkana on the boxcar with Tin Can Mahlee after my daddy's tumble into the Mississippi River.

"Get down from there. Annie Grace, you're pushing it."

I twisted my head, staring at my husband who had stormed from our house which sat two blocks away. "I'm taking a break. I'll come down when I'm ready."

He yelled, "Who are you today? An investigator? Oh wait, you're a writer! No, I'm sure you're going to say a photographer. What is it with these photographs?"

"I think they're pretty. Don't you?"

"Annie Grace, how many women climb trees? And how many wear overalls and red PF Flyers?" Crush positioned his hands on his hips, huffing after each breath, glaring up, his neck stretched like a giraffe.

I wiggled my toes. "I love these shoes. They're my thinking shoes. I've worn PF Flyers forever." I peered at my husband from the highest branch, wrinkling my nose and holding the next round of not-so-kind words inside—those prone to making me apologize. "I only wear these overalls when I'm in my creative mode."

"You must wake up creative, especially on Sundays when you forget to change shoes and wear them with your dress to church. Did you know the entire congregation gawks at you—laughing?"

"I don't care. People love to make fun of me. I'm an easy target. They're waiting for you to leave me, again."

"Me? Leave you? You've got your story backwards. I gave you some space a few years ago. And you took a trip to Old Washington in Arkansas to see Tin Can Mahlee's niece, Hope, before she left on her mission trip to Haiti. I let you search for meaning, but you came home with more questions."

I countered his words. "But you're the one who insisted we could use a few months without arguing—so I could get my anxiety handled and under control. I was thrilled to see her, she's as cute as ever, same blonde hair—like mine, but she's confident, unlike me. She loves sharing the Bible with children. I would never get such an option—no one would trust me with their children."

"Well, when you act like this, it's hard for me to trust you."

"But staying with Hope helped calm my nerves, but whenever I phoned you to come home—you put me off."

"You're wrong, Annie Grace. You have your facts mixed up."

"So you keep telling me." I swung my legs, unsure of how I mix up stories, but either way, I'm thrilled Crush let me move home considering I cause chaos and drama. Even a recent date night turned ugly, thanks to the usher at the theatre who shown his flashlight in my face. He triggered an onslaught of horrible memories and I charged from the theatre, running all the way to this tree. I can't even go the movies without crying, let alone drive by the Saenger Theatre.

"Annie Grace, come on, get down. Your creativity is playing out nicely for the folks headed to St. Edwards."

"I love sitting here. It's safe. It helps me remember."

"You could use more time living in the present."

I examined the face of my troubled spouse who's endured our early years of marriage. I'm sure he's prayed that my bizarre behavior might end. And yet he's stood by me, except for that one short time when we did split, which was more of a break of peace. Either way, we're together now, even though I have disappeared on unexplained outings. Which might make some folks say I have left him. All I know is he longs for less tree-climbing and more lady like behavior.

His gaze pierced me. "Annie Grace, come down."

The wrinkles around the middle of his forehead appeared longer and deeper, especially when anger rises up in his voice. His freckles flashed a circle of brown spots next to the scar on his head too, from when I caught him on fire by the fireplace in Old Washington back in '48. His injuries stemmed from the fire, from the accident of my carelessness. Most of the injuries

I've received or given—come from accidental creative moments.

Crush yelled, "Come down from the tree!"

I smiled, the words I longed to spout steeped between my teeth, and I struggled to keep my manners intact. The opinions lurking, forced my mouth wide open. "You don't understand me. You believe I'm short a few boxcars since I'm mentally lost in this tree. But I'm working on a plan to solve the madness and the continuing crisis of mixed messages bouncing like ping-pongs between my ears."

"Seriously, this must stop. I need peace. You need peace."

I leaned around the arm of another branch which held dozens of photographs, story-photos, each tied by white shoelaces. I held onto the trunk of the tree. "Stop yelling at me. You're making a scene. All those people walking to church are staring at us. You don't have to follow me."

Crush flared his nostrils with a shake of a fist. "Annie Grace, I'll come up there and get you."

"Since when do you climb trees?" I giggled under my breath, knowing I loved his chasing me. His pursuit of me reminds me how much I'm loved. But I do press him, and his patience runs thin, as does his temper.

He pounded the tree. "This is beyond normal. I've put up with your behavior for ten years. How many women tie photographs of all the people from their childhood in a tree? How many? Come down. Let's work this out at the house in private!"

I tied the last shoelace, and the photo dangled in the breeze. "I've put my sister, Lizzy Beth, on a branch and a photo of my brother, Willie. They're dancing in the wind."

"Come down. Or I'm dragging you from the tree."

I changed the subject. "When can we go visit them? Memphis is five hours away, it's not too far. We could stay a few days. I need to see my brother and sister."

"They won't answer the phone. I'm sure they're mad at you from last year. You nailed the windows shut in their houses to protect them from imaginary killers. And you changed the locks on their doors to keep out the night criminals. They were unable to open their doors, and you meddled in their affairs. First, you hammered the doors shut at Lizzy Beth's house, and you had Archie drive you to Willie's house—hiding the hammer in your purse."

"He wouldn't have taken me otherwise."

"No kidding. You are always up to something—and we worry about you."

"But I'm their big sister, and I told them I was sorry. I sure miss them."

My mind drifted to my childhood in Jefferson, Texas, where sunsets dropped a golden color across the landscape of playing with a brother and sister. The branch became my memory-moment as I leaned sideways, and I went back to those sunrises and seasons, of living with Ms. Susan and Mr. Boyd. Those days were near perfect. I loved being adopted. But, I bucked at fitting in, with going to school and with behaving. I resisted following rules and listening to the teacher but loved recess—most days. Except when I hit the boys, and they hit me.

I caused chaos at home too, at the library, at the bayou, at church—peace eluded me. Which meant peace eluded my family as they exhausted their patience with me. I sensed a feeling of being lost in the family; but loved at the same time. Often I spent my days walking on the tracks, alone.

The photos zapped with a whip, bringing me back to my world. Whispering, I spoke to my siblings. "I miss you both. I will see you soon, won't I?"

The photos dangled, not answering, but swaying with the possibility of hope, like a breeze blowing in from the river.

"Annie Grace, come on. Must we do this? The tree is filled with dozens of photos. It's time to finish this chapter. To move on."

I responded with my not-so-grown-up reaction. "I have my whole life up here. I needed to hang Lizzy Beth and Willie. Now, the tree is complete. Look at it, I picked one from when they were eight and fishing in the bayou in Jefferson. I'm creating a storybook tree before you cut my tree down."

"I've only threatened to cut the tree down, to keep you from climbing up it."

"If you don't do it, the city of Texarkana will probably whack it down like they did with the manor. There's only rubble now. But fortunately, I own the lot. There's nothing here to remind me of my grandma. All I have are my pictures."

"You have your memories of her and you have me." Crush circled the tree, his red hair falling across his brow. "The city moved quickly to rid our town of the rats, remember? The manor held hundreds of them and Texarkana made the news. The infestation took over several properties. Besides, her manor became vacant years ago."

"But it's not fair. Everything changes. The end is the beginning, and the beginning keeps ending. I'm stuck on replay, and I can't live like a regular woman. I feel like I'm ten years old. I keep going back. I know I'm forty! What's wrong with me?"

"I understand how some days you're the little hobo girl who used to ride the rail. But it's time for courage to break away the shackles of your childhood. Maybe you're all stirred up because they're shooting the movie about the Phantom Killer. It must bring up hauntings for you. After all, the killer lurked in town when you lived with your grandma right after you lost your dad. Your nightmares landed in your sleep—after you and Taddy wrapped yourself inside the case of those murders, too. You were a small girl. It had to be hard."

I swung from the highest branch, screaming, and leaping to the ground. "You have no idea how hard. I've suffered so much inside this brain of mine." I tapped my head as if Crush had no idea I had a brain.

Crush yelled, "Stop it. I went through losing my parents, too. The flood took their lives. You aren't the only person who suffers or goes through horrible things."

I jumped around Crush like a rabbit. "You think I'm overreacting. You think I'm scared. Well, I'm not afraid of the dark. Or of masks. Or of walking alone at sunset. I'm not a hobo girl anymore, either. I'm Annie Grace Raike and I'm married to Taggart Raike." I announced our names like I needed to be reminded and continued my rant. "But Taggart's an atrocious name. Your mama should have given you a cuter name. I'll always call you Crush, from when we were kids. And I'm fine. I am. I'm working through my memories. I develop photographs, and it helps me brave the day."

"Will you brave the walk home with me to the Ahern House? We'll go slow beside the old school, so you can tell me how you colored the tree in the playground with the crayons. How you clobbered the Blanton Brothers. And we'll move faster around the Miller County Courthouse because the building reminds you of the day when the police arrested the car thief and accused him of being the Phantom Killer, and how you don't believe it for one second."

"I need a nap. I need to rest. I need—"

"You need breakfast. It's barely seven in the morning. And it's going to be a scorcher. This June is already hotter than most." Crush reached for my hand. "Come eat breakfast with me before Clara reports to the upstairs, to answer our phones which never ring. I'm not sure why we have an investigation business. We have no customers. All she does is eat oranges all day. And the incessant typing. What does she have to type anyway? And why does she insist on working on a Sunday?"

I scooted across the street alongside the side building of the Catholic Church, holding his hand as I twisted my head to peek at my dancing photos in the tree. "I've hung newspaper clippings too, of the people the Phantom Killer attacked and killed. I don't think we should forget their names. Martha and Jack. Reed and Patti. Peyton and BayJo. Victor and Kacey."

"You're right. They had families too, and their whole lives ahead of them. Their families suffered too, Annie Grace."

"See, you get it. You see how they might feel and yet, you can't see how the Phantom Killer affected me."

"But you're always telling me you're fine. Your world is perfect, right?"

I almost tripped on my words. "I am fine. Never mind." I went back to discussing the photos, changing the subject. "I've also hung photos on the branches of growing up with Ms. Susan and Mr. Boyd. And of my daddy in high school. And of Timmons and Tak. Of the triplets. Of Matthew. And Thomas. And of Grandma Kree. And Tin Can Mahlee when she made the news in Arkansas. When she died." I yanked my hand from his grasp. "I miss my daddy so much."

Crush touched my arm. "What is it? Why are you in turmoil? Is it the filming of *The Town that Dreaded Sundown,* or is it something you're not saying?"

"There's a boiling in my soul, deep inside me. Something I can't remember but somehow, I will remember. And I will make a good investigator, you'll see."

On our two-block stroll home, Crush fell silent, like he does when he knows I'm more trouble than children fighting on a playground. He's afraid I'll run again. Or disappear. Or maybe, he's the one who runs from me. I clutched his hand. "Don't worry. I'll gather myself. I'll be the wife you deserve."

"You're already the wife who makes me complete. You're the one who needs answers for the trauma from your past. It's those questions I can't answer."

"I'll be better. I can do better. I've got to get better."

"You're perfect. Now don't forget we're meeting Pastor Toby for lunch today. We have time to make it to church. He would love to see you there. And please, change your shoes. And don't come up missing. Pastor Toby is guiding us to trust God, so we can both get better."

"I'll get dressed for church. It will be nice to sing some hymns and sit in the sanctuary where it's safe. Where God can speak to my soul, and afterwards we'll have lunch."

He smiled. "Yes, let's linger. We could use a little peace."

I squeezed his hand, choking on the words, knowing I would find a way to skip out early. After all, the filming is taking place downtown by Union Station this afternoon, and I must listen to the actors and what they say in the script. And see if the boots appear on any of the spectators. The Phantom Killer might show up. And a good investigator must be ready to solve the crime. Even a crime from thirty years ago.

As we moved up the steps to the yard and faced our house, I counted the columns. "One. Two. Three. Four. Five."

"You count the pillars every time we come into the yard."

"I know. It's nice to see some things don't change. Maybe we could go see Marion Kane in the nursing home in Jefferson soon. He's been like a daddy to both of us. I would love to see him. He gave us this two-story gray mansion, with the L-shaped porch, and he could use some company. I'm sure of it."

"We'll see him soon. I'll make sure we drive over his way one weekend."

"Good, I need to see his face." I whispered to the wind. "I'm a grown woman. And it's 1976. The time is at hand. It's time to stop with the photographs and time to move to the typewriter. I've written five novels in my mystery series. It's time for me to finish the sixth book. I'll solve the murders from 1946, once and for all."

"Seriously! Do you need to write another mystery?" Crush added, "Our home is nothing but offices. Maybe we could remodel the upstairs and make it more like a home. Your dreams are plastered on the walls with your investigation service and your photography."

"But that's my world."

Crush kissed my nose. "I would love to be your world, but Shoelace, your preoccupation with murders and crimes is wearing me down."

I waved my hand, pointing my finger. "Don't call me Shoelace. My name is Annie Grace. I don't use my rail name anymore. I am civilized now."

Crush waved his arms. "Civilized? Have you noticed the upstairs? The walls are covered in photographs of everything from you past. Like your tree. Goodness, it's 1946 on the second floor. With newspaper clippings. And notes. And scribbles. Your memories have taken over. I can't see the plaster for the maze of tragedy tacked on the walls."

"I'll clean it up. I will. When I solve the case."

"No, no more cases—it's time for this to stop."

"It will stop and soon."

"You have manuscripts stacked in the hallway at the top of the stairs, and a typewriter for your desk and one for Clara." Crush threw his hands to his mouth, as if letting out the truth overwhelmed him.

His temper became more than I could stand, too—his way of telling the truth made my nerves worsen. I apologized, "I'm sorry. I don't mean to cause you all of this heartache."

Crush sighed, "Your photographs send us down the same old railroad tracks. Where we end up in the same rail yard. Derailed from enjoying today."

I cringed. "Stop reminding me how broken I am. I have to solve the murders. Or the nightmares won't stop."

"You mean, solve the murders by writing about them, right?"

"No! I have to figure out who the Phantom Killer is for real."

Crush shouted, "No, you can't keep doing this every time something reminds you of the case."

"But you don't understand. I cry out to God to silence the nightmares, so I can face my future. But I need to rip the mask from the killer's face."

"Annie Grace, how long will I have to cry, too? I cry out to God, for His help. How long are we going to do this? I'm forty-two. I'm getting tired." His hands went to his face again, and he ran his fingers through his hair. "Look at us. The Phantom Killer is causing us to argue and fight, he's stalking us. We're trapped in the past—and I feel like he's killing our future."

I wiped the sweat from my face. "Stop yelling at me. One minute you understand me. The next you turn on me." I charged inside the house, stumbling over the rug, crashing into the wall—and the picture on the table next to the phone shattered into pieces as the glass splintered to the hardwood floor. The long hallway extended to each side of me like a tunnel of darkness.

Ring. Ring. Ring.

Crush called from the front door. "Annie Grace. Don't move. There's glass by your leg. Be careful."

"But it's the phone."

"Clara will answer it."

I rolled over, picking up the photograph of Crush and me and blew the pieces of glass from the paper. "I love this photo. It's from our wedding day. *Ouch!* A piece of glass cut my knee."

"Be careful. I'll get a broom. And some Band-Aids."

I waited, and the tears came. Not because of the cut, but because everyone's expectations of me are higher than I'm able to reach. I stared at the photo. "Oh, my sweet Crush in his suit, and me in my white gown. A day when we were both happy."

"Annie Grace. Let me help you up."

Tears dripped in a stream from my chin, and I dreamed of happier days and less chaos. But it seems my days are like shattered pieces of wrong choices and a lack of self-control. I remembered our wedding, and I wore new red PF Flyers from the Sears Catalog beneath my gown at Marion Kane's ranch. Taddy was the Best Man even though he rarely spoke to me. Timmons and Tak stood in as Groomsmen. Lizzy Beth dazzled everyone with her beauty as my Maid of Honor. But I had a meltdown before saying my vows—and dealt with sheer panic before walking the matrimony aisle. I knew I'd disappoint Crush—and now I have!

I peeked at my PF Flyers. They're worn, torn, and faded now, like the way Crush must feel from tracking me down. I turned to him. "I'm sorry. Please, forgive me."

From the top of the staircase, Clara cut loose with a shrill as I grimaced at the blood oozing through my overalls. She lit up with excitement. "We've got our first case. You're going to be an investigator—and change Texarkana!"

I screamed, "No way! A real case?"

She pranced on the stairs, her white Keds tiptoeing like she danced at a party. She leaned over the rail, her curls dangling. "And maybe I'll get my first real paycheck—it's long overdue. I've worked here for peanuts. I'm free help."

I wrinkled my nose, correcting Clara, and hung to the staircase railing at the base of the stairs. I balanced myself like a wobbly broom, my blonde hair waved from my tremors as I shook. "You've worked here to pay a debt for hitting my car with yours. You're not working for free."

She frowned. "I didn't mean to bump into your car at the Grim Hotel, my bumper found your bumper. I'd forgotten to pay my car insurance and had to ask my daddy for the money to fix your old Rambler. After all, I'd driven in from Dallas after visiting relatives for," she coughed, "for nine months." Her hands rubbed her tummy. "And Daddy's used to taking care of everything. He does get tired of bailing me out. So, I plan to pay him back."

"I expect we'll be even soon. Maybe you'll get a check when I solve our new case!" I couldn't help but notice, Clara's eyes turned sad as she held her belly, it's as if she stopped listening to me—and disappeared to somewhere. But where?

Rose Hill Cemetery

I whirled like a top and gazed at the maze of tombstones. I told Crush my head might burst from the throbs, using the sick headache fib on him, and left church early—like I planned. I raced like a cat escaping from a wild dog to meet the mysterious caller who gave Clara instructions for me to come to Rose Hill Cemetery.

I searched the grounds. Where is he? I've walked in and around the tombstones for more than ten minutes. I've counted the World War hero markers twice, but no one has met me or driven into the cemetery. I'm so hot, the sweat is soaking my back, and my dress is sticking to my skin.

I'll wait at my family's bench, the one I've sat on throughout the years. I've circled this bench and wept over the loss and talked to my grandma when I can't cope. The bench rests next to my daddy's empty spot, next to Grandma Elsie and Grandpa Otto.

Swallowing, I regretted the way I treated Crush. The way I carried on like a stubborn girl of my youth. I'm acting like the child whose daddy kidnapped her, sending her to the rail for five years. Messy and argumentative. I have leftover issues. I've survived being a hobo girl, and yet, I live as if my hope remained inside of a jail cell where daddies sleep it off.

I have hope on my good days. But why do I pursue the pain? Why do I let go of the promises of God?

I hope I haven't run to this spot to meet an enemy. I pray I can solve a real crime. And become a real investigator. I'm worn out too, from hiding inside the layers of stories upon stories. I want the nightmares to end, and I want to live. The fight for life is running through my veins and in my heart, and I'm running—but to what?

"Hello? I'm here. Anybody out there?" I twisted around, jumping to stand on the bench, and the massive memorial statue of Otis Henry caused me to lose my breath. "Sorry, Mr. Henry. I know you didn't mean to scare me."

I pinched myself and corrected myself. I know for others to believe in me, to take my writing seriously, to hire me to solve crimes, and to be taken as authentic, I had to stop talking to the dead.

My heart is full of broken dreams. Full of lost rain drops. Full of stormy memories. And yet, dry as sand. Why do the arms of relief seem out of my reach?

Fa-lap. Swoosh.

"Who's there? Hello? I'm on time. I walked as fast as I could from First Baptist Church on Pine Street. It's a good bit of a jaunt, and yet, I'm here. Show yourself. I'm ready to take your case. You told Clara you had clues. Clues to the case. But which case? I need you to tell me more."

The dust swirled around my head as if my questions were being stopped by the ghost of yesterday. I decided my words wilted like dead leaves. "I give up. This is one big joke. It's probably Lester playing a joke on me. Or maybe it's Gilbert this time." I screamed at them. "It's not my fault your daddy got shot when Taddy and me celebrated his birthday—"

From behind the statue in the circle drive, a familiar voice smarted off. "Stop it. Why are you picking on me and my brother?" Gilbert called, stepping around a new grave, holding a shovel. "What is your problem? We're not joking around with you. I'm working a Sunday after I received a call from the funeral home." Gilbert's caramel-colored hair flipped like wings, straight out. And he leaned up against a tree. "What brings you here?"

"So, you're not playing a joke on me? You and your brother have picked on me since I was in the fourth grade." I brushed my ponytail from my shoulder. "Are you sure you're innocent? Hey, where's your truck? I didn't see you drive in."

"My trusty Ford is over there by the back gate next to the tracks." He swung his arm wide, pointing. "I'm positive about playing a trick. We haven't played one on you in months. I loved locking you out of church, last winter. I laughed so hard. It was hilarious, though—since you sang a hymn of panic when we dropped a plastic snake from the roof. It's time for you to grow up. Let it go. We aren't kids anymore."

"Sure. Whatever. Grownups don't drop rubber snakes on ladies. You both acts like kids with the silliness. And the crankiness." I folded my arms and turned my back to Gilbert.

"You're one to talk. And I don't think of you as a lady." He trooped off a few feet, the thud of his work boots on caked dirt gave way to a hollow sound. I watched him dig, and he advised me, with one more order. "And stop posting help-wanted signs at the cemetery. It scares everyone. When folks come to say their goodbyes, they don't want to read: Hire Annie Grace Raike. She'll solve the crime or it won't cost you a dime."

"I haven't posted any signs. Not one. What are you talking about?" I stormed to his side, my arms flailing. "When did you see such a sign?"

Gilbert reached into his pocket, pulling out a piece of rumpled paper, tossing it at me. "Read it yourself. I found this note over there by the back gate."

I read the words on the paper and gasped. "I never posted any signs. I don't even run ads at the *Texarkana Gazette* because Ernie Surratt still works there and as long as he does—"

"Stop it. You're not right, Annie Grace!"

"I never put this up." I wadded up the paper and shook my fist in front of Gilbert's teeny nose.

He pushed my hand away. "I see them every few days. If it's not you, it must be Clara."

"She's afraid of cemeteries. She's not doing it."

"She's braver than you think. She's witty. Knows trivia. And her way with words—she could be a writer. And she's kind." Gilbert stopped talking, licking his top lip. "Well, someone is posting signs, so people will hire you."

I changed the subject. "How well do you know Clara?"

"What? I've known her all my life."

Puzzled by his defense of Clara, I planned to quiz her about Gilbert later on. "And by the way, I would never advertise in a cemetery. These people don't need me. They're dead." I marched off, my loafers stirring up the dust of a new round of questions—as if I should get to know Clara more—and take notice of her whispering on the phone. Of her scribblings. Of her attraction to Gilbert.

He interrupted my wandering mind, shouting as he tossed a pile of dirt to the side. "Over there. See those papers. There's a new batch tacked on those tombstones. I didn't see them earlier. You better remove them before my boss gets here."

"Your boss? It's your brother, Lester. What's he going to do?"

"He's in charge now. He wants the history of our cemetery preserved. And it doesn't include advertising for you."

"I'll get them. But I didn't put them up!"

I sprinted across the cemetery to the tombstones, reaching for the taped paper on the angel marker, snatching it free. "What? This isn't a sign about me working for someone. It's a riddle of sorts."

I jumped to the next tombstone and the next. And ended up grabbing five notes—all the same. Each had the same words. The same riddle. The same frightening letters pasted with cutouts from a magazine to form the words—to make the sentences.

My head swirled. My hands sweated. I trembled with fear, trapped in a world of emptiness, a place no one goes—or wants to go—where joy escapes like a train headed out of town. I crumpled to the ground, crying. "Crush won't believe me when I tell him about these papers. I have too many stories. And too many tales. I've poured too many lies down his throat, causing distrust and making him follow me around—all over town."

I've gotten lost in the pain of what ifs, the lost years, the ugly and horrible. The good and safe years are squashed, buried in a coffin of sadness. Each year becomes another thousand miles of no peace, no real joy. It's time to face the truth. I'm not good at anything. I've got nowhere to run.

Since the age of ten, the nightmares have hovered over me, and consumed my life for too long. I can't see beyond the face of my own mask. Beyond the fear. Or beyond the tombstones of today.

I glanced at the sky, the sun baking my skin. "Dear God, will you catch me if I run? What if I fall? Should I take this case? Can I solve it? And what kind of person hires someone at a cemetery?"

Gilbert's voice cut through my prayer. "What are you doing? I heard you yelling and crying, sort of like a hollow squeal. Are you sick?"

Turning, I faced Gilbert and held out the scrunched-up notes. "Read this. Someone called my house to hire me for a case. And now—I've gotten the same note on each tombstone. What do you make of it?"

Some of the papers floated to the ground, but Gilbert held one, reading it first to himself. He backed up, dropping his shovel. "What have you gotten yourself into? This is—"

"It's a clue to help me solve the case of the Phantom Killer! But who sent them? And why five? Why now?"

"It's the movie. It's got some folks riled up." Gilbert's top lip twitched. "And why would they post these notes, unless—"

"Unless, I was supposed to find them." I bent over, picking up the other four notes from the ground, and pulled the fifth one from Gilbert's fingers. "Never mind. This is a joke. Someone left these for me. To poke more fun. Everyone knows I've always said I'll solve the case. It's another cruel joke. I'm Texarkana's Crazy Woman."

I pressed the papers to my chest, raced from the cemetery, across the tracks, behind the feed store, zigzagged along the tree line and faltered when I reached the edge of Swampoodle Creek. I yelled at the bridge over my head. At the tracks to my right. At the spot where I'd tumbled after chasing the Phantom Killer—so many years ago.

Exhausted, I slumped to my knees, the wound on my leg a reminder of the cut from this morning. I took in the words from the notes. Each letter jumped as if slicing away skin, to expose my heart so I could bleed. The throb in my neck confirmed the veins were tight, my pulse inside my temple pounding with the same heartbeat.

I shouted the words from the papers, letting them escape from the dry spot in my throat. "From Lover's Lane to Spring Lake Park. From Highway 67 to Union Station. To solve this case, you must wake up from your past. And the boy with the yellow hair holds the answer to helping you solve the murders from 1946. He can be found—where they are filming the movie."

I brushed dirt from the hem of my dress, folded the five notes, but couldn't decide if the truth was about to give way— or my life. I moved up the road, along Broad Street. Panic set in. "Oh my! There's Crush. He's looking for me. I missed another counseling session with Pastor Toby."

Our green station wagon rolled up next to me, and Crush sighed, shaking his head. Beads of sweat poured from his temples, but he didn't say a word. He only motioned through the opened window for me to get into the car.

The march in front of the Rambler lasted for a thousand steps. The glare of Crush staring at me made me want to run, a need to flee made my feet itch, especially since this is something I've created due to my choices.

I shoved the papers inside the pocket on my dress, which could hold the entire contents of a purse—knowing full well the pocket hid a cemetery secret. I melted into the seat, sighing, "I'm sorry, Crush. I had to meet someone about this new case. If I told you my appointment meant going to the cemetery, you would have forbidden me to go alone."

Crush hit the brakes and we skidded through the stop sign. "And yet, you went anyway. I've been driving around for an hour. You weren't home. Clara said she hadn't seen you. You swore her to secrecy, didn't you?"

"I threatened to fire her if she spoke a word."

"You can't fire her. She doesn't get paid much."

"I knew you'd respond this way. That's why I didn't tell you."

"So you lied about being sick. Well, did you get the job? Tell me. What's going on?"

I gulped, the now curdled milk from my breakfast gurgled upward in my throat, ready to blow like a volcano. I touched my pocket. "I don't have a case. I'm sure it's Gilbert and Lester. They've resumed their pranks again. You know how they play jokes."

"A joke? I'm beginning to think our entire marriage is a joke to you." Crush spun ahead, up Broad Street, but we were met with road blocks at Main Street. "Great. They're filming for the movie at Union Station, aren't they? Get out. Go. I'm sure you need to see this. Maybe it will help you get through this rough patch. I hope the bleeding of your past and the future of our marriage makes it to the other side of the tracks—to a place where we're not suspended in the continued bleeding from your wounds."

I sucked hard on my lip. "Are you sure? I won't be long. I promise." I grabbed the handle on the door, leaning toward Crush to kiss his cheek, but he moved, forcing me to kiss the air. "Honey, I promise. I'll be home in a bit."

"I know. I've heard it before."

I slipped from the car—the call of the notes and of my past became a shout of shrills booming between my ears. I wiped my brow, the sweat dripping from my bangs, and watched Crush drive away.

The tug on my heart called too, the one telling me to chase him—until I heard the commotion on Front Street. The man's words echoed in my ears. "Ready. Let's take this shot on the stairs. Over there."

Jogging, I hurried around the corner, and crossed the street where a crowd of people hoped to see the film crew and actors get to work. I too must get to work because I'm the unstoppable Annie Grace who will solve the mystery of the Phantom Killer.

I took a deep breath and prayed the things I kept telling myself weren't all lies. I also prayed the case isn't filled with sheep in disguise or wolves ready to kill me. I pray I'm not losing control. And I pray I'm not headed to the thunder of nowhere.

Rounding the Hotel McCartney, I rushed to get a glimpse, but too many spectators blocked my way. I glanced at everyone's feet, looking for boots—in case the killer had joined us, but found only regular shoes and regular people hoping to catch a not-so-regular taping of an anything but regular movie scene.

I spotted the fire escape which would plant me across from Union Station. "I could see from up there." I grabbed the bottom rung on the dangling chain, pulling, and the rusty metal left orange marks on my hands.

Like a rabbit, I jumped onto the stairs, climbing up the ladder-escape. I plunked down, holding my dress around my knees, trying to appear respectable on a fire escape, which is virtually impossible. I'm not graceful like the other women in this town and should stop trying to imitate them.

"Ready. Let's roll." The director called for action and the crowd glued their attention on the actors and actresses, those from our hometown and those who were famous.

My untied PF Flyers dangled as I swung my feet, and both my shoes dropped to the sidewalk. One nearly hit a man in the head, but his near-death shoe injury went unnoticed as he gazed at the crew.

My toes loved the fresh air, and I wiggled them from my escape-balcony seat. It's too hot to wear socks in the summer—too hot. The seat became a movie theatre moment— with the best view in the balcony. "This is great. I've got the best seat ever. The end to my past is beginning. Now to find the boy with all the answers. With the yellow hair."

"Let's take it from this angle." The director moved the people around, got the camera at the spot he wanted, and the camera man took some shots after his men hushed the crowd.

"He must be Charles B. Pierce. I love how he's in charge and using his creativity." I stretched my neck to see, taking in the action.

The replay of history came to life from the actor's lips. Same story but different in parts. I disappeared to 1946, to a place when the horror landed on my heart like pieces of letters from a magazine, where words like sadness, sorrow, and suffering stuck like glue. I sighed, wiped my eyes, and toppled—tipping over, my dress caught on a piece of metal.

I fell backwards against the rung of stairs, toppling and falling, yet holding onto the fire escape like a trapeze artist. I reached for the rail before I crashed to the sidewalk and caught a glimpse of a small blond boy around ten or so, as my body hung in the air. "Is he the boy with answers? Could it be? I've seen him at church."

The boney youngster in blue jeans and the unbuttoned, dark-blue T-shirt, skipped with excitement around the director. "Hey, Daddy. I wish I could be in this movie. I've acted in *The Legend of Boggy Creek*. You know I can do it. Please, Daddy. Please."

He patted the long-haired boy. "I expect you will make plenty of movies with me. We'll see."

I balanced myself on the rung of the escape. "No way. It's the director's son. And he has yellow hair!" In a body slam to the concrete, I busted my chin, grabbed my shoes, rubbed my face and hobbled to the set. I slipped my shoes on before the hot sidewalk burned my feet. "Where is he? Where did the boy go?"

I pushed my way through the crowd of shoulders, and rushed into the center of the action, and a tug on my arm sent me running in place. The man with bulging muscles, wearing the white T-shirt stopped me. "Ma'am, we're filming. Do you mind?"

"But I need to see—"

He squinted his brown eyes, looking at my head. "You're bleeding. Someone, please help this woman. She's hurt."

I faded, losing myself to my wobbly legs and someone catching me—like falling from a boxcar into arms of saving grace.

One Good Reason to Hide

"Annie Grace, wake up. You took a fall. Sweetheart, it's me, Crush. I'm right here. Can you hear me?"

Blinking, I focused on the mirror above the dresser and the tan rocker with the footstool by the window. And the flowered and black afghan. And the chest of drawers with Grandma Elsie's wash bowl. I ran my fingers across the patched quilt on the bed, where a thousand colors shot up at me, as if a rainbow had landed on top of me. I focused on my surroundings. "This is one of my grandma's itchy ones. I'm in my bedroom. I'm home. How did I get here?"

A gentle shove sent me back to the pillow. "Quiet, your head has a bruise and your chin has three stitches. I suppose you'll be one giant scar by the time you're sixty."

"I'm at home?"

"Yes, how do you feel?"

I stared at Crush, realizing his ability to find humor in most anything made him more handsome each year. He's never lost his joy in spite of having me for his wife.

Crush quizzed me. "Would you like to tell me how you hurt yourself?"

"Well, I charged toward the action at Union Station, but I tumbled off the fire escape. And I tried to talk to the boy!"

"You climbed a fire escape?"

"Yes. I couldn't see."

"But tell me about the boy."

"He holds the answer to the answer behind the clues." I popped up, my head throbbing with a pulse in my temple, deep inside and under my forehead, too. "My dress. Where's my dress?"

"I tossed it in the laundry. It's not stained, a little summer dirt never ruined a dress."

"No, I need my dress."

"You can't have your dress right now. The doctor said you'll need to stay in bed the rest of the afternoon. You passed out downtown."

"It's my favorite dress from Belk Jones, and the only one they had left when I bought it. Clara shopped with me, and she planned to purchase the dress too, but I snatched it from her. I couldn't let her outdo me."

"When are you and Clara going to stop competing for everything? Life is not a competition."

"It is with us." I wobbled from the bedroom in my orange pajamas, hurrying and stepping over manuscripts. Barreling, I hopped downstairs, each step a lopsided bounce as my legs jiggled. "Whoa! I'm not all together." I reached for my head, grimacing.

From behind me, Crush called, "Wait, I'll help you. Can you please let me help you?"

"I need my dress!"

"What's so important about your dress?"

Twirling around on the red-carpeted stairs, the softness of the pattern, along with the firmness of the wood pressed on the soles of my feet. I shouted at him. "You have no idea what happened today. I'm getting my dress!"

Crush passed me with a whiz, stopping me in my tracks, blocking me halfway, in the spot beside the window where the stairs twisted to the right. He pulled some papers from his pocket. "Could this be what you're looking for? I have no idea what's going on, but it's going to stop."

"What do you have there? Those are mine." I jumped forward to grab the papers. "Crush! Give those clues to me."

"What are these? There's five. They're the same message with the same type of pasted letters. Is this what you received at the cemetery? And who gave them to you?"

I snatched the papers, holding them close. "I never met the person who left them. Don't you see? It's the Phantom Killer. He's alive and he wants to get caught."

Crush inched closer, right up to my face. "So this is your new case. You're going to catch the killer and you think this is the same person from 1946? Why would he set himself up? Who does such a thing? Who wants to get caught after all these years? He's would be at least fifty now or older. This is a hoax!"

"Maybe he's remorseful. Maybe he's ill. Maybe he's crazy and not thinking rationally. Maybe he's trying to set things right."

"Are you serious? This is how you investigate? You assume? What happened to facts and truth? You are not taking this case. We're turning this information over to the police. You're getting caught up in something which could be life threatening and dangerous for you."

I shoved Crush like we were teens. "Who do you think you are? You can't tell me what to do. You can't decide which cases I work or don't take. I have always wanted to investigate crimes. You've known my dreams. I've never made a secret of my goals."

"No! This is where I put my foot down. I love you. I care too much for you. I am not letting you risk your life with nonsense clues. Especially since the person who left these notes for you—called this afternoon."

"What? He called?"

"Yes, right as Clara prepared to leave for the day, she grabbed the phone in the hallway by the front door."

"What did he say? Tell me."

"He said he watched you take each note, and he knows you showed your friend, Gilbert. And now—

"What? Is Gilbert in trouble? Is he in danger?"

"He's come up missing. So, it must be related to these notes. I called him at his place, and his brother, Lester. No answer. Then I drove to each of their houses and finally found Lester back at the cemetery. He told me Gilbert worked late digging a grave. He found Gilbert's truck at the tracks, but he's missing."

"No! When I left the cemetery, Gilbert was there with his shovel!"

"Well, he's not there now."

"I had no way of knowing what would come of the notes or talking to Gilbert. How could I have known this would happen?"

"Exactly! This is why," he grabbed the notes, "this is why you're off the case. And you're to stay home and out of sight."

"You've got to be kidding. I need to do this for Martha Long and Jack Hall. For Reed Gordon and Patti Malvern. For Peyton Mars and Bay Jo Baxter. And for Victor Stamps and Kacey Stamps."

"Listen to yourself. Are you really wanting to chase the killer to help them? Because it sounds like you're in this for yourself. You are obsessed with this case. You have never gotten over the ride on the boxcar with Taddy. Or breakfast with your grandma. Or the night at Spring Lake Park. Or the ride to the Stamps farm. You're caught in the graveyard of yesterday."

"I know! I know! I have to see what this is about." I rubbed my hands together, my heart racing as if it might pound itself to death. "But, what about the boy? What if he's in danger? Let me help the boy! What else did the man say on the phone?"

"He said the clues you need are a secret. But the hiding must come out, so his wife can sleep. I had no idea what he meant. So I called Officer Teacup. He's a seasoned cop. He'll know what to do."

"There's no way you're dragging him into this. Officer Teacup nearly arrested me, years ago. I was only a kid when he caught Taddy and me making suds in the fountain by the post office. He's the one who knew we rode the boxcar on Taddy's birthday, on a Friday night in February when Taddy and I witnessed the first attack. Which is also the night I met Gilbert and Lester after their pa got shot by accident."

"That was a long time ago. He'll want to do the right thing. He's for us, not against us."

"He's against me. He's never liked me, and I've never liked him." I stumbled to the stairs, my head swimming. "I've got to sit down. My head's throbbing."

"Come to the front room. I've opened the windows. There's a cool breeze drifting in from the west and bringing nicer weather for tonight." Crush paused, sighing deeply. "We're going to cooperate with the police."

"No! You've made all these decisions without me. I had no say in this. Not one word."

"Honey, I was protecting Gilbert. And you! Don't you see?"

"I see how you've overruled my first case, by giving it away. I can't believe you'd do this to me." I plowed past Crush, bumping into his shoulder, and tangled my toes with the cuff on his pants leg. "Get out of my way. I'll never forgive you for this!"

Crush reached over to help me untangle, and I shoved him off to the side. He scolded me. "Annie Grace, stop pushing me. You can't push your way out of this."

"I can, too." I lost myself, forgot my name, and everything went black—like disappearing inside a boxcar late at night.

I shouted at someone, but not at Crush. I screamed at the memory forcing itself into my present day. "Get away from me. You shoved me from the ... boxcar. And I recognize your eyes! I will remember your face. I will."

Crackle-clump-thud. Crackle-clump-thud. Kaboom!

The thuds thumped with the rhythm of my losing track of where I was, of who I was. And, like waking up, I sat with my arms around my legs, rocking. The bottoms of my pajamas were covered in blood. My hands were coated, too.

I knelt at the base of the stairs, sitting right where the glass had cut me earlier, beneath the chandelier. I pondered the reality of my capability to lose touch—and realized, I'm staring at a limp body.

"Crush?" I leaned over the lifeless, red-haired man, my husband. "Crush! What happened?"

His chest went up and down.

"He's breathing. But his head is trickling blood like a water faucet left on. "Crush? Did I do this? Could I be the reason you fell?"

Panicked, I phoned for an ambulance. "Hurry, my husband's unconscious. I have no idea why. No, hurry."

Slamming the receiver down, I charged upstairs, washing my hands in the bathroom, while crying. I wiped the sink with a towel, acting like a criminal, ready to dash into the night. I tossed on some overalls and a shirt, tied my shoes, and rushed downstairs.

I opened the door, sliding across the hall, to Crush. "Honey, it's not safe to be with me. I'm not sure I did this. But I'm not sure I didn't. But you'll be fine. The ambulance is on its way."

I scrunched the papers into my pocket and darted to the porch. "One. Two. Three. Four. Five." The columns were there. They never change. I charged up the road, hurrying to my grandma's tree, and climbed to the highest branch, hiding in the sunset, surrounded by the photographs. "I'm safe. No one can see me. I'll stay here for now."

After time dragged and the minutes cranked into what seemed a million hours, my questions zipped inside my head. What about the boy with the yellow hair? And what about the man who called the house? And where is Gilbert? And is my husband alive? What woman runs away when her spouse is out cold on the floor?

Full of Self-Pity

The breeze swished through the bare branches as the photographs swung back and forth. I cradled the branch as if my embrace might send me back in time—to a place before kidnappings, before boxcar rides, before whiskey bottles, and before the time when the night life called to my daddy. To a season with a normal family, with two parents. Where we ate chocolate cake and fried chicken and drank sweet tea. In that order.

I flinched, wobbled, and reached for a limb with one hand. "What am I saying? My family never sat together at the table. I never knew my mama. And I never knew my daddy when he wasn't ready for a card game or for a night at the bar."

Weeping, I cried, "God, what is wrong with me?" I twirled around, leaning against the main part of the tree, balancing myself. "I should go see if Crush is alive. No, I should stay. I've gone and hurt him. Who will I injure next?"

The cycle of chaos unraveled in my head as the sun lowered itself behind the tall buildings. Behind the Grim Hotel. Behind Union Station. Behind the Hotel McCartney. Behind State First National Bank. Behind the *Texarkana Gazette*.

I sighed. I yawned. I scolded myself. I argued with God. I apologized to Him. And I heard a voice in the shadows. "Remember, the person in right standing before God who is loyal and steady—will find herself—fully alive."

I twisted my neck, unable to see the face of the wanderer. I pulled my legs up to my chest, pretending a grown-up woman can turn herself invisible when she's up a tree. Besides, this person had no idea I hovered above his head on a branch, especially since he crossed his legs, and sat at the base of the tree.

I glanced down, peering at him. Who was this stranger? Who was this man? And why was he sitting under my tree? In the dark? I held onto my questions, the illusion of a lie louder than the truth.

The voice below broke the silence. "You've engineered the ruin of your own house because you carry shame and feel ruined yourself. You are undermining the foundation God has given you, and the rotting of your soul is at hand."

I made a face, whispering to myself. "Rotting of your soul? Who is this person?"

The man rose from the ground, held up a flashlight and switched the light on, shining the beam into my face. "And you are the one I speak of, as you suffer like a child instead of walking tall like a woman. Go to your husband. Go and start anew. He needs you. It's time to wake up and stop being the victim. It's time for you to hold your head up. You are braced for the worst, when you should climb to the lookout tower and scan the horizon. Stop being silent. You know the truth. You know the way. It's time to pray and rid yourself of this self-pity."

I shimmied down the tree, my eyes seeing spots from the light. "Wait, I know you. You speak as if you know my deepest parts."

The man with dark hair, wearing the trench coat, who switched the flashlight off, smiled. "Hi there, Annie Grace. The time has come for another handkerchief."

"Archie Gabs? Oh my! I haven't seen you since forever!" I ran my fingers across his cheek, taking the handkerchief. "You're getting older."

"I'm older and tired. But when a friend is in trouble, you come."

"How did you know to come now? I've been in trouble before. And you've never showed up."

"Well, actually Crush asked me to come. He phoned me two days ago, worried you might leave him again."

"I seem to remember he leaves me."

Archie shook his head. "Crush is out of options. He can't figure out how to help you live."

"I've hurt him tonight and didn't stay at his side. I ran like I always do. I always run away and hide."

"So, this is how you hide? Right in plain sight?"

"Yes, this tree makes me feel better."

"Maybe we should go to the hospital and see your husband. He's worried about you. And by the way, you didn't hurt him—someone bashed him over the head from behind."

"No, I was right there."

"Crush said you passed out on the stairs during your argument, and he went to help you, when the front door creaked, only for him to end up—landing on the floor."

"Are you serious? But why?"

"Well, I'll show you at the house. Someone scribbled a message for you on the vanity mirror in your bedroom. Officer Teacup found it, and now they're worried you're in danger and being stalked!"

"I don't understand. This isn't happening. Why would anyone want to hurt me?"

**

I cuddled with Crush in his hospital bed. "Honey, I'm sorry. I was positive I had lost myself completely and hurt you."

"I've got a pretty bad headache. But the doctor said I can come home tomorrow. I'll need to call in to work. We'll be busy at Kings Row Inn, but I'll get another cook to cover for me. The crew from the movie is staying there." Crush pulled me close. "Will you be all right at the house? Or will I have to worry you'll be running around?"

"I'll stay at the house. I've already called Clara to come over, too. And Archie can sleep on the sofa downstairs."

Archie hovered like a tower on the other side of the bed. "I'll be here for a few days. I can keep watch. And ..."

"But, you can't follow me. I'm capable of taking care of myself." I snorted at Archie. "Promise me. You're here to be a friend."

"I'll be your friend. I'm closing in on sixty next month, I'm not as young as when we rode the rail. So don't make me chase you." He chuckled, like he meant it.

I sat up. "You never rode the rail. You were trying to find me, and the journey took you to the rail. You found my sister, so she could know her twin brother. And you helped me find my family." My body tingled with a warm, good memory worth thinking on, instead of the achy ones which send me off to self-pity land.

Knock. Knock. Knock.

Crush answered the tap on his hospital room door. "Come in. I'm awake."

In walked the uniform of a police officer, the man I've avoided for years. Who now seemed thicker, and his face puffier. And much older. "Mr. Raike, I've posted an officer at your house, to be safe. Will anyone be staying there tonight?"

"Yes, my wife will. And Ms. Clara. And our good friend, Archie."

I moved to the other side of the bed, standing next to Archie. I announced, "This is our friend from Memphis, and you might remember me. I'm Annie Grace. I was a young girl when I lived with my grandma at the manor. I stayed there for a short time."

He cocked his to one side. "I'm surprised we haven't run into each over the years."

I laughed. "Well, I haven't put any soap suds in the fountain in a long time."

"Well, it's great to see you and it's nice to see you didn't become a delinquent after all." Officer Teacup nodded, "But, we do need to see if you have any idea what the message on the mirror might mean."

Archie nudged me. "I'll drive you home. We'll meet the officer there and get this behind you."

"Let's go." I leaned over the bed, kissing Crush on his cheek. "I'll see you in the morning. I'm so thankful I'm not the reason you're in this bed."

"Me, too. I love you, Annie Grace."

At the house, I paused in the yard. "One. Two. Three. Four. Five."

Archie asked, "What are you counting?"

"I always count the columns on the house. They never change. It gives me a sense of stability."

Officer Teacup waited for us on the porch, and the officer who stood guard reminded me of Gilligan from the television show, *Gilligan's Island*. He was skinny and frail and a little goofy. He's in that show with Dawn Wells and she's here in town, doing a part in the movie.

"Shall we go up to your room?" Officer Teacup asked, but his tone sounded more like an order. "This may rattle you some, but we need to see what you think it means."

"I'm coming. But first, give me a second."

Archie offered to wait downstairs. "I'll get these windows closed. We can't be too careful."

Upstairs, I inched along the piles of paper, following Officer Teacup, but stopped shy of going into my bedroom. I rattled on with nonsense words, nervous on the inside, jittery with tingling lips. "I always wanted the last room on the right because it faces the front of the house. And I'm close to the balcony where I drink my coffee and sit—except for facing the dreadful courthouse."

Officer Teacup sighed. "Shall we go in?"

I leaned on the wall, stalling. "I know Marion Kane gave us this house, but the view has kept me focused on the wrong part of my life and now someone has come into our home. I'm not sure I need to see this."

"But you do need to see this. It's personal. It's for you." Officer Teacup moved inside my room, leaving me with the decision to run or to stay.

Thud-creak. Thud-creak.

I peered over my shoulder. Archie's pooched-out stomach and slumped shoulders spoke of his aging. But his eyes sparkled, and he joined me, surveying the disaster in the hallway. "I decided to come with you." He glanced at the manuscripts. "It seems someone's writing a lot about life and leaving it scattered."

"I've written a thousand stories; I disappear inside of a story—hoping to find the answers to life. To living. To find my happy ending."

Officer Teacup stuck his head into the hall. "Please join me in here. I need to see if this means anything to you."

"Yes, I'm coming. Archie, take my hand. Come with me."

I scuttled to the center of my bedroom, observing like an investigator to see if any of my personal items were missing from my room. I'd left the bed unmade. The cross on the wall next to the mattress seemed bigger tonight. The tissue box on the dresser sat on the left corner with the white figurine behind it, and the three orange candle holders sat in the middle. The praying figurine rested to the right, her hands folded like always. Two hair brushes rested on the right corner. One face down. The other face up. All my things were in place.

I moved my eyes upward to take in the red scribbles on the mirror and my hands went to my throat. My eyes were stuck on the letters, words I'd tucked inside my heart since 1945—in a special pocket deep within, where shadows go to hide. "Oh my! Why that phrase?"

Archie read the words out loud, "Tie them shoelaces!"

I shook my head, "This doesn't make sense. My daddy hollered those words to me when he fell into the Mississippi River in Memphis. I had on my first pair of PF Flyers and they were untied, and he called to me for the last time with those words."

Tripping like my daddy when he was drunk, I tumbled to the rocker, falling to the edge of the seat. "I don't know what to make of it. I don't understand. First, the notes and next Gilbert disappears. Someone knocked Crush out, and it wasn't me. And now, this phrase is written on my mirror. In my house!"

I charged to the tissue box, pulling out as many wads of tissue as I could hold. I smeared the words and the blur of red lipstick spread like blood as my hand wiped the mirror. "This isn't happening. I wanted to become an investigator. To accomplish something and make a difference. This it too much!"

Officer Teacup grabbed my arm. "Stop. Don't tamper with evidence." He yanked the tissues from my grasp. "And what notes were you referring to?"

"Nothing. Nothing at all."

"Are you sure?"

I raced to my office across the hall, plunged into the floor between the two desks—sitting in the middle like a girl holding onto the coal car when her daddy fell.

A shadow stood in the doorway, holding out a handkerchief. Archie switched the light on. "So, this is your office?"

I rose in slow motion, running my fingers along the typewriter, the one nearest to me. My tears falling from my chin. "It's my investigator business. I've never solved one crime."

Surrounded by the memories of death and suffering which I'd plastered on the walls, I trudged across the room and stared at the stories written in the paper by Ernie during the search for the killer. I had the entire series and all the photos from the papers all taped on the walls about the attacks and the murders. "I've read these so many times, I can nearly recite them."

"But why do you recite the things you cannot change. Recite the hope in today, by changing as you move in the moment of now."

"Archie, you have this way of bringing me back from the pain. I can't believe we don't see each other more often."

"Life's taken us on different paths. But I think of you every day when I see Lizzy Beth and Willie at the office. We're helping so many families adopt children. It's rewarding to see the smiles of the new parents with their baby or toddler. And seeing the children run to their arms is so rewarding."

Sighing, I nodded. "They're mad at me. Willie's wife won't let him come see me. But Willie's three boys think I'm fun. Boy, I miss them. They're all in elementary school now. And Lizzy Beth holds grudges longer than I do. She protects her husband from me, like I'm contagious. He's the one with the weird name, Maxwell Thackeray."

"Don't make fun. Be kind. And they'll get over it. Give them time."

"I'm trying. It's lonely being the woman the others whisper about when you come into a room. When I shop for clothes, I see the glares. I hear them talk. I know it's about me. I've given everyone in Texarkana reason to think of me as the crazy woman on Laurel Street. So, I hide in plain sight."

Archie lifted my chin. "Rise up. Become more than a whisper. Become the voice of hope. Change this town. Change a life for God. You'll find your peace by serving God, too."

"Change a life? Now that's a great concept. When I try to change something for good, the good becomes bad. I have this knack for ripping and tearing and destroying."

"Maybe it's because you see yourself in such a way. You've worn the wrong labels for too many of your adult years. Dress yourself in the goodness of God. He will lift you with His righteous right hand."

Officer Teacup interrupted our chat. "Excuse me, I'll check back tomorrow. Lock up. And stay put."

I nodded like I do when I agree, knowing full well I could change my mind. I followed him downstairs, noticing his neck had four giant moles. "I'll be fine. Archie's here." I stopped at the base of the staircase. "Wait! Clara hasn't arrived. She's not here yet."

Archie called from the top of the stairs. "I'm sure she'll be here soon."

I shut the front door, putting my back against the glass, staring at Archie who joined me in the hallway. "Thank you for being here. You keep showing up in my life at the right time."

48

"I have a certain knack of showing up when you need me. Come sit. Let's talk. Maybe it's time for you to write a letter to yourself."

"A letter? What? Now?" I shuffled into the front parlor, touching the piano, the one from the orphanage in Jefferson. The one with the etching marks to me from Tin Can Mahlee about her love for me. I choked on the memory, and another warm moment slid into my heart.

Archie walked to the piano. "Mahlee wrote you a love note on here. She did the best she could in spite of her broken walk. Maybe it's time for you to write God's love on your heart, too."

Ring. Ring. Ring.

I picked up the receiver, stopping short of saying hello, afraid of who might be on the phone. Archie grabbed the phone and I pressed my ear next to his, listening in. Archie answered, "Yes, this is the right number. No, Clara's not here. What? She left an hour ago?"

I whispered, "She lives on Highway 67 next to her daddy's mansion. He built a small house next to his. It's ten minutes from here. Who's on the line?"

Archie asked, "Sir, tell me who this is. Hello?" He glanced at me with his chocolate eyes. "The caller hung up."

"Oh my! What's going on? We must find her!"

Clues to Clara

I shouted at the stars. "We've driven in circles. I'm going to run out of gas. She knows the way to my house." I debated my answers with more questions, unable to figure out why or where Clara might go.

Archie fidgeted in the passenger seat, the way I had earlier in the day when Crush picked me up after my escapade to the cemetery.

I wrapped my fingers on the steering wheel, stopping the car beside an abandoned building. "What is happening? I'm getting the oddest calls. These notes. Even on the mirror. Gilbert is gone. And Clara is missing. It adds up to absolutely nothing that I can pinpoint. I have no idea what it all means. Maybe I'm not cut out to be an investigator. I seem to wander without purpose." I put my head on the steering wheel.

"So sitting here in the dark makes sense? Does it help clear a person's mind to wallow? Does it get rid of the crust of the day? Does it help you seek God's direction?"

Peeking under my arm at Archie, I called to him. "You send me in circles with your questions." I straightened up, remembering something from Clara's desk. "Let's go back to the house. I need to check my office. I think we'll find some answers."

I pressed the gas pedal, spun backwards, and skidded around the corner. "This isn't such a mystery. I know what's going on."

"So you say. If you knew the answers, you wouldn't have kept me up most of the night searching in the dark."

"But Archie! That's it! It's the crust!" I ran the stop sign, turned left and came to a halt in front of the house. "Come on.

I need to look in the office." I stopped in the yard to count the columns, but instead I heard the snore of the guard who sat asleep with his head sideways. The wooden rocker on the porch his makeshift bed.

We rushed inside like kids, like when Taddy and me used to play. Only this wasn't play. The investigator in me rose up, ready to fulfill my purpose and I charged upstairs. Digging in Clara's desk, I pulled out files and tore into her cluttered desk. "It's here. I remember."

Archie hung near, shaking his head. "What are you searching for?"

"I'll show you in a minute. I'll know when I find it. It will help me know if I'm on to something."

I pulled out a thick folder, the papers scattered to the hardwood floor, and I knelt to gather them, only to stop, frozen on my knees. "Archie. Look at this. It's a manuscript. Clara's writing a book."

He joined me on the floor by her desk, moaning on the way down and uncurled himself. "I'm a little stiff. I'll sit in her chair."

I passed him the papers. "What do you make of it? She's writing her book on my dime."

"Your dime? How much do you pay her?"

"Well, she's working for nickels. Her daddy's high and mighty and he figures we need to work out our differences. He thinks she rammed my car a couple years back after we fought for the same dress at the store. But I'm sure she was in hurry since she'd returned home—after leaving unexpectedly for a few months. She seemed preoccupied when she hit my car."

"You two are so much alike."

"We are not. I rode the rail. I was kidnapped. I slept under bridges. In barns. In old houses. Clara had everything poured into her life. She had the nice house with the columns. Her daddy has given her money as if he has a vault in their cellar. She's never had a reason to move out on her own."

"You have a nice house, too. With columns."

"Well, her family has all the money."

"You have plenty to eat. A bed to sleep in. Crush provides for you. You lack for nothing. You are loved. Crush stands by you in all things."

I squirmed, grabbing more paper, shuffling them like cards. "Well, she has those frilly dresses."

"You have dresses now. But you wear those overalls."

I touched the bib. "But they're comfortable. I've never forgotten how Clara pranced around me at my daddy's funeral, on my grandma's porch like I was a nobody and she was a somebody."

"I've heard this story a thousand times from you. She offered you a piece of her orange, and you spit the seeds on her dress."

Swallowing hard, I continued, "Anyone could have written the note on the mirror. I've told everyone how I received my rail name. It's in my books, too. Goodness, solving this clue-case won't come easy. As for Clara, I did spit at her. And I'm still pretty good at spitting."

"Annie Grace, you were ten. When are you going to live in the present? You are allowing the seeds that stuck to her dress to stick to your eyes, clouding your view. To keep you on the porch where you stagger in your world of disappointment and rejection."

"But she received everything and anything and was given so much—life fell into her lap like a present. I longed for trinkets and gifts—those I could never touch."

"And if you'd had everything you dreamed of, you wouldn't have found your sister or brother. Or Crush! Or have known Tin Can Mahlee. Or Pastor Cody. Or met Taddy. Or lived one special year with your grandma Elsie. Your treasure box of memories is unique to your walk. God ordered your steps. You are called and chosen by Him."

"I don't feel so called. Except called Crazy Woman by so many in town."

"And look at your memories of a life many couldn't have survived. You are strong. You are on a mission. Hold on. When you look at others to find your peace, you lose your way. When you look to things to fill the void, you lose your day. I'm praying you find a way to fight for hope and peace, and when you feel like you have nobody to turn to, hold onto God."

I sighed, letting out the pain. "But it's harder for me. My shoes take me on a path filled with suffering."

Archie placed a stack of papers on the desk. "God is with you in this chapter of your life, too. Draw near to Him."

I leaned on Archie's leg, hungry for the wisdom he gave. "How long are you staying? I could use your guidance for more than a couple of days."

He patted my arm. "My time here is short. The lessons you've learned are inside your heart. Trust yourself to walk in confidence. To not lose one more day to the past."

I stood, clutching the papers and adding them to the others on the desk. "I can't get over the fact that I never knew Clara was writing a book."

"We're all writing a story about life. What will yours say in the end?"

"I don't know. Right now, I'm only on page three of my final novel."

"No, I'm talking about your story. You ricochet and fall away. You bounce like a ball from extreme highs to the lowest of lows. You struggle to ride the day with hope. You act as if

God has a 'no access' sign posted on you—as if you're still a little girl who rode into Texarkana on a boxcar. A broken and scarred girl with big blue eyes—longing to find her life."

I held out my arms. "But I do have more scars than most."

"So you do. But you also have scars on your heart and they are affecting how you see life. Crush believes in you. I know I do. But more importantly, God created you, a scarred-beautiful mess of a person. You were sent to Texarkana to change lives. You can give God glory in the new days ahead. Do it before it's too late."

I ran my hand over the manuscript one more time. "Did you see the title on Clara's book?"

"No, missy. Tell me, what does it say?"

I shuffled through the stack of papers in her manuscript. *"From Nobody to Somebody."*

"What do you make of it, Ms. Investigator?" Archie smiled, his eyes squinty like he could fall asleep while talking to me.

"She's on a search for meaning. She's struggling, too."

"When you take the time to look, you can see past the darkness."

I swung with a jerk. "But that's why we're here. I scolded Clara for eating her toast at her desk the other day. She dropped crumbs on everything, and I don't like crumbs."

"But what does this mean tonight?"

"I remember the scribbles on her yellow pad. She had drawn hearts around Gilbert's name. I asked her about it, but she stuck the pad in her desk and left me standing there wondering."

"So, she's dating Gilbert? They're a couple?"

"Maybe, but I still don't know why they're gone."

**

A familiar voice called to us from downstairs. "Hello. I've got some news. Annie Grace? Mr. Gabs?"

"We're coming." I turned to Archie. "It's Officer Teacup." I charged downstairs with Archie behind me, running smack dab into the officer on the last few steps. "What is it? Why are you here in the middle of the night?"

"It's not good news. We received a tip at the station about a car and two bodies on the road. We've found Gilbert and Clara."

"And—where are they?" I squinted, my tiredness causing me to move slower, my skin tingling with a numbness.

"They've been found at the lake."

"What are you saying?"

Archie stepped between Officer Teacup and me, leaning closer to him, almost whispering. "Tell me they're alive."

"I'd love to tell you this, but they've both been shot."

I shoved Archie aside. "It's not true. No!" I collapsed, unable to breathe, caught between a crushing feeling of suffocation and the need to scream. "Clara and Gilbert aren't dead! They can't be!"

The officer from the porch stumbled inside. "What's going on? What's all this noise about?"

I rose, charging him like a bolt of lightning. "You are worthless. You have slept through it all. You haven't watched my house for intruders. You're not worth the badge they gave you."

Archie pulled me from my onslaught of ugly words. "Annie Grace, it's not his fault. He didn't shoot anyone."

I wiggled free, bolted from the room, pounded out the front door, darting outside, across the yard, down the front steps to the sidewalk—and hurled myself in the direction of my tree.

The two blocks of charging into the darkness landed me in the middle of the street where all my strength tumbled to the abyss where little girls cry and ask why. Where grownups cover their ears and eyes. "Dear God, tell me the words I heard were a lie. Two friends didn't die tonight. It can't be true."

I curled into a ball on the asphalt in the middle of the street, hoping to get run over by a car. Not that anyone was still up—except for the moon—because the people in Texarkana were sleeping safely in their homes while two people lost their lives to a killer.

Closing my eyes, I stared as the stars fell from heaven and I prayed the sunrise of tomorrow would never come.

Copy Cat Murders

"Where am I?" I unfolded myself from beneath the blanket, my head aching, my neck stiff. My chest throbbed like my veins were threads of unraveled rope, like my heart might stop from the drum-like hammers booming inside my body.

"Rest, dear. You're exhausted." The familiar and soothing words of Crush sent me straight up.

"You're home? We're safe. I had the worst nightmare."

"Honey, it's Monday afternoon. I'm home from the hospital. But—"

"But, the part about Clara and Gilbert is true, isn't it?" I choked on the hot, dusty air and my throat stuck like glue, my eyes burned. I couldn't get my words to come together without stuttering. "Tell me. What … what happened?"

"Honey, we've learned they were dating. But we've also heard rumors of how Clara's father wanted better for her, not one part of Gilbert measured up for his daughter." Crush sat next to me, holding my hand.

"Good enough? She was forty, like me. She's run off every available man in Texarkana. She can't be too picky, at her age." I coughed, wanting to swallow my harsh words.

Crush patted my arm. "She and her daddy struggled to see things clearly. She was a good friend to you."

"She was? Well, we had some great adventures, like when she took a road trip with me for research on my books. She hated to get up early though, so I always told her the wrong time. Eventually, she caught on." I held onto my memory for an extra second. "She was kind to me more than I was to her. We laughed and argued. We met each other half way."

"She loved you. And longed to be more like you. Strong. And independent. But you were a challenge to her."

"No! She challenged me. We were like night and day."

"You were, but together you made this house full of passion and life."

Sniffling, I added, "The upstairs got pretty loud on certain days, for us not to have any customers." I snickered, knowing I'd miss the smell of oranges and watching her put lipstick on, of her primping. Sorrow rested on my shoulders, her absence real and horrible. "Crush, where did they find them? What do the police know? Who did this?"

"We only know they must have gone out to Lake Texarkana to be alone. And someone shot them."

"You meant to say, they were at Wright Patman Lake."

"You know what I meant. I've called it Lake Texarkana for too long."

Shaking, I hit my legs with my fist. "I'm not ready to say goodbye to either of them. We've been friends and enemies for most of my life. I adored them. When I wasn't mad at them."

"I know. You love more people than you admit."

"Oh, Crush! I've got to solve their case. Someone came into our home. And now, Clara's dead. And Gilbert."

"You aren't solving anything. This is out of our hands. I'm not letting you get any closer to trouble than we already are—and with the filming of the movie about the Phantom Killer we've got to keep this quiet."

"Why would we keep this quiet?" I stormed around the coffee table, dragging the blanket around my ankle.

Crush met me by the fireplace. "What if this is another serial killer? Or the Phantom Killer is back."

"We must tell everyone. We need to call Ernie Surratt at the *Texarkana Gazette*. He loves to write stories with his name in print. What if the Phantom Killer came back to strike again—to make a statement?" I put my hand to my mouth. "Or to get caught?"

"So, you think the notes you found at the cemetery are related to all of this?"

"I definitely think so. Clara gets a call. I get the notes. Clara's on her way over here. She doesn't make it. We have yet another clue. And it's on a mirror. This is the next chapter in a horrid case."

Crush called to the ceiling. "Lord, what am I going to do with Annie Grace? She's unreasonable, and I can't control her."

The voice from the back of the house answered, "We should let her put the pieces of the puzzle together. She'll heal. She'll be made whole."

"Not if she's in danger," Crush said.

I countered with my reasons. "I'm always in danger. It's how life falls around me. I've got to figure this out."

Archie walked into the room, placing a tray of sandwiches down. "I've made some tuna and apple with mayo."

"I hate mayonnaise. Always have." I snubbed the food, knowing I had to get busy or lose my mind. "I'm going upstairs. I need to get dressed. To take a walk. To think."

Crush talked with food in his mouth. "I should go with you. I will go with you."

"I'll be right back. I need to wash my face and pull my hair up. You can walk with me." I rushed up the stairs, knowing I'd fibbed to Crush, knowing I'd sneak out the back door, to the alley, to walk—alone. To find a way to handle the fog of pain. To see if the sky would turn blue or offer up gray—before I knew what to say.

Once in my bedroom, I saw the blurred red on my mirror, and the echo of my daddy's voice called to me from the boxcar on the bridge. "Annie Grace, tie your shoelaces." His final words before he died. Or did he die? I've always wondered. A deep sadness sent me spinning with confusion. I had to go. To do something.

I tossed on my overalls, forgot about my crusty eyes, grabbed my Minolta camera, and slipped like a ballerina on the stairs, or more like a mouse on a hunt for cheese. Or in this case, a hunt for the boy with yellow hair. He's the answer to something. But I'm not sure what his something might be.

My heart kept a perfect rhythm with my feet and I hurried toward the kitchen wearing my favorite PF Flyers. But first, as I moved beside the counter, I grabbed an orange for Clara from the fruit bowl. In her memory.

In the yard, sniffing the orange, the smell of the fruit sent me to the days when Clara snacked on oranges nonstop. How she slept in hair-rollers to have some extra curls in her blonde hair. How she fought to make her daddy proud of her. How she struggled to have friends. How she once said she'd become an old maid if fate had its way. She gave her heart to any guy who looked at her for more than a minute. And she bounced from job to job. And now, she'll never sit in my investigator office again.

I charged like an elephant whose trunk carried the heaviness of a thousand worries and sorrow. Like I weighed a million pounds from all the horrors I'd seen. My feet were heavy with the mud of yesterday. My broken hallelujah wasn't ever going to sound in tune. Or like a beautiful song.

I ran and ran and ran, my chest hurting from the overthinking and short breaths. Huffing, I rounded the corner to the spot where the film crew prepared to capture another scene. A wedding scene at a small white church played out as the camera filmed the action. Had I walked this far? Was I on Bowie Street?

I watched as the actors moved into place, a boy on a bicycle rode by, and two women emerged from inside the front part of the sanctuary, one wearing yellow and the other wearing pink. Each with bouquets of flowers tied to their wrists. The bride, a young woman in a wedding gown holding her own bouquet of white and yellow flowers stopped talking mid-sentence. "I mixed up my words. I forgot my lines."

The film crew didn't halt the action, and the director kept the camera rolling, motioning with his arms. I noticed the man who played the groom had the biggest ears. I'm sure I've seen him in the produce department at the grocery store stacking tomatoes. And yet, the group of actors appeared like a family as if they were happy. As if they unaware a killer lurked in their midst.

My foot kicked at the street sign, and I wanted to replace the man playing the part of the pastor. He didn't fit the role, as something about him seemed fake. I noticed how someone had taken the sign with the name for this church off the metal rack. Now it could be any ole church. In any ole town.

My jaw dropped, and I wondered if Gilbert and Clara had made plans to marry. To have children. A sour spot thickened in my throat, burning my nose. Poor Crush, he had always wanted us to have children, but after three miscarriages I knew my chances of becoming a mother slipped away with each winter, and with each January birthday.

The director repositioned his actors and took another shot. He tried an angle from the left and the right. The actors smiled and repeated their lines. If only they knew, their lines seemed to mimic the future Clara and Gilbert had planned.

The blonde boy shadowed his daddy as if filling those shoes might be harder than one might think. He hung close, his hair dancing with each move. He checked out what his dad created on film—soaking it in like a sponge.

I rocked side-to-side in my comfy clothes, and waited across the street, standing across from the black car with the streamers and the words "Just Married" on the back window. The camera cut to the smile of a small girl who grinned bigger than Texas, the final person with a part in the scene.

Like a streak of gloom and doom, Ernie drove up in his cream-colored Studebaker. The one from my childhood. He jumped from the driver's seat, calling to the director. "Have you heard? There's a copycat Phantom Killer murder. We've lost a young couple last night out on lover's lane by the lake."

The cheerful actors who pretended to be at a wedding, became talkative. And Ernie, slower and older too, much like Archie, announced, "I heard it was Old Maid Clara. And one of the Blanton Street Brothers."

I barreled across the street. "Clara wasn't an old maid. She was engaged to Gilbert. They were going to get married and I planned to take their photographs. They were in love!" I stretched the truth to make Clara and Gilbert more special, because they were—as I had ignored her for too long.

Ernie took his trusty reporter-pad out. "Tell me what you know about this case. Are you involved? Usually if something bad happens in Texarkana, Annie Grace Raike has the scoop or has caused the trouble."

"Clara loved Gilbert. He loved her. And she was my best friend." By saying she belonged in the best friend category made Clara sound nicer. Or did it make me sound nicer?

Mr. Pierce-man moved toward us. "Excuse me, I'm shooting a film here. Can this wait?"

I nodded, smiling at the boy peeking from behind his daddy's trousers and ignoring the director. I spoke to the boy. "Hi there, what's your name?"

He twisted like a rubber-band ready to snap. "I'm Junior. I'm ten. I'm going to be a movie star."

I bent toward him. "Good, but I need to ask you a question."

Ernie slid between us. "I've got a story to do. We're going to press. I need to update the readers, so they know what we're up against. So, what do you know about the murders at the lake?"

Grabbing his arm, I shook my head. "Seriously, Ernie. In front of the boy. Is this necessary?"

The boy corrected me. "I know about murder. This movie has a killer. He wears a pillowcase on his head."

Mr. Director announced, "Everyone take five. We've got some distractions to tend to." He marched closer to Ernie, using his inside voice in the outside yard, which made me step closer to listen. "Ernie, what happened? Is it something we need to worry about? We've got another few weeks of filming to do."

Ernie scribbled, tearing a sheet off. "No sir. I'm sure it's isolated." He turned to me, handing me the paper. "Call me later. Let me get your take."

I wrinkled the paper up, tossing it to the ground. "Clara was my friend. I'm not giving you a story at her expense."

Ernie scratched his nose. "At her expense. We need to catch the person who did this."

Junior showed up next to me, picking up the paper. "You might need this. We don't litter on the set."

"Sorry. Can I ask you a question?" I moved closer to the boy. "Have you been told to give me anything?"

"Why would I give you anything? Who are you?"

"I'm Annie Grace Raike. I live on Laurel Street on the Arkansas side. I go to First Baptist Church on the Texas side. I write poetry and books." I touched my camera. "I snap photographs, too, and I'm an investigator."

"I don't know you." He spun around to join the actors and the crew, and the man who first stopped me at Union Station stepped up to me, making it clear I needed to move along. I shuffled across the street and Ernie grumbled as he marched to his car.

The girl from the wedding scene with the giant grin skipped up to me, glancing over her shoulder, her long blonde waves bouncing in the air, and she looked at me. "Hi, I'm supposed to give this to you. It's from Junior. He said it's clue number one. There's four more."

"What? Four more?" I shoved the paper into my pocket, not wanting to let someone or anyone see the clue. I glared at Junior and caught him watching me like a chicken hawk. I mouthed silent words to him. "What are you doing?"

He slipped his finger to his lips, shushing me.

Crying Softly for the Way It Was Before

The funeral is today. On a Saturday. At Rose Hill Cemetery. And I'm saying a tribute in remembrance of Clara. But I have nothing nice to say about Gilbert, since I only knew him for his pranks. I never gave him the time of day, he rubbed me wrong—seemed to set me off. I never spoke to him about his life, his dreams, or what he longed to see happen in the future. Time ticked away like taps on a typewriter. Wasted words never spoken. His life's manuscript cut short.

The streaks of sadness and regret zapped my strength, and the long endless summer days boiled into a waterfall of scorching lament. I've never perspired so much, and now a small river dripped, burning my eyes. The dirt stuck like peanut butter to my shoes. The sting of two goodbyes yelled at me with a hollow ache of nothingness.

The spillway drew me closer, and I hovered near the water's edge at the dam. I touched the ripples near my feet, pondering how death had engulfed Clara and Gilbert. And I found myself interrogating the rushing water. What did I miss? What secret life did Clara and Gilbert live? And who would want to hurt them?

I stomached the guilt pouring over my soul, unable to cry or smile. The dirt under my shoes crunched with the shattered loss, and I staggered across the spot where the car's glass must have shattered on Clara's Volkswagen. Where someone pounded the hood before taking their lives.

Lingering, I could almost hear Clara's last scream, but I hoped she collapsed with a quick and silent farewell, without suffering.

"Lord, pain penetrates our lives with suffering. How do people kill each other? Why do they do the things they do?"

I bent down, holding a sliver of glass. "I'm sorry Gilbert. I'm so sorry, Clara. We never treated each other like true friends. Our arguing tangled with our past and in the insecurities of our humanity. God, if you will, please let them know, I'd love to be friends with them in heaven." I coughed from the dust swirling in the afternoon wind, realizing I never shared my faith with them. I hoped they were Christians— they did go to church with me.

Tossing pieces of glass across the rocks, I disappeared into the sadness like a broken sliver of shattered hope. "Lord, help me live more open and with understanding, and let me reach out to others who may hurt—the same as me. Help me fight the battle to live and to survive—to love and to give to others. I'm selfish and self-centered. Crush has emphasized my need for thinking outside of my world, to love others. I know he's right, but I argue with him anyway."

I jumped from rock to rock next to the rushing water at the edge of the swirling foam, sniffing in a fishy odor. I wiped my nose, mumbling to myself. "Ernie wrote his story without making the article sound like a copycat murder, and he used kind words. But for me, this copycat case shouted louder than a whisper, more like a church bell clanging with noise and chatter. With rumors and fear. With worry. And anxious days."

Reaching into my slacks pocket for the note from the girl, I wished to have answers. "How will I get the rest of the clues? I have one. And what is so important about a boy having yellow hair? I expect someone is manipulating me and sending me chasing the wind."

Back at my station wagon, I quizzed myself with more questions jumping around in my head. And kicked a pebble with my loafer. "What shall I do next? The days with Clara were wasted, the shame of how I treated her will haunt me. Is this the work of the Phantom Killer? Or is someone else murdering my friends in my town?"

I read the clue with similar cut-out letters as the ones from the cemetery, same but different. Could the person who left the notes in the tombstone be the same one who left this one? Something feels different. I can't pin point it. What am I missing? I yelled. "I'm missing the other clues. This one only has two words: baby gone."

Sighing, I marched to the water's edge again, and fixed myself like a statue on a boulder, reaching to the sky with my arms outstretched, holding it for God to view. "Did you see this? What does it mean?"

I staggered, and sat on the rock, shoving the note into my pocket, and grabbed a handful of pebbles, tossing them at random into the water. I skipped a rock across the top of the water, plop, plop, plop, and the sinking of each rock made me think of someone losing a breath and suffocating.

My heart trembled from the heartbreak with each skip of a pebble and I stumped my toe as I flipped a flat rock with a whip. "Stupid boulder!" I tossed more rocks and more, unto I could find no pebbles within five feet of me. Tears streamed from my eyes and a whirlwind of dirt spun around me like a tornado, leaving my face gritty and coating my clothes. "I'm sorry for not being nicer to you, Clara. And to you too, Gilbert. I pray I never forget either of you."

A dusty cloud drifted over the water as a car drove up, parking next to mine. I squinted, thankful to see Pastor Toby, not only my grown-up pastor, but my longtime friend from Jefferson. He once desired to become an actor but opted for preaching and moved to Texarkana after Bible college. He holds a church service for the homeless people by the creek when he's not at our main church. "Hi, Toby."

He waved, climbing from his hatchback. He believes in becoming the best you possibly can, and he's great at leaving a trail for others to find God. He's a modern-day Paul who holds prayer meetings and hopes the Lord opens a heart to hear about Jesus.

"Annie Grace, are you ready for this afternoon? You haven't returned my calls this week. Crush told me you plan on going to the service. But he wasn't sure if you were prepared to give the tribute and he said you came out here."

I fell over a rock, tearing my dress slacks. "Oh my, now I'll have to change clothes."

Toby rushed over to me. "Are you cut?"

"No, I'm fine. These rocks are out to get me."

"Let's go to the shade over by the cars. Your face is red. How long have you been in this heat?"

"A couple hours. I'm trying to figure things out. But it's not working. I can't get past the words on the note. The one about a baby being gone. Whose baby? Why a baby? I don't understand. I can't focus and have nothing for the tribute."

"I never could stand the sun, let's sit." We hiked to the shade of a group of trees.

I wiped the grit from my face, using a hanky from my pocket. "I hope I pass out."

"You do not."

"I won't have to say anything at the funeral if I'm out cold."

"If you don't want to speak, you don't have to say a word. I'll take care of the service. It's not like you connected with them like I did—you argued with them nonstop. I knew their hearts."

"Thanks, I'd rather not talk. You're right, I treated them horrible. I picked on them like they were kids, acting childish

68

myself. I have too many crusty layers to deserve any friends or a husband. Crush puts up with my nonsense. And I give everyone a hard time."

"He's the reliable one—except for—"

"Except for?"

"Oh, nothing. He struggled a few years ago when you two split up."

"We took a break. We didn't split up." I put my hands on my hips.

"So you say. You know me. I'll tell you the truth. Hiding never works. Neither does beating around the bush." Toby unbuttoned his coat jacket.

I helped him slide his arm from the sleeve. "No wonder you're hot. You're wearing a suit in June." I scolded him, as if he were my sibling, something I've done pretty much my whole life.

"I had the windows open on the drive out here, so I wasn't soaked until now." He dropped the jacket to a small bunch of bushes, standing tall in his white shirt which seemed pressed with extra layers of starch. The shirt could stand up on its own if he took it off.

Quizzing him, I threw out my words. "So why are you really here?"

"I'm trying to share some insight about Clara and also Gilbert. If you know a little about them, you can console their families better today."

"I'm not sure I'm the right person to comfort them. Gilbert's pa hasn't gotten over the wheel barrel incident from the night Martha ran to his house for help. Which is the same night he shot himself with a ricocheted bullet. Which he blames on me."

"You were a child. I'm sure he's forgiven you. Your offering kindness today would be a good time to reconcile the past."

"I have nothing—"

"Let me remind you how Gilbert served at the church services with our folks at the Bridge. He played his guitar and led our song service most every Saturday. He gave of himself to others."

"He did serve with a kind heart to many."

"And he cut firewood for the homeless during the winter. He was a friend and expected nothing in return."

I choked on the dust swirling beneath my nose. "I never knew he liked our friends at the camps."

Toby swung his jacket in the air. "Oh goodness. Ants. There's ants crawling up the sleeves."

"Give it to me." I pulled the jacket from his grasp, flipped the sleeves inside out and slammed the coat into the bark of the shade tree. "This will get them. They'll fly out or die from the blows."

"It's not a rug. You're not beating out the dust. You'll tear the fabric." He yanked the jacket from me. "Stop tearing up my clothes."

"Sorry, I tried to get the ants off for you. If you get bitten, it's your own fault." I chuckled, noticing a small rip on one sleeve. "Hey, the tear won't show. It's on the inside."

Toby moved his jacket to the hood of his car. "Shall I go on? I hoped to calm you with our chat, but as usual—it goes awry."

"Go on …"

"I remember how Ms. Clara tagged along to sing at the Bridge when she wasn't working on Saturdays."

I countered his remark about her working. "She had Saturdays off. She worked on Sundays but went to Sunday night services."

"She never came to church on Sunday night."

"She did, she told me she went."

"Well, she might have met up with Gilbert. He never came on Sunday night, either."

"I bet they had a secret rendezvous. During the week, Clara loved to sing and belted out those words to 'Amazing Grace' upstairs at her desk. I'm convinced she practiced her bellowing to annoy me. She didn't know her voice grew on me, I wish I'd told her."

"We all have regrets in life."

"She loved the old hymns and she made music bounce with her notes and swirly sounds. I'll miss hearing her sing in my home."

Toby shuffled next to the tree, leaning. "I probably shouldn't tell you this since I counseled them. But they planned to marry."

"I knew it. I told Ernie they were getting married. I didn't know it was true when I said it, though. But for once, my gut was right."

"They were hoping for a fall wedding when it cooled off. And they wanted to marry at the Bridge, so they could be surrounded by the community they love. Since our congregation is family."

"Family? But Clara's daddy would have challenged them on the location. He would have pressed them to have a proper wedding. He wouldn't have approved." I nodded with myself on what I said. "Her daddy was hard on her. He might have run Gilbert off."

"He was strict as they come. He always wanted a boy. But got a girl."

"How do you know?"

"Clara told me in one of our sessions. She also told me, since her ma died a few years ago, he's gotten meaner. She worried he might kick her out of his house if she didn't marry into money. He built her a house next to his, to keep her close but tossed the deed up whenever she failed him."

"No way! He's disgusting. I'll have trouble with speaking kindly to him today."

"People don't always love their children the way they should, as you know yourself—your daddy lost his way, but he had some good moments, too."

"My daddy loved me, but I couldn't fix his brokenness. He drank the whiskey, hoping for life's answers, but the liquor only complicated his life and kept him lost."

"What am I thinking? I'm giving out information which should remain confidential. But I guess, it's fine. They aren't here now. And I won't be officiating their wedding." Toby wiped his brow. "I'm heading to town. The funeral's in an hour. I need to meet the families when they get there. Have you reconsidered? Might you say a kind word?"

"I don't think so. Someone who knew them like you did should be the person to remember them." I fumbled for keys, but they weren't in my pocket, only a hanky and the note. "What have I done with my keys?"

"You had to have them when you drove up." Toby glanced at the ground, stepping off the trail we'd taken to move to the shade.

"Oh no!" I ran to the water, glancing at the glassy lake. "I tossed rocks and yelled and screamed, and I might have thrown a tantrum, letting my anger blow across the water. Do you think I tossed my keys into the water by accident?"

"Surely not." Toby winced.

"It's me you're talking to. I tend to do the opposite of most people, and the wrong things at the worst times. Can you give me a ride into town and drop me off Kings Row Inn? Crush covered the lunch rush for the crew, so they could eat before they shot the next scene. He'll have the other set of keys on his ring. He's in the pickup, and the ring has the extra key. I came here to think on life and now I've gone and delayed you."

"Think? I can't believe I forgotten to give you this. With the funeral, I forgot to give you this note. You remember Junior?"

"Well, sure."

"He rode up on his bike earlier at the church and handed a paper to me. He asked me to give this to you at the funeral. I should give it to you now—though."

As I sat in Toby's car, I unfolded the paper, bending the edges back to look at the note. "It's another clue! Another one! It says, 'never held'. Two notes and they say, 'baby gone, never held'."

Toby went into preaching mode. "Whose baby? And why wasn't he or she held?"

The Rest of the Wrong Clues

The funeral for Gilbert and Clara lasted longer than a swim across a dry desert—and I was confident I lost ten pounds from sweating. A ghastly display of tears poured from the families as if everyone crumpled from the weight of losing Clara and Gilbert. Most people used to make fun of Clara for her snooty ways, but I discovered she tutored children in math. And she volunteered at the orphanage on most Saturdays. Which blew my theory of her meeting Gilbert for romantic interludes.

Gilbert's family took the brunt of disgruntled and cocky words from a group of men who meet for coffee at the cafe. They told of his pranks on them—of the plastic roaches in coffee mugs and the mouse inside glove departments in their vehicles.

With the sun burning like a broiler from an oven, my stomach reeled, gurgling, and my head spun, and standing made me queasy. I had to hold my head in my arms more than once.

The chairs littered the cemetery around the trees and sitting in those metal chairs turned everyone into a wet dishrag. The sun cooked our skin—not much shade in June. My skin stung, as if I'd fallen into a giant frying pan of sorrow.

I listened to the stories of those who paid tribute to Clara and Gilbert, even though some tales sounded puffed up, causing head shakes.

Pastor Toby discovered he wasn't the only person paying a tribute, and his shoulders slumped as he crossed his leg in the chair, off to the side, fiddling with the pages in his Bible. The minutes turned into two hours. Lester shared his brother's love for rock'n roll music, like Elvis, and gave his final words, speaking to the waving paper fans and sweaty faces. His tribute landed like a cheerful goodbye more than a final farewell and the four cousins from Oklahoma shared their summer vacation stories from when they were kids—of swimming at Crystal Springs and swinging from a tall rope. Of how Gilbert hated those fish when they nibbled at the moles on his legs.

All of the Crush Boys came: the triplets, Tripp, Thor, and Thicke. Along with Thomas, Timmons and Tak, and Theodore. They rode up together from Jefferson. I was sad Marion Kane's health didn't allow him to leave the nursing home. The brothers promptly left after the service—however, each one promised to visit Crush and me soon.

Crush hugged them as if they'd never hug again—caught in the sadness of how families don't make time for each other. Until they meet at funerals.

Back at the house, I've let the breeze swoosh through the hallway from the front to the kitchen while I sat in the middle of the house on the staircase. My heart sputtered in the sadness of losing Clara and Gilbert, the nightmare real, the loss unspeakable. The darkness settled in, a sign of another day ending.

My car's in the garage now, even though Crush wasn't thrilled at having Pastor Toby run him to the lake to retrieve it. He's asleep on the sofa—snoring like a walrus caught in a sandstorm. He's worn out from working long shifts, and from my carelessness with my keys.

Archie booked a room at Kings Row Inn, to stay for another week and didn't want to eat up my food—or to keep me from resting. But rest is far from what I need to do. I can't shut off the movie reel inside my head.

Moving from the hallway, my feet heavy like a robot, I marched out the front door, rounded the courthouse, and hiked the four or five blocks to where Mr. Pierce lives—to where the boy with yellow hair resides, too.

Crouching like a criminal, I knelt by the brick wall in front of the two-story brick home on Grand Street. I learned Mr. Pierce's residence sat on this corner lot, thanks to Ernie's ongoing stories in the paper. The picture made the house appear smaller—but this house swallows up half the block.

I rocked side-to-side, listening to the wind, and scuttled to the swing which swayed in the shadows next to the oak tree. Its towering branches hung next to the upstairs windows like arms protecting the home.

The driveway in the rear looped the yard toward the carport. And a small wrought-iron fence added décor to the backyard. But the fence was too low to keep trespassers away and the brick-like gazebo took up the whole corner near the driveway. I wiggled around the yard as if I had permission, knowing most folks were readying for bed—but my night revealed my need for answering the clues, like an article of tomorrow's edition of solving crimes.

I sauntered back to the tree, talking to the bark. "I could climb you and take a peek inside the window and tap on the glass. And see if the boy might talk to me."

Scolding myself for talking to a tree as if it might answer, I whispered, "What are you thinking? Here you are in the dark and in the director's yard. And still climbing trees. As for peeking in the window, you could get arrested for doing such a thing."

Creak. Creak.

A padding noise stomped toward me. "Can I help you, miss? Wait, I've seen you twice now. You climbed the fire escape by Union Station and fell, hitting your head. And you interrupted our wedding scene at the church. Now you're on my property?"

I jogged up to Mr. Director. "I'm here to speak to your son. I believe he's supposed to help me solve the case of the Phantom Killer." I said my words as if everyone says such things. But I knew it came off as not so normal.

Circling the tree, using it to keep a little distance between me and Mr. Director, I almost ran when his face grew firm, when his lips pursed. "Do you realize what you're saying? My son is ten years old. He's not a part of any investigation to solve a murder. We are simply shooting a movie."

"But, you don't understand. The face of the Phantom Killer haunts me." Pausing, I swallowed hard. "I remember bits of his face. Well, mostly his eyes. I fought with him and tumbled from inside the boxcar to the rushing water under the bridge, back in 1946. I couldn't swim, but someone saved my life. I can't remember parts of the night, but I locked eyes with a killer. And now, he's in Texarkana! Or maybe, he's been here all along. I believe he's using your son to reach out to me! He wants to get caught!"

I pulled the cemetery notes from my pocket and the two notes from Junior, passing them from my hand to his fingers. I dropped part of the papers before I could get my final words out, and we both scrambled for them on the ground. "Can I talk to your son?"

"Please, stop shouting." Mr. Director gathered up the papers—placing them in my hand. "You need to leave my property."

"But my name's Annie Grace Raike and I need your help."

The flashing lights made both of us jump, and fear rose up in me. The wind tangled the rope swing around my neck, my throat tightened, and I put my hands to my ears. "No! This can't be happening. You've called the police?" Unraveling, I squirmed away from Mr. Director.

"You need to leave. You're causing a scene. The neighbors are peeking from behind their blinds at you. Two called me to tell me you were out here. You need to be reasonable. Go home and let me make my movie."

I backed up, inching toward the swing, collapsing into the wooden seat like it cradled me from pain. My ears heard the sound of the piano—from somewhere afar, like the pianist jabbed the keys with all ten fingers. "Do you hear the music? I hear it. It's coming from inside your house."

Pushing the swing backwards, I lifted my legs up like a girl might, if she played in this swing. The high pitch of a violin offered a tune, along with the music on the piano. "Do you hear the music? It's haunting!"

Mr. Director squinted his eyes at me, not saying a word.

As the swing went back and forth, I hummed, and I contemplated running since the policeman made his stormy march toward me. Instead, I asked, "Does anyone hear what I'm hearing? The boxcar of confusion is swinging. And I'm a thousand miles from the truth. I'm scattered pieces of me and I'm littering up the tracks. I need to pick up the answers. But I can't get out of this swing."

The officer tracked across the yard, halting in front of me, and the music inside my head stopped. He grabbed the rope on one side of the swing, jerking me to my feet. "Annie Grace, what are you doing here? This is private property."

My insides shook. "Oh, no! What have I done? Where am I? I need to go home. I'm sorry." I galloped closer to Mr. Director, dropping some of the notes.

He gathered them up, holding the papers in front of my nose. "I'll give them to Officer Teacup."

"No, they're mine. I need them for my investigation. Not for his." I peeled the papers from my palms, shoving them into my pocket.

The lights from another car blinded me as I followed Officer Teacup to his patrol car, hoping he'd not arrest me. I whined, "There's my husband. Let me ride home with him. Sometimes my memories bother me in the present."

Crush moved slowly, crawling from the driver's side of the station wagon, as if he wished to hide, to disappear. "Annie Grace, what are you doing? We've got to move on. This craziness must stop."

Kaboom! "Wait, stop her. Mama said I must give her the other three clues." Junior darted with a whiz, the screen door slamming behind him.

My heart raced and I prepared a thousand questions all in two seconds, ready to interrogate him. But he poured out his answers like a ripped sack of potatoes without my saying a word. "Mama said Ms. Clara's funeral happened today. You're the woman she worked for, I've seen you at church. But since you're the crazy woman from the tree—I'm not allowed to talk to you."

"So, everyone does call me crazy?"

"Sometimes they do." Sniffling, he added, "Ms. Clara taught my Sunday school class. She shared her oranges with us, and she loved to sing with all the kids. Two Sundays ago, she gave me an envelope after class, asking if I could keep a secret, which I told her I could."

"Wait? Why would she give it to you?" I countered.

"Because she worked for you. She said you investigate stories even when there's no story." Junior backed up, cocking his head. "She told me to give them to you, Ms. Raike—if something happened to her. I hoped this was all a joke, but now she's gone!"

Officer Teacup and Crush stood on each side of me. And Mr. Director pulled his son to his side. "Junior, what's this about?"

"Daddy, I promised Ms. Clara. I have to give these clues to the investigator lady. We have to let her solve the crime." He turned toward me, "I'm sorry. I like to write stories like my daddy. So, I cut up her phrases and made five notes. Like it was five movie scenes. I was only playing. I had no idea the clues would become evidence."

I sighed as if the truth rested somewhere between the moment Clara wrote the notes to the moment when she took her last breath.

Junior gulped. "I'm sorry. I had my own script for a scary movie with these clues. I was only pretending!"

Mr. Director turned his son around, glaring at him. "Son, what were you thinking?"

I charged at Junior, shoving his father to the side. "So, you have the others?"

"I have them in my pocket with my trusty cassette recorder." He smiled, "I tape all my daddy's directions from the set, but the papers are in my pocket. I'm sure of it."

"Please, give them to me."

He dug in his pocket. "When the phone rang tonight, and the man said he knows who killed those people, I got scared. I almost tossed them in the trash, but maybe Ms. Clara needs to speak to you from her grave. Here, I hold the answer to solving a part of her crime!"

"Son, we're not filming a movie. This is real. Give Annie Grace the notes."

Junior prodded inside his pocket, digging, and he handed me several pieces of paper. His sobs cut the night air as if a broken tune from a piano from way off—along the tracks hitting sour notes.

I clutched the clues in my fist, ready to peek at the words, but I needed to put them in order. "Junior, tell me how they go. They're mixed up. I know the first two. But the last three don't make sense, the way I put them."

Junior recited them in order, without reading the papers. "Clue one says baby gone. Clue two says, never held."

"Go on." I fumbled with the notes.

"Three says, if I'm dead, keep watch. Four says, if Gilbert's dead, keep watch. Five says, there's no doubt, it's Lester who took our lives."

"What in the world does this mean?" I trembled, as if this were a movie, but somehow, I knew the certainty—a killer lurked in Texarkana. Could Lester be a murderer? A prankster, maybe. A sarcastic man, surely. But not a killer. I reread the clues, speaking as if my voice might fade from the horror.

Crush caught me as I staggered and collapsed into his arms. He whispered, "Honey, hold on. Let me take you home."

I puffed long breaths, crying, "Clara knew her life was in danger—and she never told me."

"She probably hoped she was wrong." Crush tried to reassure me, but I was beyond comforting. I repeated the words from the notes under my breath, as I toppled into the front seat of the car.

Before Crush shut the door, Officer Teacup pulled on my door with a yank—opening it wide. "Can I see those clues? This is evidence and Ms. Clara's speaking to us. I need to take those to the station with me."

I tugged on the car door. "No! I'm going home."

Officer Teacup bent over. "I'm pulling rank on you. I need those clues. All of them. They're evidence to a double murder. You can't keep them for yourself."

"What? They're mine. Clara clearly left the notes for me. Don't you get it? For me?"

Crush touched my arm, squeezing somewhat, soothing me, more like a nudge. "Honey, you must give him those papers. Even the ones from the cemetery."

I covered my overall's pocket with my free hand. "No, these were meant for me, too."

Teacup growled, "Don't make me take you in for trespassing, which," he pointed to Mr. Director's house, "Mr. Pierce isn't pressing charges, but I can change his mind."

I shrieked like out-of-tune keys on a piano. "It's not like you'll solve the case. Remember the murders of '46? Nothing came of your investigation even with the help of the Texas Rangers—and a killer got away. I don't need these clues to solve my case!" I tossed the papers to the curb. "I don't need your help to solve the Phantom Killer cold case, either! I'm going to solve both cases before you can file those notes as evidence!"

Shovel the Dirt

"Unlock this door, Annie Grace."

"No! I'm sleeping in my office tonight. I'm going over every newspaper article and every story. There's something in these photographs. I've missed something."

The muffled words of Crush filtered into my room from the other side of my door. "It's not your responsibility to solve an old murder case. They couldn't solve it, and now, too much time has gone by. Or maybe the killer is in prison—the car thief they caught had plenty of opportunity. And the murders did stop after he went to jail. So, let the officers do their own investigation of Clara and Gilbert's case."

"You don't understand. With Ernie writing all those newspaper stories again, it's like the attacks and murders are happening now. Wait! They are!" *Thud.* I had leaned forward, hitting my noggin on the closed door. "I can't ignore what I witnessed in the boxcar any longer. I need to remember the face behind the mask. I pulled it over his head. I had the mask in my hand. Don't you get it? I know his face. But whose face did I see? And why can't I remember?"

I slipped to my knees, falling to the floor like a worm, unable to wiggle free from the past. From the hallway, Crush continued pleading with me, his pushiness shifting with each tick on the clock and he raised his voice. "Annie Grace. Please, open this door. Pastor Toby dropped by."

Wiping my brow, I whined, "Sure, he did. It's ten o'clock at night."

Archie echoed in the hallway with his own words and the conversation grew tense—Crush yelled, his voice cracked, and Archie spoke with a low tone, which caused me to press my ear to the door. "Crush is worried about you. Open this door, honey."

"Go away, Archie. I'm not in the mood for your wisdom or insight. Or for any words from the pastor, either. Unless you're both ready to help me figure out motives and movements of those attached to both crimes."

Archie offered his wisdom. "I'm ready to help you. When the sun goes down, we miss its rays. When the darkness comes, we long for light. When you stare at the past, it keeps you from the present. You're longing for answers and they aren't pasted on the walls inside your office."

Standing, I twisted the lock, opening the door, peeking from my cage of sadness. "Where do I begin to find answers? I'm trapped in this coffin of death. And I am smothering."

Pastor Toby stepped up, taking my hand. "Come sit with us."

Like a puppy following its master, I tagged along with Crush and Archie, and with Pastor Toby, step by step down the stairs. I watched Archie's gray hair bounce and Crush with his red hair, swirled in waves on his head. Their heads bobbed up and down. For now, I'm safe. I'm surrounded by men with wisdom who trusted God, who made me long for the same confidence and strength.

With Pastor Toby next to me, his grasp firm, his way of sharing insight into walking with God came easy for him. But for me, I longed for God to give me such understanding, but I struggled to sense peace. Either way, the three of them are mentors in my life. And they believe in me. Like Marion Kane from Jefferson.

My daddy missed my high school graduation when I surprised everyone and wore a dress. And my daddy missed my wedding, but Marion Kane didn't, he even paid for my ring—so Crush could give me a diamond. Marion Kane's taken care of so many people throughout his life—I would love to be kind like him. He saved me from me—in Jefferson the year after my grandma died, the year after the Phantom Killer attacked and murdered those people. He became my father figure—more like a grandpa and father all in one.

My fingers touched the small diamond on my wedding ring, and a memory of when Crush asked me to marry him jumped into my mind. Of how he proposed on the tracks by the bayou in Jefferson in the rain when we were seniors in high school. We had strolled along the railroad tracks, when lightning struck a tree near us, splitting the bark apart. And it became two trees. One side of the tree died. The other flourished.

So I made Crush wait twelve years before saying yes to his proposal. The dead tree represented me, and what I'd bring to a marriage. I believed Crush would flourish without me—but over the years, he convinced me, he loved me more than anything with his constant attention and affection. And hounding!

He never left me alone and followed me to Texarkana when I left Jefferson after high school—where I worked at Guy's Orange Stand as a car hop. Crush loved to bake and cook, so he took a job flipping Texas-sized burgers on giant buns. One time, another cook took a fancy to me, and Crush pulled a pocket knife on the guy—and told him we were dating. He told the other man I belonged to him.

I shouted at Crush in front of the customers who sipped on their orange drinks, the ones with the recipe using fresh oranges and another secret ingredient. I quit my job right there on the spot and stormed to my apartment. But the next day, I begged the manager for my job, which he gave me back. I learned a great lesson, do not quit a job with the rent due.

Crush stalked me forever, and I fell in love—no one ever cared for me like he has. And after sitting in church services behind me on a million Sundays, Crush captured bits of my heart—and I remember how he winked at me the first day he strolled in the burger joint as if to say—you're mine. He loved to flirt with me, something he had done since we were teens. So, I called him Winky under my breath for months before telling him I gave him a nickname.

As for his singing during worship, he belted out horrible notes and ruined the lyrics of those hymns. One Sunday, I caught him at the sanctuary door and invited him to sit with me, on the same row, but with one request. He couldn't sing, he was required to hum. Humming became his new way of singing—in the kitchen, at breakfast, in the yard, or whenever he fished.

His humming made me feel alive on the inside. And I hummed, too. I suppose we wrote the lyrics to our own song, as we danced toward marriage. My love grew. And I finally said yes to his marriage proposal.

A hand went in front of my face. "Hello, where are you?" Crush waved his fingers in front of my eyes. "You've stopped moving, frozen on the bottom of the stairs and you smiled, and your eyes watched something in another place. Was it a good memory?"

"Yes, I remembered how I used to call you Winky—for flirting with me. Don't you remember how you hummed more when we were younger, too?"

Crush grinned. "I'm still your Winky, and I still hum. You're busy with your life and miss most of my humming—when you're preoccupied." He pursed his lips, squeaking a hum to a song with a catchy tune.

"What song are you singing?"

"It's the song I drove you crazy with in those early years. It's by Elvis Presley. Remember, how I sang this to you when you brought me my morning coffee, when we first got married. It's 'Are You Lonesome Tonight?'"

"Oh, Crush, I've forgotten how much I love that song. And I love you, Crush. You're my Elvis!"

Crush touched my nose with his finger. "I love seeing you smile. You stole my heart when we first met, even though you were only twelve. I knew you were going to be my wife."

"No way! You didn't like me one bit. You were too busy being a bratty teenager."

"Taking care of my brothers took most of my time. As for you—you were mouthy, brazen, and wild. You needed some taming."

"Taming? And how's my taming going?"

"Some days are better than others."

Pastor Toby interrupted us. "Archie's made a fresh pot of coffee. It's rather late for a counseling session, but I have the time—as you both have some unresolved issues."

Together, we said, "We do not."

I smiled again, as did Crush. He took my hand in his, and we agreed to behave. I turned to Crush. "Come on, Winky. Let's drink some coffee."

**

After three cups and plenty of caffeine, I'll stay up half the night, and now Pastor Toby and Archie are chatting about how they plan to go watch the filming tomorrow since Mr. Pierce is taping the first attack scene.

I perked up, like coffee in a percolator, twisting and bouncing and pacing. "Do you mind? You men bring me in here for coffee and we've taken a road trip with our memories of how I met Toby and the Crush Boys at the Bayou, how we all slept in the empty house next to Marion Kane's home. Except Toby used the house to practice his preaching. Crush bragged about all the boys he shooed away from asking me out in high school, which I think is a lie. And now, we're back to talking about murder. Can't we spend one second without going full circle?"

Archie apologized. "We start with regular talk, but you take us to the path of broken chapter, to topics you're caught inside with tangled rope around your heart. We do our best to keep you from taking the wrong road in your conversations, but you're consumed, and you have a limited reservoir of subjects to discuss."

Crush stirred in the rocker, half asleep. "What's wrong? What now?"

"Sorry to bother you three with my life and my problems." I stormed to the hallway, prancing to the back, to the kitchen, circling the dining table, leaving the long hallway, and wandering to the front door. I rubbed my hands together, knowing I flip personalities faster than pancakes on a griddle. I can't control myself, I'm a wreck.

I peered through the glass, thankful we had no guard to keep watch. Crush convinced Officer Teacup to keep the sleepy officer away, since he dozed off on the job.

Twisting the handle, I pushed the screen door open, glancing back to the front room, and not one of those brave men came for me. They were back to their bragging, their tales, and upping each other with another grand story from their youth. The caffeine wound them up, except for Crush who can sleep anytime and anywhere. Pastor Toby tried to impress the aging Archie, who had a knack for listening, and he can engage, even when stories are boring.

The midnight sky appeared like an upside-down lake full of droopy stars. Dark. Glassy. Like a mirror. Except for the full moon. I sat on the porch steps between the columns. Strong and sturdy. Like the men inside who love me. Pastor Toby cares for my spiritual needs. My husband cares for my physical and spiritual. And Archie has a way of making my heart long for greatness.

Ha-ha! Ha-ha!

Their laughter trickled from inside and would last into the wee hours of the night, long enough for me to check on my tree—where the photographs live. The sun may have baked them by now, and faded the black and whites, along with the newspaper photos. The oven-like temperatures weathered me, and the memories of my life were scorched, for sure. I should clear the branches of the photos before they litter the street with broken dreams of those who've died. Or those who've left me. Or of those who've stopped talking to me.

I approached the corner, beyond the side of the school, and a huffing sound like someone out of breath grew louder.

Huff-hee. Huff-hee.

The sound intensified, like a mixer-blade from the kitchen, a tangled gruff sound coming from a person's throat.

Huff-hee. Huff-hee.

I bolted up the tree, gripping the branches as if they were arms rescuing me. Holding my breath, my nose tingled, and fear seeped into my veins. I exhaled and held my breath again.

Squinting, I tried to see if angels were flying above the Catholic Church, and if they might find themselves dispatched to save me. Or maybe, up a block, Beech Street Baptist Church might have some late-night angels to send my way.

I focused on the noise, peering into the shaded area across the street at Taddy's apartment, where he lived when we were kids—where he lives now. We used to climb trees together.

But I never played with Taddy again, not after his being attacked in Millerton, Oklahoma. The ordeal left him traumatized after his mama, Priscilla, nearly died on the trip. When you're eleven and trauma happens, it's hard to recover. The scars left Taddy afraid, too. I should know, I'm not quite over my tragedies even now.

The huffing sound evaporated, and I waited to make sure someone wasn't looking for me. Or after me. I'm paranoid right now. I better head home before I'm missed.

My mind wandered, taking me to how Taddy and I never worked on becoming friends again after he moved to Jefferson. He excelled though, and became valedictorian of our high school class. After his college days in Marshall, Texas, he accepted a position at Texarkana College. He teaches English, but I never see him unless he comes to church, which isn't often. Not because he's absent, but because I am. He wears thick glasses, and his gait's purposed with short steps. He remembers everything, and his brain is like a photograph, snapping images. He has the best memory.

Huff-hee. Huff-hee.

The breathing returned, but this time—I knew the face in the shadow when it ambled into the street light. I shouted, "Lester, what are you doing out this late?" My insides gagged, as I digested the ugliness of what Clara's note implied, wondering if she could be right.

He halted his jogging, stumbling over his sneakers. "I could ask you the same thing. You scared me to death."

"What are you doing? You're breathing as if you're exhausted."

"I've finished my three miles and I'm winding down." He wiped the sweat from his chin on the collar of his shirt.

"So, do you run all the time? I've never noticed you coming downtown to run."

"I run late at night in the summer. It's too hot during the day. I like to keep in shape. I've been a runner for all my life. I made the track team back in the day and running helps me work through things too—so I can think."

"But running at midnight? It's not safe." My quizzing continued as I analyzed Lester.

"You're one to talk. Folks are saying you've lost it, especially now—with Clara and my brother gone. They think it's the final straw for your sanity." Lester offered less than kind answers, his tone laced with bitterness and with fighting words.

I accepted the challenge, tossing my ugly responses at him. "I'm not insane. I've struggled with living up to what most of you call normal. I do overreact. You have no idea who I am, or what I've gone through."

"Your life entertains the people in town, and your normal speaks anything but normal. Even Clara talked about you and how you treated her. She used to tell me how you picked on her. How you used your sarcasm to make digs at her for being so pretty. You were jealous because Clara held the corner on classy. She possessed everything you lack, by the way. And now she's gone."

"So because I'm plain-looking, I'm not worth anything?"

"You said it. Not me." Lester smirked. "Clara had the prettiest curls and a cute pudgy nose. And the way her dresses swayed when she walked caused men to adore her."

Shaking my head, I argued, "Are you serious? A person's value begins on the inside—not in the clothes they wear." My words stung since I didn't offer Clara much in the way of friendship and judged her myself.

I finished my lecture to Lester. "Now she's dead, and all you can talk about is her beauty? What is wrong with you? You never were a compassionate person. You are the most superficial man. You are worse now—than when we were kids. I've never liked you, and you've confirmed why I hold this opinion of you."

We launched our torpedoes at each other as if we were back on the playground in the fourth-grade slinging mud and our fists. I launched my pain at Lester, the need to injure greater than my need to be kind. Since we had no answers to why Clara and Gilbert were murdered, except for the notes, I hoped to trip up Lester's answers.

One second, I attacked Lester and the next moment, I remembered how he'd lost his brother. Torn between accusing him and being kind, I chose to argue with Lester, to see if he said something incriminating.

I spouted out another round of wounded-hate. "It sounds like you were attracted to Clara." Taunting him, I asked, "You weren't jealous, were you?"

Tying his shoe, Lester bolted closer to me, his lean and slender body a sign of his training, and he gave me a forever-goodbye glare. "You, my friend, aren't worth talking to anymore. Why I bother to speak to a no-good crazy woman like you, I'll never know."

"Don't worry. I have nothing more to say to you, either. You may have some folks snowed, but your secrets will be found out. I know something about you, Lester."

"What do you know? Nothing, I'm sure."

"I know Clara was afraid of you." I covered my mouth, swallowing the rest of my accusations.

"Seriously? Me? You have no clue. And don't worry. I'm leaving town soon. There's nothing here for me. I'm working a dead-end job at a cemetery. Someone else will have to keep the place mowed and clean and taken care of—but it won't be me."

"I'd let someone know where you go. The police may need to talk to you."

"Crazy woman. Go home. You may need to weep before the night's over. The loss you feel isn't anything compared to how it feels to lose your brother to the girl—"

My hand went to my mouth, but the foul came out. "Do you mean the girl of your dreams? Is that what you were going to say? Were you in love with Clara?"

"Never mind. You bring out the worst in me."

I egged him on. "So, you and your brother both loved the same woman?"

"Get out of my way." Lester pushed me aside, almost like he could have pounded me and left me for ashes on the ground. He bolted like lightning into the darkness.

"Wait!" I jogged to catch up, but Lester shot up the hill and around the corner, and the smell of whiskey in the air contradicted his leading a healthy lifestyle.

I stared into the black sky, shuffling home. "Lord, what is wrong with me? Pastor Toby tells me that out of the abundance of my heart I speak. Can you please find me a new heart? This one needs so much work. I have no right to accuse Lester of any crimes? But he did smell like—"

I slumped, carrying the weight of regret with each step, playing back the words on the note from Junior, clues to something—and nothing—and everything.

A glare up ahead made me stop. "What's with the flashing lights? What are the police doing at my house? What is going on?"

Too Long, Too Much

As I charged, the trees surrounding the courthouse leaned in towards me, almost as if the branches poked fun at me for even thinking of becoming an investigator. The beads of water on my hands and the river of sweat on my back dripped like drops of fear. "What is it now?"

My eyes burned and I tried to focus, but the blur of people running, sent me storming ahead. My tears let loose, soaking my face, as I drowned in worry. Each jog sent a pounding to my heart. Why can't I have a season without death, or pain, or sorrow? I wanted to go back in time, so I could offer Clara my friendship. I longed for another chance to forgive Gilbert for his pranks and my distrust of him. I wished for the day when I could be a loving wife, to a day with my own children.

My feet thrashed on the sidewalk, and my heart drummed with booms from the forest where the death-lion waits to prowl, to consume. Time has stolen so much from my life. I must not let the past outrun me. I must persevere. I must run my race. I must finish well.

I've survived Taddy sneezing when we first witnessed the horrible scenes on his birthday when he turned ten. I've survived witnessing a crime scene where two people were murdered, when they were left outside the café on the muddy road when Grandma and I went for breakfast. I've survived going back for my shoes at Spring Lake Park when a masked man hovered across the lake. And I've survived going to the Stamps farm to find my daddy's treasure when a chicken hawk nearly killed me. I'm still alive!

Halting across the street in front of my house, shouting, "I can survive! With God, I can go forward."

The next few steps toward the front door played out in slow motion. Fast sounds and slow movement. Loud talking. And then whispers. Officers on my porch. Two police cars by the side of the house.

Pausing, I caught a glimpse of Crush through the front door and his presence caused my faith in new tomorrows to rise up in me. I reassured myself, "He's not hurt. Nothing has happened to him." I hurried to him. "Honey, if it's me you're looking for, I'm right here! I didn't mean to scare you."

I moved up the steps, hurrying along the walk to the stairs between the columns—to hug my husband on our porch. He raised his hand like a school-crossing guard. "Stay right there! Don't come any closer."

"What? Why not?" I stopped in my tracks, my eyes growing larger as if big eyes helped me see in the dark.

"There's a misunderstanding. You need to cooperate with the police. You must explain the reason—"

Shaking my head, I cut him off. "The reason for what?"

Officer Teacup marched up to me. "We received a call. It came in after your little incident on Grand Avenue. It appears we have a witness of someone who claims you threw something in the lake before the funeral today. So, why were you at the lake? Were you disposing of something you may have left behind?"

"Left behind? Are you serious? I can account for my time. Crush can vouch for me. I have nothing to hide." I waved my arms like I might form a fist with both hands.

Crush put his hand on my shoulder. "Honey, they want to talk to you."

I screamed, "Are you kidding? It's after midnight. This could wait. I live right here, and I'm not going anywhere." I pointed to the police cars. "And are those flashing lights necessary? You're making a scene and giving my neighbors more to say over coffee in the morning."

Officer Sleepy coughed, "I'll turn them off."

Teacup stroked the pistol on his waist. "Let's go inside."

Crush gave me a gentle shove. "Honey, where have you been for the past hour?"

Teacup interjected, "See! Your husband doesn't know where you were tonight. Let alone during the day. I'd say he has trouble keeping up with you."

Bolting inside, I trembled at how fast a truth can become a lie. "Honey, help me. I'm not responsible for killing Clara or Gilbert. You know that!"

Crush embraced me. "Come inside. We'll sit."

"Sit? That's your answer. You want me to sit down?" My head spun, and I heard voices talking to my soul. They told me I'm not a person anyone should believe. Another voice countered the lie and said I'm strong. Then to quiet the voices down, I screamed, "I'm a force to deal with, and a cop who can't catch a killer who murdered five people and attacked three others from thirty years ago—he won't stop me from living. This is crazy. I'm not the one who needs a talking to."

The commotion inside the house lessened, as I sat with my lips pursed, and my arms folded. My heart dropped to my stomach, and the heaviness of the night couldn't end fast enough. My nose dripped like a broken faucet from the crying, and layers of snot coated my lips. But I didn't care.

I disappeared to the place where I ignore those around me—to a place where imaginary things seem real. Like my dream from the other night, where I floated to a world full of laughter and hope. To where children played. To where coffee tasted like chocolate. To where everyone lived in peace.

But the reality of my pretend world turned cold and dark, even though I sensed a fire burning inside my belly—a spark of resilience which had been tucked away. I'm no killer. I can solve both of these cases—if the police will leave me alone. But right now, I'm shackled to this room with invisible chains on my ankles—along with the continued glare from Officer Teacup. He's asked me a hundred questions and I've grunted at him, offering him my evil eye stare to counter his tired gaze.

I wanted to go to bed, so I could wake up and find out this night never happened—that it was one of my nightmares. Not only has the face behind the mask taken over my life, but now someone has spread a lie about me. And the police think I'm a murderer. How could anyone come to such a conclusion?

The fight for hope eluded me. It's like winter dropped into Texarkana in June. I can't move. I can't wiggle. And this isn't a dream. I jumped to my feet. "Where's Crush? Let me speak to my husband."

Officer Teacup sat back, calling, "She wants you, Mr. Raike."

Crush slipped into the room from across the hall. "Honey, talk to the officer so we can go to bed."

I leaned close to his ear, whispering, "I had a flashback. I keep seeing the eyes!"

"You say this when you get stressed and exhausted. And you always forget what you see. So, before you say a word, let's get some rest." He turned to Teacup. "Can we come by tomorrow and let her visit with you? I'm sure she has nothing more to add, but we'll be happy to help."

Officer Teacup sighed, "Have her at the station by ten."

The blur of uniforms left, and I hovered near the fireplace. I lost myself to the memory, the one fresh in my mind. To the face of the person who dropped me from the boxcar. And just like that, the flashback came and went—like it's done before. I regretted saying a word to Crush—wishing I could take back my untimely announcement. Wishing I could make lives come back from the grave.

I'm tired of running from this man in nightmare after nightmare since he's trapped inside my head. His eyes appear one way on certain nights when I sleep—like in the murder at Spring Lake Park. And then I see another set of eyes in the boxcar. I have no idea if he's dead or asleep in a bed—or somewhere in town. But I hold the key. I hold the truth deep within my soul. I've taken the pain and the hurt—and allowed the killer to chase me and haunt me for most of my life. He's ruined my nights and most of my days!

On some nights, when my head hits the pillow, the nightmare morphs, and I try to escape from two Phantom Killers. One reaches for me before I fall from the boxcar, while the other peers at me with eyes like lightning bolts. And I always jerk away, sweating!

Screaming, I came back to myself. "I want to live. I want to change. I want to believe, that I can believe. If I build the wall high enough around my heart, I could keep the killer away. Brick by brick though, I find myself trapped. I've become a shadow, who never truly lives. A ghost with insomnia."

Officer Teacup rushed into the room. "Annie Grace, tell me what you know. Why are you having all this anxiety if you're innocent?"

"I thought you left."

"I came back for my keys. I left them on the piano."

I struggled to stand. "I have anxiety because of the craziness surrounding me. And by the way, I'm innocent. I would never murder anyone. I tossed rocks into the lake and talked to God. I accidently threw my keys into the lake, too. I had nothing else to toss. See, you left your keys. It happens!"

"We'll talk more tomorrow. We are combing the bottom of the lake to see what we might find."

Pam Kumpe

Clues from Above

I retrieved my Bible from the office floor after bumping it from the shelf—knowing I should open the pages more often. I do listen to Pastor Toby's sermons, unless I'm grimacing at the ladies in the second pew who twist their heads and whisper about me during service. It's not like I don't carry my Bible to church—but I'm not in the habit of soaking up what it says, unlike Crush. He loves reading verses to himself and to me.

I flipped the pages, digging for a scripture and crossed my legs on the floor. "Aha! This verse reminds me not to grow weary while doing good."

A call from Crush drifted upstairs. "Annie Grace, we must leave now. I promised Officer Teacup you'd visit with him this morning."

I stretched my neck toward the hallway as if my voice might travel faster along the stairs. "I'll be there in a minute. I'm trying to find Clara's manuscript. I placed it here myself the other day. Now I can't find it." I stood and touched the top of her desk as if the papers might magically appear.

"I'll pull the truck around front. You have five minutes."

"I'll be there in a second. I need some evidence for the case." I covered my mouth, hoping my voice faded before Crush heard me. I placed my Bible on the desk—and the pages flipped with a ripple as dozens of verses waved at me.

I touched the opened page and glanced at the highlighted words, those pointing to the possible in the impossible. "God, help me trust you with the impossible Officer Teacup." I shook my head, knowing God rolled His eyes at my request. So I recited a better phrase than picking on an officer of the law. "With God all things are possible."

Ring. Ring. Ring.

I jumped to the other end of Clara's desk, picking up the receiver. "Hello."

Echoes of silence traveled through the phone and the person on the line snorted.

I repeated my answer. "Hello, who's there?"

The female spoke, giving me instructions. "I have clues for you."

"What? What is this about?"

"I have the clues, and I know the name of the Phantom Killer. I've heard this case is high on your list to solve, and we must share our family secret with you. It's actually a part of your secret, too."

"My secret?"

"Yes, my husband called Ms. Clara and he planted the riddles for you at the cemetery. It may have seemed strange, but we wanted to stay out of the spotlight. So, please return to the set when they resume their filming. I'll be there soon, when I know it's safe. You'll know me by my son. He has yellow hair. He's two."

"So the child with blond hair is *your* boy? But he's a toddler?"

The woman on the line rattled off the instructions as if I could swallow them whole. "You'll find peace, and we'll find peace if you have the evidence. Your heart is bruised and bleeds of sadness. This information may heal you from the ashes of your childhood. And it may heal our family, too."

Click.

"Hello, don't hang up. No! You can't hang up!" I tumbled like a weed, sorting through the clues caught in my head, those trapped in my throat, those gagging me. I pounded the receiver on the desk. "Who is this couple who can help me solve the case of the Phantom Killer? But what about Clara and Gilbert?

Clara gave clues to the actor boy, about her safety and of Gilbert—and about a baby who's gone. I'm so confused."

Crush touched my arm. "What is wrong with you? I'm confused, too." Crush answered my one-sided conversation. "I've called and called and called for you! We're late. Do you understand? This is not going to look good. We can't even arrive at the police station on time." Crush stopped yelling and took the phone from my hand. "And who have you been talking to?"

"No one. I lost my temper with everything going on, and beat the phone on the desk. I do hit stuff when things fall in around me. You know that." I sighed, struggling to keep the latest bit of information tucked inside. The clue burned in my stomach—all the way to my lips, but I kept it from sneaking out. "I'm ready. I can't find Clara's manuscript though. I must have hidden it from myself."

Crush picked up my Bible, holding the book to his chest. "Annie Grace, you may feel afflicted, but remember, with God you are not crushed. I'm perplexed, as I know you are, but I pray we are not driven to despair. You may feel the ladies in town persecute you, but don't be struck down. Remember, with God, you are not destroyed. I do pray you know this."

I embraced Crush, as I tried to believe God wouldn't let this chapter in my life destroy me.

**

"Annie Grace, this isn't going well." Officer Teacup slammed his fist on the table in the small room at the station.

I flinched, clamping my folded hands tighter. "Are you charging me with anything? The walls in this room are closing in around me, and you're drilling me. I want my husband in here with me."

"He's outside waiting. He's not leaving. We're only talking. I'm trying to figure out why you would receive cryptic notes from Clara? Why there's mention of a baby? Why you have a riddle about a boy with yellow hair? But what I don't get is why you are the person to solve the Phantom Killer case?"

"You've asked me these same questions as if you think I'll budge or share what I know. I only know I didn't kill Clara or Gilbert. I've told you. I lost my keys there. We're done here. I can't help you. You're asking your questions to the wrong person." I flared my nostrils, to get a good breath. "Besides, you aren't terribly good at what you do for a living anyway."

"Some criminals get away. But not all of them." Teacup rose to his feet, moved to the door and called to Mr. Sleepy Officer, the man in a uniform who needed to retire—whose bushy eyebrows grew like weeds, whose wrinkles cut into his face like small rivers. "Bring it to her. Show Annie Grace what we found in the lake this morning tucked under a big rock at the water's edge."

The tall, unsteady cop carried the item and placed it on the table. A rusty handgun slid inside the plastic bag.

I bolted from my seat. "I have no idea why you found a gun. I had rocks, I'm telling you." I charged for the door, running from the room, crashing into Crush. "Honey, what is happening? I never hurt Clara or Gilbert. Now they're showing me a gun. Who is this person who said I tossed something into the lake? I'd like to know why this reliable witness is hiding. I haven't broken any laws. I've never so much as gotten a speeding ticket."

Crush soothed me, "Stop yelling. This is a good moment to gather yourself, to use your inside voice. To remain calm."

"Calm? Are you kidding? No one is accusing you of murder!" I pushed Crush away. "Please, I need you to stand with me, but don't patronize me."

"No one is accusing you, either. They have a witness. When there's a witness, it must be checked out. I'm sure there's a reasonable explanation." Crush cradled my head against his chest, but my pulling away made it hard for him to hold me.

I backed up, inching towards the front door of the police station. I slid my shoes across the tile, like a roller skater doing a trick and going backwards, but I kept talking, fast and erratic as I shouted at Crush. "Reasonable? It's me, the crazy-tree-climber you're talking to. I'm the never-going-to-be-an-investigator woman who never gets hired."

"Calm down. You're yelling. No need to raise your voice."

"What? I yell with the best of them. Because I'm the wife who argues with the ladies in church. I'm the woman who shouts at the produce man about the fact his scales are off—and how the grocer charges too much for his bananas. I'm the woman nobody asks for lunch. If I invite the other wives to our home, they won't come. They all have excuses! I'm the horrible-not-normal woman!"

"I know you didn't murder anyone. I know your heart." Crush inched toward me.

I found myself beside the double glass doors which led to the street, and I kept my eyes on Officer Teacup and Sleepy Officer who were hunched behind Crush. He kept waving them off from pursuing me. "I'll get her calm. I'll bring her back to the room. I'll sit with her."

I shouted, "No more sitting. And no more talking."

Crush looked at me, holding my hand. "Come back inside and let's work this out."

I whispered in his ear. "I can't, honey. They're going to lock me up."

"No, the officers are here to gather information."

"I'm sorry, honey. I can't stay." I charged out the door, rounded the corner, and ran smack dab into a fire truck in the driveway at the fire station. I assumed someone followed me, and climbed to the top, became a pancake, burning my face on the metal and wishing to evaporate.

Officer Teacup drove by in the patrol car, followed by Crush in our pickup—I dashed from the firetruck, headed toward the tracks, racing to Hobo Jungle. To a place where I'm welcome. To where I can drink coffee steamed through a sock. Where I have a friend whom I need to ask forgiveness from, so she'll let me stay with her to keep away from—the Texarkana police. She'll help me figure out what's happening and keep me safe!

The camps are my second home—away from home, where Crush has often hunted for me and brought me back to the Ahern House. He's uncertain around my friends but is always kind to them. He knows I fit in there, when normal eludes me. Since this world is comfortable to me.

While here, I must organize myself and get a plan. Someone is making it appear as though I'm involved in the death of Clara and Gilbert. I must also find a way to find the toddler with the yellow hair, whose mama and daddy know secrets they must share. They might know more about the Phantom Killer than anyone—more than the cops or journalists, or even me—if they're telling the truth!

Pam Kumpe

From PF Flyers to Keds

I shoved the shrubs out of my way, my breathing fast and heavy, exhausted from dashing down the tracks and up the trails. I've ducked beneath a set of boxcars, and crossed the creek, and since I'm not under arrest—I'm not evading anyone. Am I? I coughed and slobbered, realizing my body is older and not as limber as when I ran these trails at ten. When I come to see River, I'm not galloping like an old mare. Or sweating like one, either.

My goodness, this trail has become an obstacle course. I'm sure Ed and River are grateful for the weeds and the snakes, since it keeps onlookers away.

The limbs poked at me, and the path narrowed. For a stray visitor, the trail would appear unused, which is a good thing as it would keep trespassers away. I pounced like a cat, wiggled between the bushes, and charged ahead to River's campsite, to her spot next to the creek. Her tent isn't much of a real tent; it's more like scraps of a covering with a tarp over it.

Her place is tucked behind a band of monster weeds, overgrown like a fence of poison ivy and other itchy leaves. Her hermit lifestyle is safe from the rest of the world, although she occasionally ventures out, collecting cigarette butts and walking to the soup kitchen.

She used to eat with me on Tuesdays until last month. We argued, not on a Tuesday, but on a Sunday—when she attended church in her rugged clothes, surrounded by women in sun dresses. Who acted as if they'd never seen River before, but they have—many times on the sidewalks downtown. Only to them, she's always appeared like a dirty rag, unkempt and not worth their time.

I stopped to catch my breath, wishing for water, as I hadn't swallowed anything—except bugs and dirt. "River, are you home? It's me, your friend." I called to alert her of my arrival, but I'd forgotten how far back the tent nestled under the trees, and how far I'd walked. The trail twisted in a zigzag, and she lived somewhere between the last tree at the end of the row of bushes, and at the bend up ahead.

I hoped she'd forgiven me, but at our last meeting the ugly words and screaming overshadowed our reasoning. However, I must disappear with her for a day or two—or until I answer the questions others are throwing at me, since they are pointing fingers at the wrong person. Which is me!

Sluck-ska-sluck.

"What in the world? What is on the bottom of my shoe? *Ugh!* River, is this pile from your dog?" I shouted with an annoyed tone toward the secret camp, confident her ears could hear me. "Your dog, Flashlight, has left his mark."

An angry tone rose up like fire from a pit of smoldering ashes. "Who's there? You're not welcome here. I have my dirt and my dog. I can talk to Ed, but I don't need you. You've stopped coming to see me. So, you're not my friend." The rough voice of my once-best-grown-up friend coughed with a grit of firmness. "A true friend would have stuck up for me."

"I am your friend. You're the one who stopped talking to me. You ran off and wouldn't let me explain." I pushed myself between the zig and the zag of the underbrush. "Can I come in? I need your help."

"No, go away. You have a life over on Laurel Street. It doesn't include me. I don't fit in your world."

"I don't fit in my world, either." I peeked around the dead bushes, where two leaves hung on.

River shouted, "Go home. I haven't forgiven you for what you did to me. You made me look stupid. You made me look like you own me. Like I wasn't a person."

I gazed at my friend, a thin woman of thirty, whose life has taken her on too many boxcar rides with her older brother. She looked ten years older, more like my age. She'd like to forget her past too, as I would—we had so much in common.

I used my soft voice. "I'm sorry. I didn't mean for you to get embarrassed at church. Ernie manipulated you. He does trick people, so he can write about them, especially when he's excited about a project. He hoped to write a story about you, about your riding the rail. And how it's the 70s, and you have lived the dangerous life—for a woman."

River growled, "Whatever! It's more dangerous to live in your world—most of the time."

I continued, "It is right now. That's for sure."

"Why, what's going on?"

"I'm in trouble with the police." I paused. "But I want you to know when you joined me for church that Sunday, I didn't give Ernie permission to invade your privacy. I promise, I never told him anything. He learned all about you from Clara. She's spent so much time with me, working for me—and she's asked questions about living and riding the rail. But I always suspected she investigated our friendship with another motive."

"She isn't as bad as you say. She gave me a ride after church, when she came upon me. After I bolted from the sanctuary."

I covered my mouth. "She had her kind moments. But I'm sure she was jealous. I'm sure of it. She didn't like our being friends. She told Ernie all about you. I never had a hand in exploiting you. I promise. And now she's dead!"

"What? She's dead?"

"Yes, she was murdered. I should have included her when you came for our secret lunches at the house on Tuesdays, when Crush worked. Now she's gone—and will never eat with us—ever!"

"Are you telling me the truth? Clara's dead?"

I parted the branches like a swinging door and shuffled up to my weathered friend. She leaned on the tree in her blue jeans and navy shirt, which hung loose. Her boney arms a sign she's not eating enough. She kicked at the dirt with one of her dingy tennis shoes, which used to be white.

I moved closer. "Yes, she's gone." I glanced up and down. "You're looking thin. You need to eat."

"I'm eating at the soup kitchen, but it doesn't taste like your food. Or I should say, the leftovers from Crush cooking for you. I do miss the extra you always sent with me."

"He is a great cook. And you are always welcome at my home. You don't have to stay away."

"I do better when I'm away."

"But I need you. I can't believe I've let a month go by, waiting for you to knock on the back door. But we're both a little hardheaded."

"We do argue like sisters."

I grabbed her hand. "I'm sorry. I do think of you as my sister. I can't believe I let this go on—and didn't come after you."

"But what happened to Clara?"

"It's horrible. These last few days are a blur of death and accusations. And of clues. And I'm in a bit of a mess right now."

"Did you make Crush mad again? Does he think you're meddling in the case?"

I sat on the wooden chair next to the tent. "Whoa! This chair is wobbly." I steadied myself. "River, it's worse than anyone getting angry with me. I can't believe I'm saying this, but I have the clues to who killed her, or I did have—but Officer Teacup took them."

River plunged to her knees, her stringy brown hair like spaghetti, and she rocked. "No! Tell me what happened. When? How? You're talking in riddles."

For the next hour, I blurted out the horror of my life and the murders. I shared how there's two cases to investigate now. One in the present. One from the past. I let River know that part of the clues mixed me up, while some information filtered through my brain with clarity. I poured out every detail as my friend listened, while she cradled herself on her heels like she does when she's scared or nervous.

I patted her on the shoulder. "You will let me stay, won't you? I'm being investigated by Officer Teacup and I think he believes I had something to do with killing Clara and Gilbert."

"Gilbert? You left out the part about his dying. What are you saying?"

I rattled off more clues. "I'm sorry. He was shot, too. And yes, he dated Clara, and they were getting married in the fall. Pastor Toby counseled them, but they kept it a secret. Her father's a tyrant."

"Where did it happen?"

"At the lake on a dirt road. I went there to think about my tribute to Clara before the funeral, hoping I could come up with something nice to say. And I threw rock after rock, after rock into the lake! I was furious at the killer for taking their lives!" I screamed so loud, the birds fluttered from the trees.

River sniffled, pausing in between rocking forward and sitting back on her heels. "I'll miss his singing at our services by the creek. He strummed the guitar like an angel, even if his brother cackled at his gift for music."

"Lester did pick on Gilbert. He used to bully him in school, too. Even though I only went to school with them for a short time. Lester was a year older than me, I think. But Gilbert was like two grades below me." I brushed my bangs from my eyes. "Time sure gets away. One minute you're five. The next you're in school. And next, you find yourself grown. And being accused of murder."

"And the next minute, you're dodging the fists of a group of angry drunk men who let the bottle tell them how to treat a woman." River added her story to mine.

"I'm sorry I haven't been a better friend, and for how Ernie treated you at church. If it's any consolation, he didn't write the story. Someone called the paper and mentioned he dated this homeless woman—the one he planned to write his unbiased story on. Seems he had a conflict of interest."

"Oh my! Did you call them?"

"I may have. I can use my Tin Can Mahlee voice when needed."

"You've told me about her. She was a tough one, huh?"

"Tough is putting it mildly. She towered over most men, even though she rocked and cried a lot, too."

River folded her arms. "I cry more than I should, and I do rock."

"You could be a mini-Tin-Can Mahlee, if you weren't called River."

River laughed, holding her stomach. "My brother gave me my nickname when I floated the river to get away from those men. I can swim like a fish."

"I can't swim at all. Never have. Never will."

River stood, turning toward the trail. "You didn't see my dog, did you?"

"No, but she's close. I stepped in her ..."

Sorry. It is her woods." River hooted for her dog. "Here, girl! Come on. We've got company!"

I peered at the near-dry creek. "How long has she been gone?"

"I haven't seen her since this morning. She wanders off sometimes. She'll be back."

"So, can I stay?" Not waiting for her confirmation, I moved into my let-me-change-my-look mode. "I'm going to need to swap clothes with you. And do you have any scissors? I need to cut my hair off short, like a boy. And a cap. I need a baseball cap to wear."

"I guess you want me to wear your overalls, don't you?"

"Unless you have more clothes. Last I checked, you wear the same ones, rinse them in the creek and you let them dry while you parade around in your ..."

"Excuse me. Do you have to be so personal?"

"It's what I do. I have a big mouth."

"Well, we can agree on one thing. You do have a big mouth and plenty to say."

"No, that's not true. I don't always talk."

"Whatever. Here ..." She pulled her shirt over her head, kicked her Keds off, and we tossed clothing in the air like we were children ready to have a slumber party. But this exchange brought no party, and the night rushed in with a gray sky, but the slumber would have to wait. I tied my tennis shoes, noticing an odor lurking under each arm on the shirt. "How long has it been since you've washed these clothes?"

"I wasn't expecting company." River glanced at her shoes. "I've always loved your red PF Flyers. And to think, I actually have them on now. But this one," she lifted up the right shoe, "it stinks!"

112

"Sorry, it is your dog's woods, remember?"

We both laughed as if humor might ease the tension of how life hung like a half-moon. I added, "You can have them. Crush thinks I've outgrown PF Flyers. Maybe he's right."

A scuffling sound came from the swinging-door bushes. "Anyone hungry? I've got supper."

River hollered back, "Ed. Come in. It's Annie Grace and me. She came out here to apologize."

Smirking, I nudged her, giving her a glare. "I sure did. It's the least I could do."

Ed towered over us, glancing at me and at River. "So are you wearing each other's clothes now?"

I smiled, "Yes, we've traded. I'm on a case and needed to hide out in town. I'm spending the night with River." I put my hand up, like a stop sign. "Don't ask. It's a long story."

Ed nodded, and motioned for us to join him. "Well, I've got plenty of fried chicken tonight. Pastor Toby gave me a bucket of food at the mission this afternoon. There's enough for all us."

Woof! Woof! Woof!

River hollered. "It's Flashlight. She's over there on the other side of the creek. Come here, girl." She slid on her bottom on the embankment, hopped the creek, and climbed up the hill. "I'll be right back."

Ed offered his assistance. "Do you want me to get her? She'll come to me. I've got the food-smell on me."

"No, she's my dog. I'll get her."

Ed and I marched our way up the trail to his camp, where the make-shift fence marked his spot. Where the dirt shines like tile. Where the table sat with some old dishes on it. Where the miss-matched coffee mugs waited for coffee. Where the bucket of chicken waited to be consumed.

Pffft. Pffft. Pffft.

Ed pushed me aside. "Did you hear that popping sound? Someone is shooting a gun." He hollered, running like a stalk of wheat ready to be threshed. "River, where are you? Are you okay?"

Woof! Woof!

A rustling sound of long strides moving between the trees made me cringe, so I tracked Ed, going with him. An orange dog with black ears dashed toward Ed, licking his hands. Ed greeted her, "Good girl. Where's River?"

I jumped to his side. "Hey puppy, where's your mama?" I bent down, gazing into the snout of the dog and charged around Ed, galloping like a horse escaping from its corral. "River, answer us. Where are you?" I dashed between branches, the limbs walloped me, and a few seconds later, I found myself on the tracks, with Rose Hill Cemetery to my left, and Union Station behind me, down the tracks.

"River, where are you? Ed has your dog." I bellowed, and marched up the cross ties to the front of the cemetery where the brick columns led to tombstones of goodbyes. "What is that? No! River, what happened?"

Across the grass, beyond a row of markers, a body lay crumpled, bent in a way a body doesn't go. The body wore red PF Flyers and my overalls! I stood frozen, weeping at my friend on the ground!

Ed showed up, pushing me aside, charging around me, and he knelt to cradle River. "No!" He cried, "Annie Grace, she's been shot. Get help!"

When the Investigator Comes

The businesses downtown were closed, and the moon disappeared behind the clouds, as I galloped like a lame horse—all the way home. I pounded the screen door to the kitchen and my arm tingled, huffing with half-breaths, hollow and short. I swayed and called, "Crush, let me in. River's been shot!" I slammed my fist on the door, and didn't try to open the door myself, until it dawned on me it might be unlocked.

Squeak!

I turned the knob, marched into the kitchen, fumbled my steps around the kitchen table in the dining room, knocking over a chair. The lone lamp lit the hallway by the phone. I darted to it, picking up the receiver, spinning the dial. "Operator. Operator. There's a woman at the tracks beside Rose Hill Cemetery. She's been shot. Send an ambulance. And hurry."

I paused to make sure she responded.

"Yes, at the cemetery! They'll see Ed, he's tall and he's holding her. I only know she's bleeding."

I threw the receiver to the floor, charged into the front room, and ran to the sitting room, and back to the kitchen. "Crush, where are you?" I clamored up the stairs, crushing the carpet with my jumping, and yelled, "Honey, where are you? You should be home. It's after dark. Where are you? I need you!"

Silence fell, and my heart thumped with an irregular beat, the pounding boomed as if an earthquake traveled from my head to my feet. I spun around, unsure what to do or where to go. I cried, "Can there be beauty from pain, God? With each death, I feel like hope gets snuffed out. If I had a candle, I wouldn't be able to light it, for the oxygen is leaving me. I'm dying inside from this pain and sorrow."

Upstairs, I fell against the wall in my office. "God, my dreams of peace have sifted through my fingers like sand. I'm slipping away from reality. I can't do this. I'm here. But I'm not. I've cried my last tear, or have I?"

Bolting downstairs, I asked questions out loud to the walls. "Who shot River? Why her? I can't understand what is going on, or what it has to do with living. I've heard there's beauty from ashes, but I'm simply standing in the ashes of no answers."

Switching the light on, I fell to the sofa, whining, "I'm at my wits end. I've got no one who can help me. I'm lost. I'm broken. I can't see. I can't hold on. I have forgotten how to win at life. Is there a dawn tomorrow? And will I stand? I don't know. I must go. I can't stay. I won't be here when Crush returns. I can't be. This is deeper than my usual chaos. Someone is shooting at me—only it wasn't me this person wounded."

I talked to myself some more. "I've caused this. I've just made up with River, and we've forgiven each other. And now, this has happened. What if River dies? What if it's my fault?"

I rose, ending up in the hallway by the front door. All the lights were now on, and I tried to remember. Did I turn them on? Or were they left on for me? The house seemed full. But no one's here. No one's here to take my fear. I must find Crush. I longed for my husband. And yet, he's exhausted, too. And I'm torn. Should I stay or leave?

Rumble-tum. Rumble-tum.

A storm's rolling into town, not just in the sky, but in all of my whys. I tripped over my feet in the hallway and raced to the front porch, standing in the changing temperature, in the shadows. The light in the doorway shot a beam to the yard like a spotlight from behind me. "Crush, where are you?"

No answer.

"Hello?"

No answer.

"I am alone. But surrounded. Life's falling in around me. I don't know why the tears are falling when I have none left." I marched to the yard, "Is that lightning? Maybe if it rains, I can stand again, and be washed brand new. The stains of June could go away. God, let the rain come down, but don't let my world drown me. Let me live."

I knelt in the dead grass, rocking like River did earlier at camp. "God, my world's crashing down. I need help. I need someone who can guide me. Who will stand with me? Who will believe me? Who will walk with me through this? God, is there anyone who will do this? Anyone at all?"

Plop. Plop. Plop.

The sky opened up and the rain came down as if someone turned on the faucet, as if a pipe in heaven burst, as if the angels all cried at once. Soaked, I hung like a wet towel in the yard, kneeling, letting the water wash away the ache.

I wallowed in the muddy grass, crying like a child who never got over her daddy's death. Who never forgot that he kidnapped her. Who struggled to let go. To live. To love. To face life with hope.

It comes easy for others. But not me. I fight. I scream. I cause so much pain. I never planned to be the person I am. I never planned to see those murders or be around the Phantom Killer. I never knew I'd never fit in with real women. I never knew I'd lose my way. And find my way, again and again.

I argue with everyone. I give in to the sadness. Then I stand. Only to fall. I feel drenched in sin. I'm a wretched person, and I'll never understand how others hurt with guns and with meanness from within. And yet, I've hurt Crush. I've hurt Clara. I've hurt my sister, Lizzy Beth. And my brother Willie. I've hurt Gilbert. And even Lester. I'm worse than most people—I am the ugly I chase. It's consuming me. And I can't get out of this horrible place in my head, and in my real world the joy gets stolen.

A voice spoke into the night like a shower of peace. "My sweet girl. What has trapped your heart now? Give God your heart. Speak of truth. Tell Him. He will listen. I'll help you, too. I'll go with you. I'll stand with you."

I sat up, wiping water from my eyes, focusing on the shadowy ghost. Or was he more like an angel, coming closer to me? I leaned on my arm, my hand in a puddle of water. "Who's there? Who is talking to me? I can't see you. Who are you?"

"You are loved. You are whole. You can breathe. I am here. It's time for me to come to you. Time for me to help you finish this once and for all." The ghost inched closer, the brown shoes splattered with rain, and the ghost wore a suit, wet with the rain of hope.

I knelt on one knee, trying to stand, my jeans soaked. "Who are you?"

"I'm the one who will help you seek what is true. I've been sent for, but I should have come on my own. When I needed you, you helped everyone find me. You endured my being tied up, beaten, and locked inside a shack—all to rescue me. I have never forgotten you came for me. And yet, I pushed you away. I pushed everyone away to keep from hurting or losing anyone."

The familiar tone of the man's voice drifted into my ears, reaching into my heart. A kind voice of a past gone by, and his words stirred me. Standing like a fountain with a million leaks, I wept at hearing his call to me. "Is it you? Could it be?"

The kind ghost reached for my hand and offered a firm grip to my arm to help me balance myself. "I know it's been a lifetime since we've talked. Can we start over? It's me, Thaddeus William Day Jr. My friends call me, Taddy."

"Taddy, you are and will always be my friend!" I collapsed into his arms, into the grown version of the little boy, who grew up. At the age of ten we became best friends, and he was allergic to cats and peanuts and about everything else. And me, too.

"Let me get you in the house." He helped me up the steps, to the door.

"Taddy, why come now? You haven't talked to me in years and years. I'm not exactly at my best tonight. What is going on?"

"Crush is missing. And you're going to need the support."

"No, he can't be missing. He helped me escape from the police station this morning."

"He, helped you escape?"

"Well, he let me go, because he knew I was innocent."

"I heard he followed you downtown in his pickup. His truck was found on Broad Street by the creek and no one has seen him since. The door was swung open. And the keys were inside."

"Wait, he probably walked to the camp to search for me. He's not missing." My heart flipped-flopped and I prayed he wasn't anywhere near the tracks where River had walked, where a killer lurked in the woods.

Taddy filled in the blanks. "Earlier, Pastor Toby and I chatted on my evening walk and Officer Teacup drove up next to us in his patrol car, asking a dozen questions. He pressured the pastor with nonsense tactics and reworded his phrases as if he tried to trick Pastor Toby into disclosing information about you. I assumed he's asking questions of anyone who knows you—or has ever known you. He's suspicious of your excuses and explanations."

"I knew he was trying to arrest me with something—any evidence he could muster up."

"I agree. After he left, and after Toby walked on home, I found myself gazing out the window of my apartment at your climbing tree. Your photographs were blown down, well, most of them. And the shoelaces dangled in the branches. The ladder Crush put on the trunk for you last year, so you wouldn't fall, became a reminder of how big your tree has gotten. Then I remembered how many times we climbed those branches together as kids."

"Have you been watching from the window all these years?"

"I have on certain times, like when you go early or sit there late at night. I've worried about you, but I haven't said a word, only prayed for peace to find its way to you."

"Peace? It's not in town right now."

Taddy interrupted me. "I remember how you were the brave girl—and you would do anything to save me."

"We used to be good friends." I sniffled.

"And I never forgave you for barging into my world. But I have to say, due to our meeting each other, I learned the truth about my real mama and my aunt. I discovered someone could be my friend even though I could spell better than her."

"That's not true. I could spell bigger words and beat you in spelling bees."

"If I remember correctly I let you win." Taddy grinned. "But I did learn how brave I could be, too. I need to do the right thing by you. I am here to become an investigator with you. But mostly, to be your friend."

"Seriously? I'm shocked."

"I'm a slower learner on a few things, especially when it comes to acting like a friend."

My smile hung behind my teeth. "Taddy, I'm not the greatest at keeping friends, either."

He helped me inside. "But you're going to need a friend if you're going to get around town—without sticking out. Officer Teacup's on a mission, and it involves you."

"I need to find Crush. He's out there hunting for me. He won't stop until I'm home. I'm here—but he has no idea. I'm sure he's fine. As for River, someone shot her."

"River? Is she your friend from the camps?"

"Yes, and tonight she chased after her dog, only for someone to shoot her on the tracks. She wore my overalls and my PF Flyers. The bullet was meant for me."

"Why did she have your clothes on?"

"We changed so I could walk around in disguise." I coughed, slobbering into my palms. "I cause so much pain." I cried with sounds which would scare off any ghosts if they'd dared to come to my house.

"Together we can make it through another day. We will find Crush. You will solve this case. Let me stand beside you."

"I don't understand. Why help me now? I don't get you."

"It's complicated. Life is too short to hold the past against someone. And someone I love desires for me to change—to make amends with those I've allowed to wound me."

"Make amends? So, this is your good deed?"

"No, it's my way of living without burdens and walls built around my life. My fiancé, Colleen, has challenged me to make a difference by starting with myself."

"Do I know her? I had no idea you were engaged."

"No, she's a new teacher at the college. I'm changing and reaching out to others. Oh, I have a cat, too. His name is Wheezer. I've outgrown my sneezing."

"You are changing. You've sneezed for most of your life whenever cats came near you."

"Well, I still won't eat peanuts. I'm not testing that premise."

"I need to make amends with you, too. We need a fresh start." I peered into his chocolate eyes. "I have to solve both cases. I have to. The one of the Phantom Killer and this one with Clara and Gilbert. And of course, this makes my life more complicated than ever—with someone shooting at my friend."

"I can help you with details. I remember most everything from what we witnessed so long ago. Remember though, you are not alone. I have spent too many years teaching and guiding others at the college, and I've let you down, my friend."

"The killer must be someone we know, at least the one who shot Clara and Gilbert. I'm onto a suspect right now and I'm trying to think objectively. As for River, I've put her in danger—and now she's on her way to the hospital."

Taddy offered his advice. "We need to pray for the person behind the crimes. We may struggle with hating the person, but I pray we only hate the actions. And I pray that you will not be a victim. We must write the ending to this story and fight the sadness from our past."

"Taddy, you have no idea what this means. I'm not standing alone in this fight. For a change."

"Let's get some dry clothes on you. And we'll color your hair brown."

"Brown? What are you saying?"

"I've watched a movie or two, they always cut their hair and die it another color."

I almost laughed, but my blonde hair does stand out like a beacon.

Taddy nodded to himself, as if he listened inside his head. "You mustn't stand out—it's time for you to appear like a regular woman who is plain and timid."

"I'm already plain. But I'm not so timid."

"You aren't timid, that's for sure. And let's get you a room at Kings Row Inn. I had coffee with Mr. Pierce earlier, and he needs some extra actors for a few scenes. Plus, since the crew is staying there, you'll blend in with everyone. And you'll be safe in case someone comes to your house looking for you."

"But Crush will come home. And I won't be here."

"We'll leave him a note where he'll find it."

"I'll put a note on the mantel."

"Whoever shot River knows it wasn't you by now. So, putting you in front of the camera will keep you surrounded by plenty of people."

Pam Kumpe

When Memories Come Back

In one hand, I held the stained towel, thanks to the hair color, while running my fingers through my chocolate hair. "I'm going to make the folks in laundry mad for ruining their towel. I'm not sure about having brown hair. But I don't look as pale, or it could be the lights on this mirror. Or maybe, it's my high Choctaw cheek bones. Those from my daddy's side of the family." I danced a twirl, swooshing the hair in my toes on the floor.

After whacking more than six inches off, I assessed my new look. "Not bad. It's pretty straight, too. Shoulder length hair fits me."

I'm grateful Taddy paid for my motel room which put me close to the restaurant and he's in a room next door—in case I need him. My body's aching from exhaustion, and my mind won't shut off. I'm to report to Mr. Pierce in the morning and Taddy told him my name is Cindy.

It's close to one in the morning, and I'm torn on whether to actually stay and sleep, or to leave and search for Crush. One second, I'm sure he's fine. The next, I don't know what to think and the worry sets in. What if he doesn't see my note? I'm a wreck. I'm not rational. I'm not myself even as I am myself.

Thankfully, Taddy made a few calls and confirmed River is stable at McMichael's Hospital. The person on the phone told Taddy a woman came in through emergency, and she has no identification. But she wore overalls and red PF Flyers.

I've prayed for her nonstop, hoping she'll live. As for me, I'm almost wanted by the police; at least as far as Officer Teacup's concerned. He's not prone to listening to my side—

124

he's hoping to pin the murders on someone and it won't be me. I whispered to the face in the mirror. "How did I become a target in all of this?"

I stared at the pillow across the room on the bed, and marched to it, pulling the covers back. I crawled into the sheets—the softness a cloud of comfort. "Hair! I have hair on my feet! And now, it's on the sheets!"

Wiping my feet with another towel, I removed strands of hair from between my toes. "Great, now I can't sleep in the bed. I'll have to sleep on top of the bedspread." I yawned, tossing the towel to the bathroom, and the heaviness of my eyes sent me backwards to the mattress.

I prayed, staring up to the ceiling, and sought answers which could only be delivered by God. "Lord, I know you're with Crush. I pray you're with me in the days ahead. I pray I find the boy with yellow hair too, and I pray I bring peace to families who have no answers. That River will live. That I will find my hope."

**

I hovered by the wall in the restaurant, barely awake since it's two hours before I normally get up. I'm mixing in with the cast and crew too. Not one person has glanced my way with evil eyes or with whispers. I touched the red dress draped on me like paint, and smacked my lips, the red lipstick the brightest part of my face. I loved not standing out like a wild woman. And for once, I didn't feel like the odd person in the room. Other than the red dress, but it's a costume, and I'm expected to wear it.

Taddy appeared nice too, wearing a vest and a dress shirt, with pressed slacks. His hair's smoothed to one side, slick and perfect. He phoned his girlfriend and she's coming later to meet me.

Mr. Pierce trooped from the back of the restaurant, putting his napkin on a table near me. His crew joined him. "Let's get to work, people. It's early, but this scene takes place at night. We'll shoot it before the sun gets up. Martha Long is attacked on her date with Jack Hall. We'll head to Blanton Road at the end of the paved part of the road and take the dirt trail used by the farmer. There's plenty of trees there. It'll look like Lover's Lane. Let's get going. The day's getting away."

He stopped moving, his son bumping into him. "Sorry, Daddy." He wiped sleep from his eyes.

Pierce smiled, patting his son's head, and glanced at everyone behind him. "So, where's my Martha and my Jack?"

Taddy motioned with a raised hand. "I'm playing Jack's part."

"You look a little older than you should." He put his hand to his chin. "Where's my Martha?"

Taddy held my arm up in the air.

I stuttered, "I've rehearsed my lines until late last night, and this morning, too. I'm ready."

"And how old are you?" He walked on without letting me answer, but he gave a request to a man close to his side. "Make sure makeup takes care of her wrinkles."

I mouthed, "Wrinkles? I have beauty lines."

He came back to me, cutting between the crew and stage hands. "Do I know you? You seem familiar."

Covering my eyes with my hand, to act like I scratched an itch, I responded, "No, I don't think we've met. I'm just a woman who loves to act."

"I see. I guess you have one of those faces."

Taddy whispered in my ear. "You have one of those faces which gets you in trouble."

"Stop it." We joined the crew and filed out to the cars outside. I urged Taddy, "Help me watch for any spectators in the crowd, while they're filming. The woman will be holding a small toddler."

"You've told me this for the fifteenth time. I'll remember. And I'll keep watch."

As we walked to the parking lot, I turned to Taddy. "No one has heard anything from Crush, have they?"

"Not a word. Not yet. But most everyone is asleep right now. He's probably at home asleep, too."

"Let me call him again. Let me try the house."

"You've called four times. We have to go with the crew or get axed."

"What's so important about our having these parts in the movie?"

"Well, Colleen wants me to overcome my shyness. She won't marry me until I conquer my fears. I have to do this for her. And you need to solve a case, and I need to overcome my fear of people."

"Taddy, don't stop being you—to become someone Colleen desires. If she loves you, she'd love the shy and quiet Taddy, I know."

He sulked like he used to when we were younger. "I need to think of others instead of just about myself. Colleen said I've gotten used to hiding inside my apartment."

"So, your tree—is your apartment?"

"You could say so."

Taddy stepped to the driver's seat of the vehicle and I ran my fingers across the curvy bumper. I remembered the car my grandma drove, and how she smiled at me holding that steering wheel. I sat in the seat, tucking another good memory away for later.

As Taddy followed the caravan, I broke the silence. "Hey, I'll practice my lines while you drive."

"Sure, go for it." Taddy held the steering wheel of the old-timey car.

But first I apologized. "I'm sorry, I didn't mean to insult you. I happen to like the old Taddy." I straightened my dress, watching the tail lights of the caravan in front of us. "Silly me, no one will be at the set to watch the filming at this hour of the morning. What was I thinking?"

Taddy rebutted, "This is a big deal in our town. There will be several who'll come. People love movies. And this one is about people from our town and a killer who made history."

I nodded. "Hey, let me say my lines to you."

Taddy held onto the steering wheel. "Why not, it's not like you don't know them."

"Let me set the scene. You stretch your arms in the car after we park, and you put your arm around my neck. I say, 'Jack move your hand.'" Laughing, I choked on those words, the irony of saying such things to someone I think of as a ten-year-old in a grown-up body.

Taddy added his part. "Why'd you turn off the radio?"

We kept role playing. "I heard something."

"Will you please concentrate on what's going on?"

"I'm not kidding, I heard something."

"Martha, that's the oldest trick in the book."

"Are the car doors locked?" I explained my next line, moving out of my character role. "Taddy, I get to scream, which is what I did when we hid in the bushes as kids, when the killer attacked the real Martha and Jack."

128

"I remember how I sneezed and ran off, leaving you there. I also remember the boots. And his giant hands. He had big knuckles. He was strong. He broke the window on the car and slammed Jack in the head with a bar. He told Martha to run." Taddy gripped the steering wheel. "That was the most frightening night ever, it ruined my birthday." Taddy unleashed a memory of horror, explaining how all the blood and screaming kept him awake for years.

Choking back tears, I swallowed hard. "I'm not sure I can do this acting thing. This feels like real life."

"You'll be fine. It's a reenactment. I shouldn't have shared all those details. Sometimes memories jump inside my head like an old movie."

"I know. It's like spoiled milk, which soured in our life. And we can't stop the smell."

Taddy followed the vehicles, inching along the dirt road, and a man showed us where to park. The camera man marched to his spot, and camera lights were placed in another spot. And we waited in our spot. Everyone had a spot—but where is my Crush? What spot will I find him in? The inner call to leave and search for him ripped at me. I should go. I should look for him. Torn between running and staying and hiding—I disappeared inside my head—unable to react or move.

I whispered to Taddy. "I don't want to be in this movie. These were people who had families. Who are gone. I don't know if I'm cut out for this."

"Well, it's too late. We've committed to being in the movie. It's who you are for now—roll with it."

"Roll with it? You've been out of my life for years, and now you offer more advice than I care to hear."

Taddy snickered, "Some things never change."

Mr. Pierce scuttled up to us. "I have some bad news. After looking at you through the camera, I have to make some changes. We did our best to cast locals in most of the roles where they resemble the person they're playing. However, when we filled these two spots with you two, after the other man and woman canceled, the casting department forgot Jack and Martha were much younger. I'm going to ask you to step aside and let our two new sweethearts take over."

Taddy spoke with a tone of relief. "We understand. Maybe we can be in a group scene somewhere else in the movie."

"I'm sure we can work it out for you."

I sighed, following Taddy toward a tree next to the car. The same man who noticed my wound the other day, rushed up to us. "I need to run you both back to the motel, so you can change into your own clothes. I need this dress," he pointed to me, "and your," he pointed at Taddy, "shirt and vest and slacks."

I did my best to keep from making eye contact, as we rode back to the motel with muscle man. Stepping from the car, I announced, "Give me a second, and I'll give you the dress."

Taddy opened his car door, talking to the driver. "I'll change in my room. I'll be back in two minutes." Taddy gave me a glance. "I'll be right back."

I smiled. "Sure, we'll take your car and go back to the set and watch the scene. Or we could go check on Crush."

The man waiting for the actor-clothes spoke. "Thank you for being gracious in how you're handling this situation. You are one of the kindest women we've had on the set. Most women would have thrown a tantrum at not getting to become an actress in the movie."

"Why, thank you. No one ever thinks of me as kind." I handed him the barrettes and the lipstick from my pocket and went to my room. "I'll be right back, too." Mumbling to myself, I decided wearing a dress and having on lipstick made me appear respectable.

After handing off the clothes, I rushed to the restaurant to find Taddy sipping on coffee, as he adjusted his collar. "Sit down. We have a few minutes. It's not like we don't know how the scene goes. I haven't eaten much the last couple of days. I want one of their Monte Cristos."

"I'm going to phone Crush."

"I've already phoned your house. He didn't answer."

"No, he must be there."

"Sit down. Let's eat first. I'm sure he'll show up. He's probably asleep on the sofa, waiting for you."

"I'm not hungry. Let's go."

"Can I finish my coffee first?"

"Sure." I pulled up a chair at the table across from Taddy. I gazed at the aging Taddy whose wrinkles were less prevalent than mine. And I took us down memory lane. "I hated how we never became friends again, even though we attended the same school. When you became valedictorian, my heart burst with excitement and I wasn't surprised you did so well."

"I do have a good mind. I focused on my studies, excelling at all costs. After Mama recovered from the wagon accident in Oklahoma, and we moved to Jefferson, she never bounced back to her happy self. She stayed home, hid behind the curtains, and never baked biscuits again. Emotionally, I lost her on the trip to Millerton when we lost Margo. Her heart splintered beyond repair, which kept my heart broken, too."

"I'm sorry. I struggled to make it work with Ms. Susan and Mr. Boyd, too. They loved me, and they were so great to Willie and Lizzy Beth. But I scared them. They never knew what I might do or where I might go, but they were the best adoptive parents."

Our talking transformed us to a time when childhoods were not always perfect—but where memories with a friend are exceptional in the retelling. I continued my recap. "I remember how we became friends, in our fight in our trees, yours versus mine. And you pretended to fall from the tree. And my cat made you sneeze."

"I wanted a friend so badly, I settled for you."

"Very funny. I wanted one too, but I didn't know I longed for a friend until I had one."

"I remember how you wrote poetry."

"I've gotten away from poetry, but I'm writing books now."

"I've read them. I have all of your books."

We sipped on our brew, and the silence filled my mind with a thousand memories of when we were ten—to laughing, to climbing trees, and to playing with the water hose.

From the side of the restaurant, I heard a voice, strong and loud, and he tugged on the sleeve of a waitress. "Have you seen Annie Grace? I've searched all night. I've been out since yesterday and walked all night—going to the homeless camps. To alleys. To bridges. To the tracks. I ran out of gas and had to leave my truck. So I kept walking. She's nowhere."

"Mr. Raike, we haven't heard a word. I had no idea. Come have some coffee."

I jumped from my chair, running to my husband. "Crush! You're alive! Honey, it's me! I'm safe. I'm not hurt. I'm ready to go home."

Crush stared at me as if his eyesight went blurry, and he ran his fingers through my hair. "What is this? What are you up to? And where have you been?"

"I slept here last night."

"And why would you do that?"

"I was afraid whoever shot River, would shoot me."

"River? What's going on?"

"I colored my hair and cut it." I ran my fingers through the bob. "I had to hide. Oh honey, I was so worried about you."

"Worried about me? Where's your room? Let's go there to talk. Everyone's watching us. What happened to River?"

Taddy shadowed us and interrupted our moving toward the exit. "Crush, this is partly my fault. She cried in the front yard last night in the storm—she was caught in her world. I brought her here to keep her calm, to let her rest. I've phoned your house numerous times, trying to find you—so you could come to her."

Crush squinted his eyes. "And when did you start coming to our house?"

"It's a long story. Colleen's working on my people skills and my way of interacting with others."

"And you need to see my wife?"

"No, I met Officer Teacup and Toby earlier, and then I came across Annie Grace in the front yard—having a, well, a nervous breakdown."

I yelled, "I'm right here. I'm not invisible. And I'm not having a nervous breakdown. Do you think you could stop talking about me like I'm not here?"

Glancing across the room as if I stood in a spotlight, I longed to hide, to fade away. A man and woman at one table who were eating breakfast held their forks in the air, their mouths wide, their ears taking in our rather loud discussion of my sanity. One waitress held her coffee pot in mid-pour, staring at me. And a small child jumped to his mama's lap, holding her neck.

"I can explain." I reached for Crush, who put his hand on my shoulder, like he guided a toddler from the building.

He moved with me. "Let's take this outside. And now."

Nodding, I slipped through the lobby and scooted to the door and out to the driveway, to head to my room. Taddy excused himself and made his way to his car.

Under the awning, I tasted the new day as the sun rose, the salty tears running like melted butter down my face, another sign of chaos unfolding with my absence last night. I prayed silently, "Lord, let me discover an answer to finding peace. Let Crush forgive me—one more time."

A wobbly man lurched from behind a parked car, bumping into me and he screamed, "Hey lady, watch out." The grouchy guy bounced off the wall, staggering onward as if he searched for someone.

I whispered, "Crush, that's Lester. He's drunk. And filthy."

"Let him be. We need to leave him alone. We have enough of our own troubles."

"No, he's a murderer. There's no telling what he's done." I marched up to Lester's backside, his pants coated in splotches of dirt. "Hey, I'm onto your ways. Don't think I don't know."

Crush put himself between us before Lester assaulted me with his response. "Annie Grace, stop this!" He turned to Lester. "I'm sorry. It's been a long week for all of us."

I gawked at the face of the runner who appeared less than healthy. Whose red eyes spoke of a horror, but was it because he'd lost his brother? He appeared more like a small boy inside of a lost soul.

The face of a man drunk from a night of jogging toward sin and ruin gave me his answer. "Why am I talking to you?"

I blasted at Lester. "What's happened to you?"

"Get away from me before you regret speaking to me." Lester's slurred speech came at me like an order. He squinted his eyes, his glare an internal assessment of my well-being.

"What happened to your hair? Brown is not good on you. I've had enough trouble for too long. Now my eyes are playing tricks on me. My life is a grave of death. I dig, I cover up, and I bury the night. But the light won't come. The grave is always there."

Crush held Lester by the arm. "Come with me. You need coffee. You've had too much to drink."

"No, let go of me!" He yanked free and shoved me against the wall, as if he shoved the truth deeper inside to keep it from escaping—as if he couldn't find a way to get out of the grave of last night.

I balanced myself as Crush cradled me. "Honey, are you hurt?"

"No, I'm mad as the dickens though. Lester, you better get out of here."

A car pulled through the driveway from the parking area, and the man driving rolled his window down. "Is everyone all right?"

Crush and I answered together. "We're fine."

Crush escorted Lester along, pulling him by his collar. "Get inside and I'll buy you some breakfast. Or go home and leave us alone."

I grabbed the door, hoping Lester cooperated, but instead he bolted, wrapping his free arm around my neck, and pulled me to his chest with my back against him. "Lester, let me go."

Crush charged for me, as Lester backed up and Taddy came from somewhere, along with some other patrons. Crush yelled, "Let my wife go. Or you'll regret it."

Lester shook, quivering from head to toe, and his right hand jabbed my back. I screamed, "Stop it. You're hurting me."

Taddy waved his arms as if he might pass out. "He has a gun. He's got it in her back."

The chaos rattled with high pitched screams as if hundreds of people hollered at the same time. Crush barreled at Lester, and they fell like tumbleweeds. Then their fists slammed to the ground with jerks and slaps, as their bodies tangled in a blow of Crush winning—his stamina taking over Lester—only for Lester to find himself on top.

Stumbling like a pebble skipping across a stormy lake, I couldn't get to my husband. "Crush! Watch out!" With each scream, and with the arms flying from the scuffle, the gun shambled from hand to hand—one second Lester gripped the barrel. The next Crush held the pistol in his grasp.

I echoed the terror of watching the brawl. My outbursts continued, "Someone stop this!"

Taddy dove into the maze of legs and arms and jabs. His body flopped in the exchange of blows. Slugging. Rolling. And blood. The slow-motion awfulness of three people bounced on the asphalt—one trying to wound and the other two trying to stop the wounding.

Launching my words at the bushy-faced man behind me, my words turned into a rage. "Let me go! I hope someone's called the police. We need to have Lester picked up. He's a public nuisance."

A woman inched closer to me, consoling me with her words, but I realized she'd picked up something from the ground.

She shouted, "Here's the gun. It flew to my feet." Shaking, she pointed the barrel, wiggling, stepping to the side. Her nervousness grew with the intensity of Lester rushing at her. She hollered, "What shall I do with this?"

I jerked free. "Give it to me. I can shoot. I'll stop this madness."

But Lester's fist found my jaw, slamming me backwards like a boulder of dead weight. Crush shoved Lester, and Taddy hurdled over Lester to retrieve the gun.

And the flux of bodies stormed like a maelstrom of chaos. Taddy came up for air, holding his head, and blood dripped from his ear. The dreadfulness of this moment sent the crowd scrambling and sirens grew louder—as if time stopped and sped up, the seconds slowed, and turned into minutes. My heart skipped with disgust at how humans turn on each other. At how, out of nowhere, a gun can show up. And an alleged murderer.

Beneath the awning, Officer Teacup and his men surrounded Taddy and Crush and the no-good Lester. Teacup growled, "Everyone stop. Stop now! Or we're taking you in."

Pop. Pop. Pop.

Three bangs ripped through the air, as darkness descended, leaving me watching my husband crumple to the ground in a pool of blood. I raced to his side, weeping and holding him in my arms. "Honey, stay with me!"

The scuffling halted, the questions filtered behind me, and my surroundings became a blur of blips. It's as if someone edited out part of my morning as I found myself sitting at a table next to a window in the restaurant after the ambulance hauled off my husband.

Taddy's face is one big splotch of red, his left eye is swollen, and he's leaning on his arm by the wall. Colleen arrived in her denim skirt and sleeveless white top—now she has blood on her clothes from loving on Taddy.

I mouthed inside my brain *loving on Taddy*—and changed the words to a shout. "I can't love on Crush, thanks to Lester! My husband might die!"

The rest of the world slowed, the sun fell from the sky and darkness swallowed me whole. My head dropped to the table, and I wept until my eyes stung as if grains of sand poured from my tear ducts.

My ears caught whispers dropping from patrons and others who stood near the check-in desk, where the motel keys hide in small slits behind the counter. I peeked under my arm as Taddy shuffled with Colleen out the door without a word—his numbness apparent by her ushering him. "Honey, I'll stay all afternoon. You have me. We're going to fine. It's going to be all right."

I grimaced to myself, pursing my lips. "Thanks for comforting me. Thanks for your kinds words. My life falls apart and you don't even say a word to me." I spewed my words at Colleen's iron-pressed, perfect clothes like I had spewed orange slices at Clara when we first met on my grandma's porch.

For eight minutes, it's like the sun exploded and the melting of my heart sobbed with bursts of sorrow.

Officer Teacup intercepted my muttering, and my spiral launch of words coated with slobber spit from my mouth as I plowed across the room.

He blocked my path. "Annie Grace, sit down. We're going to take you home." His firm grip pressed my shoulders to a halt, and his eyes—those eyes. They pierced my soul as if he held answers to most of life's questions due to his training to protect our city. But nothing he knew had stopped this horrible and terrible and troubled morning. When a person sets out to destroy, he takes others with him—those we love.

I obeyed as if I couldn't find the strength to muster up any more words. But I'm sure they're inside, blocked by the clogged arteries of this worst day ever. The terror of seeing my husband ripple to nothingness swirled in my veins, and my hope of a happily-ever-after became a fog. I disappeared into an oblivion of questions—without question marks, for it was one long series of words, never ending.

I'll never get the painful moment from my mind, of my husband's breaths rocking inside his chest with deep gasps for air. Had death knocked at the door of our marriage—in this way, offering a grave of no return?

I whined to myself, "Crush, I love you! I'm so sorry. You're the best of me. I need you. Who will catch me when I fall? It's always been you."

Crush believed in me. He wished I believed in myself, and wished I trusted God for wisdom and true hope. I sighed, "I'll be waiting for you. Thank you for loving me through everything. Please don't die!"

I withered, shivering, and lost my ability to do one thing more, except I had to get out of this restaurant, no matter what—or I might suffocate. I called to my husband under my breath. "I'm sorry. Crush, don't leave me! You're my Winky!"

When a Kitten Meows

"Come downstairs, Annie Grace." Archie urged, his words skidding into my bedroom beneath my locked door.

"No, I have nothing to say. I don't need anyone, but my husband." I wallowed in my pity, trapped in the ache deep inside my heart, a place where all pain lives until it's released. These four walls keep the world away, but alone doesn't feel so good right now. I placed my hand on the doorknob, knowing I should open the door since Archie stayed all day with me. But hiding is my best attribute. Or my worst!

The house rocked with visitors all afternoon with people bringing food. Like Lea and Dora, two women from church who packed my refrigerator with casseroles—kindness in calories. I never spoke to them, but I peeked at them from my upstairs window through the blinds—they wiped tears as they strode to their car, as if they had regrets in life, too. As if they were wounded hearts with cries of sorrow—longing for hope like me.

Archie answered the phone a dozen times, and I listened in on my end—picking up the receiver in my office, each time, darting across the hallway. Most calls came with comfort. Some calls came with nosiness. Other calls were whispers of sadness. One call came with word Crush was in surgery—nonresponsive—not doing great. Which sent me here, but not doing anything is haunting me. I need to hold Crush and feel his heart beating with life. But they won't allow me to see him.

I put my hands over my ears as if this might keep Archie away. I called to him. "Why do you want to come in?"

"To tell you, you're loved—to hold you. To wipe away your tears. Hiding isn't the answer. Truth is the answer. It may hurt, but you can heal."

I soaked up the words of one of my dearest friends. He's a gift to my life. I can't imagine how life might have gone for me if God hadn't allowed Archie, a skinny man in his early twenties to amble into my life when I was ten. He held me inside a passenger train when my grandma collapsed from her heart attack in Oklahoma. He rode the rail with me when I needed comfort and guidance—he listened to me. He counseled me.

He showed up when I ran away after my grandma died. He knew my daddy stole me to sell me, but he also knew my daddy changed his mind back in Memphis.

I turned the doorknob, falling to the floor at Archie's feet like a puppet without strings, picking at a splinter on the floor next to the wall. "I don't know how to handle this pain. It's more than I can bear."

Archie wrapped his fingers in mine. "My child, your walk may overwhelm you, but the Lord is still our refuge in times of trouble. May you find comfort in Him."

Wiping tears, I stared at the gray around Archie's ears.

He whispered, "Jesus wept. He's with the brokenhearted. He is holding you, even now."

"Archie, I've longed for joy in the morning, for hope to come. My life is filled with too much suffering." I jumped to my feet, leaving the aging Archie on the floor, bounding to the dresser, picking up my wedding ring from the dresser. Placing the ring on my finger—after taking it off earlier when I longed to stop thinking—I knew I had to think of my husband. "Archie, what will I do if Crush dies?"

**

Pam Kumpe

The last three days have declared signs of life in my husband, but so far—he's not opened his eyes. I'm headed to see him later, for a few minutes, but those nurses will rush me out of his hospital room before I'm ready to leave.

I've come home to sleep, to pace, to wonder, to worry. I try to pray, but the words are caught in my throat, but God knows I long to have my husband home with me. I've made new promises I plan to keep, those which bring me alongside Crush, to be his wife, to be his friend, to stop the running, to not bail when life tumbles in around me.

I plopped on the edge of the bed, unsure how my nightmares have overtaken me. My rest comes in spurts, bits of time carved out like slices of an orange. I caught a glimpse of myself in my mirror on the dresser. "What has happened to me? This brown hair must go. I'm changing it back to blonde—and now. My hair will grow and get long, but this color is not me!"

Brushing my hair, I sat at the vanity where the smudges of the lipstick on the mirror kept me staring with a frozen gaze. The clues from Junior's notes whispered to me, while the shouts of the clues from the woman I've yet to meet rang in my ears. The reality of this horror picture reflected in my soul with each breath, as if blood-red and sorrow surrounded my heart.

I shuffled to my balcony porch, ready to change my hair color—ready to see the world with clarity, with hope. I must change. I must grow. I must see the day as a gift to live—to rise up. To win at life.

I melted into my rocker, the song of the redbird in the treetop next door, whistling, and I spoke to the day. "I can't believe Officer Teacup figured me into the murder equation

142

with Clara and Gilbert. Just because his men found a rusted old gun doesn't mean it's the weapon. Then he discovered the gun might have been there for years—thus, removing me from his suspect list. And they did find my keys—as if that mattered."

Standing, I placed my hands on the wrought-iron rail, as a group of blackbirds soared across the sky. A taxicab came up the street to my right, coming toward my house, turning, stopping in front of the house. "I'm not up for visitors."

The back door to the cab swung open, and two black-headed people emerged. A man wearing a blue shirt climbed from the backseat, while on the other side, a woman with the same hair but curlier, twirled with a dance like she planned to run—to scamper up my sidewalk.

Frozen, I stared at Lizzy Beth and Willie, the twins! They carried totes and marched across the yard and onto the sidewalk leading to my porch. I held my breath, moving away from the edge, to hide from them in plain sight, to take in the moment from above them.

"She's not herself. Remember, her friend's doing better, but Crush isn't doing so great." Willie spoke, his voice soft. His way of soothing a heart, came with his presence.

"But the last thing I told her—left scars on both our hearts. I lashed out and got so mad at her. She's always so full of drama." Lizzy Beth added her two cents. She often sounded like me—ready to give an opinion.

My skin itched, ready to react, but she told the truth, 'drama' could be my middle name. Lizzy Beth added, "But she's the reason I have you, Willie. And we have her, but we aren't the best brother and sister. We need to show her our love. We need to do better. God has given her to us. And us, to her. We're family. We need to support Annie."

Lizzy Beth's way of saying "Annie" made me smile. She's the only person who never says my middle name. She's told me forever how *grace* is something I've not possessed in my lifetime—ever. Hearing her voice meant I needed a real hug. I bounced along the hallway from the balcony, rushed down the stairs, and ran to the porch to meet my brother and sister.

Opening the door, I stopped short of hugging them, since they both reacted with a pause. Lizzy Beth glared at me as if I looked different with short brown hair.

I grabbed a stand of hair. "This new color's not working for me. I'm dying it back to blonde today."

Lizzy Beth nodded. "Good, I love your blonde hair."

We embraced as if we might not ever let go, a reminder of how we often hugged each other for no reason growing up in Jefferson. When we worried, got in trouble, or were asked by Ms. Susan and Mr. Boyd to forgive each other—we hugged as children. We hugged at breakfast. Before bed. And in between.

Mr. Boyd required his family to not end the day with anything between us. Yet, as adults, the three of us harbored ugly chapters in our seasons of growth, more bad than good. But this moment, this embrace, would have brought a smile to Mr. Boyd if he were alive. This type of healing for my soul could only come from a brother and sister who understood me—even on days when they don't—they do.

"Come inside. Archie's here. He's somewhere in this big old house." They placed their bags by the door.

Lizzy Beth moved her hands across the top of the old piano as we scooted to the front room. "We're here for a week. We've put others in charge at the society while we're gone. We needed to see you. To hold you."

"So Archie called you."

Willie smiled, "He did. But it's true. We need to be here for you."

Lizzy Beth spoke, "We're processing lots of adoptions these days—with children finding their smiles and finding forever parents. Maxwell will oversee the office while Willie and I visit."

"Sit with me. I haven't seen you in so long." I patted the sofa, and Lizzy Beth plopped down beside me. "Maxwell's not mad at me—still? Is he?"

"No, he struggles to understand his sister-in-law. But we all need to work on loving you, for you." She giggled, putting her arms around me. "I need another hug. I've missed you so much."

Willie meandered around the room, touching the fireplace mantle, briefly touching a key on the piano. He moved to the bookcase, running his fingers over the spines of the books. He sighed, turned to me and unloaded his questions. "Annie Grace, when will this stop? When will you stop chasing the past?"

I popped up like a weed taking over a garden and mouthed, "Willie, I don't do these things on purpose. I don't!"

"I know you don't. I know you think we're supposed to watch and allow and never ask questions. Yet, you ask questions of everything, of every … one!" His tone shrieked, his face stretched, and my brother marched to me, ready to explode. "What are we supposed to do? The next phone call we get will be news of our big sister's death!"

"Death? I'm not going to die. I'm right here. I'm always right here."

"No, you're not. You're living your life in the past when you were a girl. When you were a hobo girl. You are not a child anymore. You are not without a home. Or family. That's not your life! Live this life, Annie Grace. Live this one!"

Lizzy Beth slithered between us. "Stop this incessant arguing. Willie, we're here to help, not correct. She must find her way with the guidance of others, but not by yelling at her."

I pulled away, folding my arms, sitting on my feet at the end of sofa. "I'm in a hard place. I don't mean to burden you. You don't have to stay. This might not be a good time."

Lizzy Beth piped in. "There you go. The conversation leans toward reality and you do your best to send those who care about you away."

I challenged her words. "Run off people who care? I couldn't even keep the kitten Crush gave me. I spooked the poor thing. It ran away two years ago. Even people are afraid of me. My life is one broken chapter after another. I don't mean to be wrecked and chaotic and jumbled in my walk."

Willie argued, "Having Boyd and Susan raise us meant everything. Don't you see? We had the best childhood you could have imagined. We ate with them every morning. Our school lunches were paid for. We never lacked for clean ears. We had more Dial soap than any family in the neighborhood. They taught us about Jesus, and serving, and loving, and being there for others. And they loved us."

Lizzy Beth countered and agreed. "We played at the bayou. We fished in the creeks and hiked the trails. And, like a ghost you'd disappear, and we'd find you sitting across the highway in a tree—watching Taddy play at his ranch in the country. You were convinced he would become your friend again, but your time wasted in trees has wasted your life."

When I opened my mouth to speak, Willie put his fingers to my lips. "We are blood. We have the same real daddy. Don't forget where God brought us from, out of darkness into the light. He used you to save Lizzy Beth and me. Sure, daddies shouldn't hurt their children. But it's been thirty years, Annie Grace! Thirty years!"

Lizzy Beth wiped the tears falling. "Annie, I need you. But I need you to recover from the past. It's like a plague! You fester, boil and blow. We want you to be whole."

I soaked in the fragrance of dandelion from Lizzy Beth's clothes, the perfume floated into my nose and into my heart. I swallowed hard, purposing to speak a word of kindness. "You were and will always be my favorite twins. I do struggle with life."

Willie nudged me. "We're the only brother and sister you have—so you have no choice but to love us."

"I do love you! I do!"

We lingered, standing in a circle, glancing into each other's eyes—as the memories flooded my mind. As I stared into their charcoal eyes and olive skin, their Choctaw bloodline stuck out. Daddy passed on his Indian genes to them—but I received the leftover genes giving me my blue eyes and pink skin. But I did get high cheek bones.

Our sharing our memories became a window into good days and happy times, as I remembered our years together. Of how they were five when they found me—or I found them.

I remembered we hadn't heard from Archie since they arrived. I called for him. "Archie? Where are you? I've got great news. We have guests."

Lizzy Beth danced to the hallway which ran from the front door to the back of the house. "Where is he?" She peeked into the other fireplace room, the downstairs bathroom and marched to the dining room. "He knew Willie and I were coming today."

I pranced to the adjacent sitting room behind the front room, meeting Lizzy Beth in the hallway. "Archie, what's going on? Answer me."

Willie called up the staircase. "Archie? Are you there?"

We twirled around, passing each other, hollering for Archie, returning from each room without finding him. I charged through the kitchen to the back door, where the steps lead to the garage at the back of the lot. Willie and Lizzy Beth bounced behind me and bumped into me when I stopped before swinging the screen open.

Lizzy Beth tapped me on the back. "A little warning would be nice."

I spun around. "Look! Over there by the oak tree. He's sitting on the top step in the shade. He tuckers out so fast these days."

We danced to Archie. I peered into his lap. "Where did you find a kitten?" I petted the kitty's ear. "He's got the prettiest blue eyes."

"I heard this teeny whimper when I took out the trash, so I followed the cry. I ended up by this tree, listening but not finding him. I watched for movement in the street, but nothing. He kept meowing and I bent down—and those teeny eyes glowed in between the bricks on these old steps. He was stuck."

Willie petted the kitty. "He's cute. His struggles brought you to his side. You tend to do a lot of rescuing."

Archie smiled. "I think it's my walk. To be where I can lend a hand. But this little guy wouldn't let me touch him—at first. I waited and waited and waited. He finally crawled up to me, skittish—until I told him I was his new uncle."

I grinned. "Uncle?"

"Yes, and I told him you're his mama. Which makes me his uncle."

Lizzy Beth, Willie and I—we knelt in the yard, playing with a kitten like children. I spouted off, "I lost the last kitten I had—or he ran away. I'm not good with pets."

Lizzy laughed, "You're not good with people, either."
Ha-ha!

Archie's laughter lifted my spirits and having my family with me did something to my insides. I was alive. I was loved. I sensed hope. And peace layered my emotions, comforting me.

The kitten licked Archie's nose whenever he grabbed the little guy to keep him from running off. Archie laughed, rubbing the kitten's ear. "What shall we call him?"

Grinning, I cuddled the kitten after snatching him from Archie's big hands. "He might be your kitten."

Archie smiled, arguing with me. "No, he came to your house to find you."

Lizzy Beth nodded. "He's definitely your cat."

"Why is he my cat?"

"He already has a scar on his belly. Poor thing."

"We'll call him Scar." I kissed the kitty on the nose, as an ugly memory from Wheelock Academy snuck into my head.

Thankfully, Willie offered a much better idea. "Let's name him after Archie. How about Hank."

Archie squinted his eyes, petting the kitty. "Hank? Are you serious?"

Willie affirmed, "Yes, you've given away hundreds of handkerchiefs throughout the years. Hank is short for hanky, which is short for handkerchief."

I agreed. "I love it. Hank it is!"
Ting-a-ling. Ting-a-ling.

Lizzy Beth hopped to her feet. "I hear your phone ringing." She ran across the yard. "I'll grab it."

Hank purred in my arms. "It might be the neighbor's phone. But if it's mine, I hope it's good news."

A Husband's Secret

Pressing the receiver to my ear, I listened—and the woman on the other end spoke with a whisper, as if she kept others around her from knowing she phoned me. When she took a breath, I took over the conversation. "You need to speak up. I have no idea what you said. Why are you doing this? What is this about?"

The woman explained, "You're not letting my family move on. We want this burden lifted. We can no longer keep quiet."

"Why me? Take your information to the police. I'm not the person for this."

"You don't understand. We have family members who won't believe a word of this—and I haven't shown them the photos or the inside of the box. It's hard to learn your family is like spoiled fruit—with horrible parts you can't cut out."

"But, my husband was shot a few days ago. I'm dealing with my own life."

"Yes, we've heard. I'm sorry. I shouldn't bother you right now. I'm sorry I called."

"No, don't hang up. You've got me on the phone, but I'll have to delay meeting you for now. I've put my investigation business on hold. My husband and my marriage are more important."

Meow. Meow.

Hank leapt from my arms, sliding across the hardwood floor with Lizzy Beth chasing him. Which meant she hovered near, eavesdropping on my call.

She picked Hank up. "Sorry. I'll mind my own business."

Back to the call, I reminded the woman. "I'm not pursuing this, not at this moment."

The woman coughed. "Your husband worked at Guy's with my husband's brother. You may remember him. Crush pulled a knife on someone, back a number of years ago before you two married."

"What? Oh my gosh! I do remember him. He cooked with Crush. So, what are you saying?"

"My brother-in-law found the clues about the Phantom Killer sometime in 1948 when he was much younger. In the house on Hickory and 6th Street, our old family home. Did you hear me? He lives with us, still does, and it's eaten at his soul—and ours to have this evidence. You have to help us. We don't want to be known. You must meet me—surrounded by a crowd."

"What? So, your brother-in-law knew who the Phantom Killer might be—years ago?"

"Yes! And we can't let this burden of lying and hiding and keeping the truth from the families remain inside the lockbox any longer."

"But why me?"

"My brother-in-law, Dennis, told your husband about what he had found—but your husband, well, he wasn't your husband when he learned this information. He said to keep what he discovered tucked away. To never bring it up again. To let it go. I'm not sure he believed Dennis. But the lies have ruined too many lives—already."

"But, why now? What's so important to making the killer known?"

"I know you're talked about in the women's circles. It's time for you to redeem yourself in their eyes. And to ease yourself of this burden."

"I'm not up to this. We've lost Clara and Gilbert and now that Lester shot my husband, I'm so confused."

152

"I understand, maybe more than you realize. Your present sufferings are mingled with your past. Please, meet me tomorrow at the corner of 7th Street and Brown. They're filming at Palmer's Grocery with Dawn Wells, and I'm in the scene."

"No, I'm not coming."

"Maybe you can become a part of shedding truth on the dark history of this town by adding light and purpose to the future."

Click.

"Wait, don't hang up. Wait?" I put the receiver to my chest.

Meow. Meow.

Hank wiggled between my legs, in and out, and rubbed his back against my slacks. I stood there numb, and yet, overthinking, and replayed the conversation in my mind.

I ran to Archie, who came from upstairs. He reached for me, handing me a handkerchief. "I listened to the call in your office. I'm sorry. But we're worried about you. So I knew I must. This is too much for you to handle alone."

I screamed, "Why wouldn't Crush tell me about having such a talk with Dennis? What else may he have hidden from me? I need to talk to him. He needs to wake up. I need to color my hair. I need to go the hospital. I need to find Pastor Toby. I need to figure out how to calm this storm. My chest is going to burst wide open. What shall I do?"

Lizzy Beth touched my arm. "Annie, let me sit with you."

Twirling like a merry-go-round stuck on fast, my world spun in circles. *Ahh!* "What's wrong with me?"

"Annie, the war you wage is inside your heart. Not all of this is happening on the outside."

Willie came to me as if walking on water. "Annie Grace, take my hand. Your future ahead includes us, but more importantly it includes God. Place your eyes on Him. Place your future in His hands." Willie held me, and I sobbed, and my shaking rattled the winds of worry and distrust, and I found rest.

Lizzy Beth helped me to the recliner, and I curled up with my kitty, closing my eyes. She whispered, "Rest here for a while. Rest and we'll be here when you wake."

Archie's voice rang from the back of the house. "I'm running to the store for some cat food. I'm taking your car. I'll swing by the hospital and check on Crush. I'll be gone about an hour."

Clearing my throat, I leapt from the chair, as did Hank, and I stormed up the stairs. "I can't rest. I need to move. I can't stay still. I have too much to do. I have to do something." My words ran together, and I spoke faster than a boxcar barreling up a hill, rattling on with each step up the staircase. "After I eat supper, and after Archie comes back, I'm going to see Crush. I need to see him. We need to talk. Or I need to talk to him. But right now, I'm getting rid of this horrible brown color in my hair."

In my bedroom with the door locked again, I yanked all the shirts and boxers and socks belonging to Crush and I tossed them to the floor, stomping on them. Throwing a fit seemed reasonable when you feel someone hides truth from you, especially since the woman's words on the phone left me with unrest and unresolved information about my husband.

"Maybe he's hiding something else. What, I don't know. Maybe he's keeping things from me. He never wanted me to be an investigator. Maybe he longed for a prettier wife. Maybe he's sorry he married someone with so much baggage and with so many emotional issues."

Convinced Crush lied to me about everything and anything, I stomped on his clothes. Maybe he's not who he says he is—he does come from a shady background.

I tumbled to the floor, sighing, the storm within me rose up and raged on. The rain of doubt, the wind of wonder, the worry of whispers telling me to run—to get out of Texarkana. To go far away. To give up. To not find hope in my future. The fear shouted like rustling leaves of death.

Cupping my ears, I cried, "Why is it so hard for me to listen to you, God? Why do I struggle to trust Crush? To trust You? To trust anyone? Crush obviously wanted what was best for me."

I collapsed into the pile on the floor, holding his shirt to my nose, the smell of love close to my heart. "Crush, I know you love me. I know you love me—"

I've spent most of my life judging my own daddy, and he left me with scars on my heart. My nights were also spent analyzing my life, leaving me with nightmares. My days were swallowed up in wishing I could have stopped the Phantom Killer on the first attack, when he chased Martha. And not doing anything has left me with no self-worth. I'm ruined. I'm no good. I didn't try and stop the murderer. And now he's killing me with one disaster after another.

Wallowing on the floor, I picked up a sock. "I've spent too many days, deciding the women and men in this town, who shop and live and eat and go to church; deciding they are mean and ugly or smart and elegant. I've made snap judgments. I've accused them of judging me. When in reality, I've judged them. I've looked at their selfishness. And yet, I'm more selfish than most people. I've witnessed greediness. Again, I'm self-absorbed in mine. I've judged those who disappointed me. Yet, I've disappointed many."

Unable to move, I sniffed the air, taken in by the smell of home as I made my husband's clothes my bed. "Oh honey, forgive me for my wicked ways. You've saved me from myself more times than I deserve. You've chased me to Old Washington even as a teen—and you've guided me and helped me find my way to your love. And now, I'm forty. And I still don't trust you? When will this madness stop?"

I crawled to the bed, kneeling beside the mattress, desperate for hope, weeping at my sin, seeking forgiveness from God for my own stubbornness. As I waited for God to respond, I heard Pastor Toby's words ring in my ear, from the last counseling session with Crush and myself, months ago from last fall—where he said, "Annie Grace, when you're desperate enough to find deliverance, please, fall to your knees at the feet of Christ. And He'll be there to pick you up."

Sobbing, I took my prayers all the way to the garden where Adam and Eve sinned, to where they hid from God. "God, I'm like them. I hide and run and make noise to keep the racket of sadness out, to hide my brokenness. I can't crawl to you, I am nothing. Please God, all those people who were attacked or were murdered by the Phantom Killer were worthy of living and of finding love. Even Clara and Gilbert were worthy. And it saddens me to see all this pain in life."

I bounced to my feet, a revelation of hope sparked my next words. "Those who died reminded me of myself. I've gotten stuck as the victim when I needed Christ to show me how to love, to rise up from the ashes of the horrible stuff, that life has thrown at me. My daddy drank too much. He lied. He left me. He kidnapped me from my grandma. He wanted to sell me."

I paused, "But, he didn't … sell me. So, he must have loved me. Or at least, he wanted to love me."

My breathing labored with gasps as if heavy bricks pressed on my chest, pushing me into a rubble of sorrow. "God, let me solve the case of Clara and Gilbert. And the case of the Phantom Killer. And I'll close my investigation business. No more obsessing with murders. I'll finish my book and write a new story—with you."

After offering my words to God, I pondered if it were wise to ask God for a deal—as if He offered deals. Or even considered answering such a request.

**

I dashed to the bathroom past the stairs, hollering over the rail to my sister and brother. "I'm coloring my hair, taking a bath, and we'll be off to see Crush. I'm ready to conquer this chapter of my life. Ready to forgive. To be a great wife. To love. To show Crush the woman he married is still inside me. She may be wrinkled and scarred—but she's chasing the dream of a happy marriage for real and for good."

Lizzy Beth's reply traveled up the stairs, but it faded, and I rushed into the bathroom, grabbing the box of hair color—meadow yellow. "Perfect. This will take 20 minutes. Not long at all."

I poured the goo from one bottle into the other, shook it up, poured the mixture onto my hair, and wrapped my head in a towel. I climbed into the claw-foot bathtub, the warm water calming. I poured extra bubbles into the water, splashing like a child, soaking up the cleansing sensation. My moods swing high and then drop low, but right now—I'm high on living free and finding my smile again.

A mumbled voice called to me through the door.

"Just a minute. I'm rinsing my hair. I have to get this off. I'm almost me again. Give me another minute or two."

I tiptoed across the tile, slipping from the splashed water on the floor, which I'd made getting out, and then I bumped my leg on the sink. Reaching for the towel rack, I yanked both of the blue towels to the floor, gaining my balance. I wobbled, dried my body and my hair, and a purple bruise took over my knee faster than I could get my blue jeans on and my purple top.

Wrapping my head in a towel, I reached and turned the doorknob. I stood facing Lizzy Beth and Willie, whose eyes were wet with tears. Archie cradled my kitty, and sighed, "Your kitty's calling for you. He already loves you."

"What's wrong? No more bad news! Please!" I shook my head. "Out of my way! Can't a girl get ready in peace?"

Lizzy Beth pulled on my arm. "Annie Grace ..."

I yanked it away. "You don't call me by my middle name."

"I do when it's serious. Come sit on this stack of papers by the wall."

I obeyed her like she held a power over me, plopping down. "What's going on? I'm nearly ready to go to the hospital. I've put my shirt on, the one Crush gave me for my birthday last January." I bent down, rolling up the cuff on my jeans. "I have some navy Keds in my closet. I think I'll wear them. They're brand new."

Willie moved in front of me. "We need to tell you something. It's not easy to say."

"Willie, hurry up. I need to take Hank outside and let the sun dry my hair. Gosh, it feels so good to have my blonde back. I look normal again. I'm ready to kiss and hug and help my husband recover, too. He's taken care of me. It's my turn."

Archie handed my kitty to me. "Darling, it's Crush. He woke up earlier, calling for you. The nurse said she phoned, but the line was busy. He requested some paper and pen, to write you a note." Archie reached into his pants pocket. "It's his final words. He scribbled this for you, before he took his last breath."

"No! Crush is alive. I'm going to see him. I'm his wife. He needs me. I'm ready to let him know our future together is free of nonsense. Free of pain. I'm ready to face tomorrow."

Lizzy Beth took the note from Archie. "Shall I read it to you, Annie?"

"Read it to me? I'm not accepting a goodbye letter from Crush. The nurse is mistaken. The doctor, too. Crush isn't dead!"

Archie wrapped his arm around me. "Shoelace, he's gone."

"Don't call me, Shoelace. She's not here. I'm Annie Grace Raike. Remember, I'm married to Taggart. He's the only man I've loved. The only one who would have me." I crumpled to the floor, my wet hair a symbol of my current status. I shot a glare at Lizzy Beth, and kissed Hank on the head. "Tell me … tell me … what he wrote."

Lizzy Beth wiped her nose as Archie guided me to my bedroom, to sit on the edge of my bed. She unfolded the paper, her nose dripping with a mix of snot and tears. "Here's his farewell." Pausing, she handed the paper to Archie. "I can't read it. You have to."

Archie sat next to me, to let me read along. He uttered, "Annie Grace Raike, you have my heart. I love you—I'd go anywhere to find you. You'll always be my wife. I'm so thankful we found each other. Love, Crush."

The room went silent, and Lizzy Beth gathered up the clothes from the floor, and I knocked the shirts from her hands, clasping some of them to my chest. "Those belong to Crush. Don't touch his things!" I sniffed his clean undershirt.

"Crush, you'll never know me as I could have been, you only knew me as I was."

Willie placed his arm around me. "He knew you. And he loved you."

I wept. "He overlooked my sin, hoping my life might turn around. He stood with me, when others ran away. He dared to believe I could change."

Lizzy Beth sighed. "He searched for you when you couldn't find yourself. He always found you—eventually."

Holding his clothes, I faded into a place where music once rippled across my heart, where birds once sang, and where laughter once abounded. My life without Crush meant a piece of me had tumbled into the abyss of a deep well, where slivers of lost hope jabbed at my entire being—like a chicken hawk clawing at my soul.

Life After Death

They've left. They're all gone. The people who eat your food and drink your tea, who attend funerals as if they're coming to a party. They've said their goodbyes to my husband as if he left town. But he's never coming back. Never!

Most of these people never spoke to me or looked my way today—it's as if I caused his pain and his death. I've resorted to judging those around me, again. And the cycle continues—I can't seem to win or fight or seek joy—not right now.

All these people who came to pay their respect, where were they when Crush was alive? Why didn't they save him from having a wife like me? I rocked in the chair on the balcony facing a life that seemed to have lost its purpose. I have no partner. I have no best friend. I have no one to snore with—or cry with—or to grow old with. I'm alone.

Earlier, Lizzy Beth met with a group of women with more casseroles who piled into the house after we left Rose Hill Cemetery. Along with dozens of others who came by to drink my tea. But the only person who came to the funeral who mattered most, in some ways was River—she's healing and staying at her camp. Even her dog Flashlight licked my face as if she knew my sorrow.

The cars littered the street, a town of friends and not-so-great friends who ate the food and shared their stories, who cried and laughed, who hugged each other. Who came inside my house—for the first time in months or for the first time ever.

I am thrilled Archie came to town, though. I'm happy my brother and sister came, too. Even Taddy and Colleen sat by me and prayed with me. But why is it that people seem to care only when life attacks or kills? Why can't we care for each other on the alive days with the same passion? I have more questions than answers and life's a blur of longing, of wishing, of lost chances, and of grief.

Four days ago, Crush died in a bed at a hospital while I talked to a woman on the phone, as I struggled with answers to my past. And then I took the time to color my hair! I had no idea that my minutes with Crush were numbered on the short end. I've dishonored him by distracting myself with clutter and with lists and with anything else, except with, being a wife—another failure in my life.

I should have known the bullets punctured his lungs, but I blocked the doctor's words out. Like most of life, I've blocked out reality and struggled to face myself—let alone face others with a true commitment.

The day after Crush died, Officer Teacup stopped by to see me when I could barely move from my bed—wrapped in a quilt of regret. I never came downstairs, but his report of the shooting based on witnesses told another version of the shooting than the originally reported account. Different than what I witnessed, too. He said the clerk claimed to see Taddy pull a gun. She's wrong, I'm sure.

And another man leaving one of the motel rooms heard Crush offer to take Lester home—to sleep it off. But that man's wife heard Lester tell him, he'd not had a drop, but his slurring and behavior contradicted his words.

But the part I remember which bothers me the most is the image in my head of this burly man hovering behind the hedge, murmuring and shouting under his breath. Did that man have a gun? Did I see the barrel poking through the bushes? Could I have seen another gun?

My brain tangled with confusion, and Officer Teacup blew the lid off the percolator of my clues by telling Willie and

Lizzy Beth that Lester's gun wasn't even loaded—which meant the bullets inside my husband's chest came from somewhere else.

So, the police released Lester. And now I need to face the truth or seek the truth or make sure I know the truth—to see if I should say something about the stranger to Officer Teacup. To see if I should report him as a suspect. Because, sure, Lester was drunk, but that's all. What did I see? What is the truth?

Confused, I rocked faster and faster in my wooden rocker, praying time would age me with each movement. That wrinkles would come with an old heart, and bring frailty, turning me into an old woman. Then my heart would fail, and the pain would leave—because right now, each breath consumed me as if a butcher knife carved at my chest.

I'm processing the information, not sure how Lester shot my husband and—didn't shoot him. And I'm losing myself in the replay in my mind, the clips of that morning played out differently each time I played the scene out, like rewriting a movie script with different possibilities.

Rubbing my eyes, I still can't get over how Taddy gave me the gibberish of showing up in my life, of wanting to reconcile our friendship, only to leave town for Jefferson right after Crush went to the hospital. At the funeral—he seemed distant and preoccupied. His statement to Officer Teacup included a story of going home to Jefferson to oversee the sale of some property. I have no idea what that meant—but it's one more confusion to add to my list of questions without answers.

Pastor Toby and Willie were clearing the empty plates and tea glasses when I excused myself to the upstairs, to this spot hanging over the front porch, which is my oasis. Crush sat here with me in times past. He was my rock. My foundation.

My voice. My heart. My hope. What shall I do next? What is the path to take?

Tweak-eek. Tweak-eek.

The squeak of the screen door behind me sent me glancing at Lizzy Beth. She asked, "Would you like something to eat? You haven't had a bite."

"No, I'm not hungry." I don't know what to do next. I'm caught on this porch with nowhere to go, and nothing to look forward to—my tomorrows are empty.

Meow. Meow. Meow.

Hank purred and leapt to my lap. "Silly, kitty. You have no idea what you've gotten yourself into by moving in with me."

"He needs you. He's alone, too." Lizzy Beth's black hair twisted on top of her head made her look older. And the loose black dress she'd worn to the funeral didn't help, either.

I stopped rocking. My own dark dress spoke of how love songs fade and how, in one second, you can lose your husband to a not-so-random bullet.

Lizzy Beth moved to sit in the rocker next to mine. "Do you mind if I sit in his chair?"

"No, someone should use it." I petted Hank.

"This may be a bad time, since no time is a good time— right now, I wanted to share this with you in person. You know how I love children, and we've considered adopting, since I'm thirty-three—and not getting any younger. Well, I went to the doctor right before Archie called, and … I'm pregnant." She smiled a grin which spoke of how joy filled her future.

I pretended to act thrilled, and although I longed for her happiness, Lizzy Beth's news only made me sadder. I hugged my sister. "You're going to make a fabulous mother. I'm sure Maxwell is excited. You should be home with him."

She rubbed her still-flat belly, a glow obvious in her smile. "I've got a few months to go. I'm barely three months along. But that's what I'm saying, I'm leaving in two days with Archie. We're taking the train to Memphis on Saturday. I have a doctor's appointment on Monday, and Willie will stay on, for as long as you need him. Or you could come stay with us for a few months."

"No, Willie should get home to his children and his wife, too. I need some time to learn how to live this way. River is coming to stay with me. She'll be here."

"Your friend who lives in the woods?"

"Yes, she's on the mend. She understands me." I put my hand to my mouth, realizing I could still be in danger. And my mind went to Taddy, not to Lester, to wondering if Taddy shot River, to wondering if Taddy shot Clara and Gilbert, too. And why? And wondering, how I could ever believe Taddy could kill anyone.

I popped up from the rocker. "Maybe I should ride up to Memphis and stay with you after all. Would you mind?" I planned my plan with Lizzy Beth, taking her on a trip of how I'd come up on the train next week once I gave River the keys to the house and car. And I'd make sure her dog Flashlight wouldn't eat my kitty.

But none of what I told Lizzy Beth would come to pass. I'll get her on the train to Memphis. And Archie, too. And I planned to talk Willie into leaving with them, so he could be with his family before the whistle on the train blew and pulled out from Union Station in two days.

My real plan included having River move in with me. Of having her help me figure out how Taddy found himself in my life and in my summer.

With River by my side, I could once again find my purpose and become a messenger of hope, which by all accounts so far has failed to manifest itself in my life.

The afternoon sun drifted low behind the house, and Lizzy Beth and I rocked without saying a word. I stared at her beauty, the classy way she crossed her ankles and folded her tiny hands in her lap. She took the bobby pins from her bun, and her hair dropped like silk. I touched her arm. "You are prettier than you know." I spoke kindness into her heart, something I should do more often.

Willie joined us, leaning on the rail, talking fast with short bursts, rattling on with reports from reading the newspaper—with how he'd love to take in a moment to go to the filming of the movie before they finished the taping.

He tapped me on the head since I was about to fall asleep. "Annie Grace, would it bother you if I went to the movie set tomorrow? They're supposed to be taping at Spring Lake Park."

Caught off-guard, I nodded, my mind rushing to the real crime scene of my past. I jumped to the night at the park, to a night when I tumbled over something breathing, with red nail polish, next to a musical instrument. I remembered how I hadn't stopped to check on the injured person because at that moment, as a kid, I figured I'd fallen over an animal.

I grabbed my chest, and the suffocating gloom hung over me, again. The triggers this movie deposits into my day are wearing me down. For every three steps ahead, I've moved back five. Those who died at the hand of the Phantom Killer left behind family. They must have suffered with horrible aches and sorrow, and now I know their horror.

I whispered to them in my head. "I'm sorry I couldn't help save your family members."

As I rocked, I kept replaying the call from the woman on the phone, about the clues from the house on Hickory. And since I missed the filming at the grocery store, I somehow knew a visit might be in order—and going to the woman's home might be the best step to take.

One thing that calls to me though, with the mingling of so many clues from both cases—is something I couldn't seem to shake off. What did Clara's note mean about the baby?

Who's Fake? Me or Them?

I called to Willie from the back door. "Willie, they're filming this morning before it gets hot. Come on. We have to drive north of Hooks, they're not using the park. Ernie wrote about it in the paper."

My brother dawdled in the kitchen, eating pancakes with syrup made by Marion Kane's factory in Jefferson. He's never in a hurry when there's food, especially the syrup we grew up having for breakfast.

I ran inside to retrieve him, as Hank scampered outside over my Keds. "Willie, you're skinnier than a fence post, and yet, you eat everything."

Smacking, he licked his lips. "This is the best syrup. Marion Kane wouldn't want me to waste a drop."

I moved from the door, pulling up a chair at the table for eight—a table that's now for one person, and I put the car keys down. I swooped my finger through the maple goo on Willie's plate, licking and smacking the syrup from my finger. "Yummy, is right. I can never get enough of his syrup."

"Me, neither." Willie showed me his food by gawking at me as he talked, as if he became a kindergartener. Which is how old he was, the summer we rescued him from the black market of the adoption ring in Memphis. He found his smile back when I was twelve. When we found the truth—and saved lives, thanks to Archie. Lots of them, by shutting down the horrible place which stole babies and children.

"Hey, are we picking up Archie at the motel? Or is he packing? He's not into watching pretend murders."

"He's not coming. He called earlier when you were chasing Hank in the front yard." Willie picked up the plate, running his tongue across the last drop of syrup, reaching for his coffee to gulp the rest down.

I acted interested in the goodbye-trip happening in the morning. "So, what time does our train leave tomorrow?"

"We leave at 8 a.m. sharp. I'll need to tell Lizzy Beth the wrong time, so we can be on time for the departure. We'll need to pick Archie up from the motel first, so I'm sure we'll need to leave here by seven. Is River going to bring your car back to the house?"

"Yes, we can leave the keys in the floorboard. I told her we were leaving by noon, but I'll let her know the plan. She'll make sure the Rambler makes it back to the garage. She and her dog will look after the place, too." I smiled. "I've missed being around you and Lizzy Beth."

Lizzy Beth popped from around the corner of the wall from inside the reading room, clutching a broom and a dust pan. "I knew it. I knew you loved us."

Squinting, I observed the clothes drooping on her body. "Where did you get that top and those cutoffs?"

She ran her fingers through the end of her silky black hair, as the mood ring she never takes off got caught in her hair. "Ouch! I do that all the time."

"You never learn."

"You're one to point a finger."

Our banter made us both smile; mine was fake, but Lizzy Beth often brings her chatty, chipper self when she thinks I need help bouncing back from things.

She danced around the table. "I didn't bring enough clothes. I'm going to wash a load while you two are gone. I borrowed this top and these blue-jean shorts from you."

I pushed her away, taking in my favorite orange button-up top with the big collar. "Did you rummage through my dresser?"

"No, I organized your dresser. You don't fold a thing. And look, we're the same size." She tugged on the shorts, pulling them up. And straightened the cotton top as it shifted around on her shoulders. "Well, they're a little baggy. And the blouse is falling off, but I'm comfy."

Laughing, I ran to her, holding my sweet sister close, so much so, she gasped for breath. This time my smile was real.

"Annie, too tight. Too tight."

"Sorry, I forget how strong I am when I love on someone."

Ding-a-click.

Willie snatched the keys from the table. "We're going to be late. Come on."

Lizzy Beth stacked Willie's coffee cup into his near-clean plate. "I'll do these." She marched toward the swinging door at the kitchen. "Oh, Annie, I cleaned up your office, dusted the desks, and swept the floors upstairs, too. And behind the trash can by Clara's desk, I found—" She reached inside the pocket on the cutoffs.

I swooped closer to her. "What did you find?"

"Well, I found the prettiest locket and I could have sworn I put it in my pocket. Darn, I must have dropped it." She dug in the other pocket. "It's somewhere. I had it earlier."

"What kind of locket?"

"It was the size of a quarter, and silver with a small engraved squirrel on the face. And a teeny brass acorn above his head, on a sliver chain."

"And why didn't you tell me? Didn't you think this might be important? And now you've lost it?" I stormed into the library where Lizzy Beth last did a round of chores, with her on my heels.

She cried, "I'm sorry. When I came downstairs, I planned to tell you after I finished dusting the piano. But the layer of

170

dust on the end tables and the coffee table called to me. Which led to cleaning the fireplace mantle, and I lingered at the family photos and went back to our school days. I love the one of you and me and Willie when we were in school—that one you have of us in junior high—and you were a senior. Time has sure gotten away."

I pinched her. "Stop deflecting with your silly rambling. The locket's not mine. It must have belonged to Clara. Where is it?" I yanked on her arm.

"Stop yelling at me. I made pancakes this morning for you two. I put the coffee on, took your trash outside. I've made myself useful by cleaning your house. I've washed the dust off the front porch with the garden hose. I'm trying to help you. I don't know how to take away your pain. Cleaning is how I cope with life. I didn't mean to lose the locket. It's here somewhere."

Willie stormed between us, shouting at Lizzy Beth. "Is this necessary? Stop listing all your good deeds. She's lost her husband. She needs our compassion right now. Let's find the locket for her."

I placed my hands on my hips, shaking my head, spouting words jumping from my mouth, those trapped in the locket of darkness, from deep within. "I appreciate your kindness. I do, Lizzy Beth. And you've both been great. I do love you. I do. More than you know. I'm in a place where one second, I'm fine, but the next it's like I slept in and missed my alarm, and I feel panicked. I hoped to wake up and see Crush. To see him talking to me in my tree—I'd love to hear him get mad at me."

Willie held me. "I'm sorry. I don't know how we can fix this for you."

"No one can. I feel like I'm a record on the turntable and stuck on replay. It's so painful." I wept, letting my hurts fall through my tears.

Lizzy Beth wrapped herself around me. "I'm sorry. I love you."

Whispering, I added, "I never imagined I'd miss seeing Clara dance up the stairs in her Belk Jones' dresses. And hearing her sing."

Willie moved toward the dining room. "Let's go for a ride. You could use some fresh air. A fresh view. Hey, we have time to check out the movie set. We'll go to Guy's and get us a Texas burger. How does that sound?"

"But you should be full."

"I am. But in a while, I'll get hungry again. I can eat anytime and anywhere."

I scuttled along with Willie, unable to argue, for fear the blank expression on my face might twist and turn and tornado into a full-fledge Annie Grace fit. "Yes, let's go take a ride. I need to put Hank inside. I don't want to lose my kitty."

Lizzy Beth touched my shoulder. "I'll find the locket while you're out. It's here. It hasn't gone anywhere."

Not saying a word, I nodded—unable to pinpoint how I should react or live or move or talk. Without my husband, I'm lonely inside this house, even with the company. I hope River's ready to be my strength once I ditch them tomorrow, because my legs are wobbly, and my heart is beating with the saddest thumps. I must have someone to talk to, to trust, to help me cope. Plus, she'll bring me back—to me, when I don't know who I am.

We marched outside and into the backyard, and by the garage, Hank clawed at the dirt next to the alley. "Here boy. Come to mama."

Meow. Meow.

Willie called from inside the garage. "I'll bring the car to the side of the house while you get the cat. I can't believe you still have this old Rambler."

"It's not old, it's seasoned and weathered and broken in." I cuddled Hank, hurried to the kitchen, cracking the screen to usher him in—when a conversation drifted my way causing me to linger and listen, to the truth behind Lizzy Beth's cleaning.

"No, she's not doing good. Honey, I'll be home tomorrow. I'm fine, no morning sickness, yet. I love you." Lizzy Beth stopped talking and motored up, again. "No, Maxwell! We'll put Annie's house on the market after we get her to Memphis. We'll need to get her settled in." Another pause. "No, she'll stay with us until the baby comes. We'll find her a house near ours. She'll be a great aunt. She won't miss this old house. It's too much for her. She needs to be near family. We'll be fine. I'm sure her crazy days are over."

I barreled around the stove, running into the chairs at the table, and stood frozen. Facing my sister, everything I wanted to say got blocked inside my head, and everything I was going to regret, exploded from my lips. "You're not selling this house. Marion Kane gave it to Crush and me. Now, it's mine. Not one piece of this house is for sale. Go live in Memphis. Go live with your Maxwell! Have your baby and be a mama— but keep this in mind." I pointed my finger at her. "You are not my mama! And you have no say over my affairs."

Lizzy Beth's olive skin turned pale. "I only want what's best for you!"

"Sure, you do! Who are you to know what's best for me?" I raced from the house, jumped from the back steps, and charged to the side steps to the Rambler, hollering at Willie. "Get out of the car. Get out of my car! I'm driving. And I'm going somewhere to think!"

Willie sighed, "What's happened now?"

"Go ask your sister. She's planning to sell my home out from under me. It's not for sale!"

Of Callie and Harper and Lester, Too

I clutched the steering wheel, skidding ahead to the next block, leaving Willie on the sidewalk next to the Ahern House, which is my house. I pulled up to the corner where my grandma's manor once stood, imagining her front porch with the wooden rockers—the ones on my balcony. I imagined the rough quilts, which aren't so rough now—they're quite worn, actually. And soft. And I imagined the chocolate cake she baked—warm and fresh—with her own hands.

The car idled at the stop sign, and I imagined the carriage house in the back where the washer and dryer overflowed when I poured too much soap powders into the water. I imagined seeing my grandma hang out clothes on the line. I imagined her humming while baking a cake. I imagined playing in the water and making the yard muddy, and hearing Grandma Elsie yell and giggle—because she had trouble staying mad at me. I imagined sitting with her on the sofa and drinking sweet tea with her.

Honk. Honk.

I glanced in the rearview mirror. "Hold your horses!" I yelled at the driver behind me who sat in the old jalopy, and for a split second, I imagined Pastor Cody being alive—but he died in the fire in Old Washington. Which was my fault, too.

Inching ahead, I drove two blocks up, stopping at the intersection at Hickory, switching my blinker on, turning left. I glanced to my right at the two-story brick house on the corner of 6th Street. Was this the house where the woman lives who has the clues?

I pulled ahead, made a right next to the house, and got out of the car. A scruffy man pushed the rocker back and forth, as a newspaper lay scattered around his slippers. He appeared around my age, with brown hair and flat nose. He sat up, folding the paper into a cylinder. "Can I help you?"

"You remind me of someone. Did you work at Guy's a long time ago?"

He rose from the rocker, which squeaked. "I may have. Who are you?"

"I worked there, too. My husband, Crush, worked there. Well, my late husband ..."

"Are you ... are you Annie Grace?"

"Yes, I am."

The man wearing his house slippers but dressed in slacks and a white T-shirt came to the edge of the porch. "I'm sorry. I heard about your husband getting shot. To think, Lester did such a horrible thing."

"You know Lester?"

"Everyone at the pool hall knows Lester. He gets drunk and talks big."

"He may be trouble. But the police cleared him of shooting my husband. They said Lester's gun wasn't loaded."

"Who do they think did it?"

"I don't know. These last few days have spiraled longer than a rooster's crow at sunrise, like an uncut version of my life. Plenty of edits. And lots of rewinding. Real and raw."

"How can I help you?"

"Does your sister-in-law have a small son? If so, she's called my house, but she won't say who she is. But refers to her boy with the blond hair."

"I live here alone. It's my old man's house. This home belonged to his father before him. Sorry, no kids. And no woman. I'm a bachelor. I'm pushing forty-five, it's me and my bird. But she tends to squawk too much." He chuckled, wiping his unshaven chin.

"Sorry to have bothered you. I'm not sure where she lives. I guess I have the wrong house. Take care." I moved to my car, falling into the seat, and drove ahead, going past the bushes, and glancing left into the man's backyard—I noticed a swing set with a slide. "No! If he has no kids, why does he have swings?"

Through my opened window, I turned my head back, to catch the man glaring at me from the side yard—but he jumped out of view.

"Wait, I need to ask you some more questions."

I put the car in park, bounded from the driver's seat, and darted to the front porch, rounded the hedge, and hopped up the stairs to an empty porch. Pounding my fist on the door, the man who lied to me peeked through the cracked door, keeping the screen closed. "Leave my property. I have nothing to say to you. I am not who you need. You need someone else."

"Could it be I need your sister-in-law? Where is she? She has a boy with yellow hair, doesn't she? Tell me where she is. I need to talk to her. And now!"

"She's across town. Across town, I tell you. She does live here. And my brother does too, he's her husband. They don't want anyone to let this get out to the news. We want you to break the case, so we can live in peace. Our family is scarred by this, and we can't keep it in—any longer."

"So, when I pulled up, you knew who I was?"

"Yes, but I don't want any attention drawn to us at the house. We only want to live our life in peace. My sister, Callie, fretted over this when her boy, Harper, found the box in the attic with all—the things I found so long ago."

"Let me see it. I'll take it with me. I'll take it off your hands."

"I can't. You must leave now. This secret mustn't get attached to my house." He slammed the door, shouting through the windowpane. "I can't let you inside. Besides, the box isn't here now. We've hidden it, until we could get it to you." He rubbed his chin, squinting his eyes at me.

"Tell me where to go. I'll get it." I shook my head, and the man's erratic behavior forced me to ask more questions. "What are you afraid of? What's wrong?"

"I'm not who you see. I'm a ghost of a man with a past. I stay here to have a place to live—because my criminal record haunts me. I would become a target." He covered his mouth, as if telling me freed his soul, and the curtain dangled and waved, and closed, and I found myself unable to move—until the door opened, startling me.

The man pushed me. "Get off the porch. Leave. You can't be here."

I scooted to the side of the porch, jumping from the end to a patch of dirt. "What is this horrible cycle I'm on? Why can't I live in peace? Why do I need to be a part of this? Why me?"

Back in the car, I drove in circles, and found myself at the cemetery, sitting on our family bench. My mind is trapped with more questions, with too much loss, and I'm lying to myself by acting like I'm not wounded. But my trust issues are worse now, and I don't know how to see when my eyes feel blinded by the horror of the tragedies in my life. I've chased perfection like Taddy, but a perfection to be someone I'm not—and I've built a safe room around me with plenty of chaos to keep others out. This way they won't know me, so maybe, I won't hurt them—but I still do.

I'm living with fear. I'm struggling with the confidence to leave the rooms in my head, where I'm safe. But I'm not safe. This world is cruel. This world is broken. I'm the piece to a puzzle, one I never wanted to take part in.

I touched my grandma's marker and leaned on her tombstone. "Grandma, I don't know what to do. My heart is tired. My hands are aching. My eyes are weary. What should I do? I hate this season. I hate this earthquake of broken steps."

Weeping, I imagined my grandma sitting next me and inside I turned into a ten-year-old girl. I heard her say to me: "Annie Grace, look in the sky. Look up. You're tired. But you are strong in God. He made you to run. He's called you to—"

"To what, Grandma?"

"You are a messenger of hope. Build a memorial for the eight—and place the statue where everyone will see—and never forget."

"What? A memorial? But, Grandma a part of me is missing. I'm tired. Can you hold me? Can you make the pain go away? Please, Grandma, hold me." I hugged the tombstone.

A voice from across the cemetery called like a tumbleweed of an impending sandstorm. "Annie Grace, are you all right?"

Standing, I moved to my car, glancing around, not seeing anyone. "Who's there? Show yourself."

"Don't run. It's me." Lester shuffled in his boots across the loose sand, holding a shovel. "Don't be afraid."

"Are you serious? Because of you, my husband's dead." I stormed right up to him, grabbing the handle on the shovel, pulling it from his grasp.

Lester raised his hands up. "Hit me. Beat me with your shovel. My brother's dead. And the love of my life."

"The love of your life?"

"Yes, I've loved Clara since we were kids. But Gilbert turned her against me."

"Maybe your drinking caused you to stumble. No one wants a drunk for a husband." Lester cowered back. "Take a swing and get it out. I'm the one who should be dead. Not them, and certainly not your husband."

"What were you doing at Kings Row Inn that morning? You were so out of it." I stuck the blade of the shovel into the ground, leaning on the handle.

"I'd spent the night playing pool, got caught up in a card game, and drank too much, and a man mocked me causing me to drop my gun to the floor. I take the gun when I go out late—on those nights when the athlete in me can't cope with losing the woman I should have had—but lost."

I couldn't help but worry that his words might be filled with truth. "So, do you carry around an empty pistol?"

"No, one of my buddies removed the bullets the other night since I was so plastered. And it's a good thing."

"But why or how did you make it from downtown at the pool hall, toward Stateline, to the motel?"

"I got a call when I was leaving, used the phone at the bar, and someone told me Crush was accusing me of murdering Clara. I took one last drink, and the world swirled. I'm convinced someone put something in my drink. I've been drunk before, many times. This was different. I got raging mad, drove there, and found myself staring at him in a pool of blood."

"Someone sent you to the motel? I don't understand. Whoever called you, probably followed you, and shot my husband. And possibly Clara and Gilbert. And even River."

"Who's River?"

"She's one of my homeless friends at the camp. Her wounds were not too deep, thankfully." I gave the shovel to Lester. "I don't know what this all means, but I do know I can't keep hating you. Hate consumes, and I'm pretty worn out."

Lester offered his condolences. "I meant no harm to Crush, but when I drink I'm worthless."

180

"The whiskey consumed my daddy's life. I hope you don't let it take yours." I processed the clues, almost like muddy water, stinky—like a dry brook with dead fish. Something smelled fishy, and the guy who took the call at the pool hall—might be the man who can tell me who shot my husband!

But right now, I'm going to Hooks—to see if Callie will let me in on the answers to solving the Phantom Killer case. Hopefully, she's there. I fell into my car, held on, and sped from the cemetery.

One second, I give up. The next I'm driven, unable to quit searching for answers. Goodness, I hope I'm not crazy like everyone thinks!

When a Clue Was a Lie

Gripping the steering wheel, I tailed the old Model-T, disgusted at myself for arguing with Willie and Lizzy Beth. I'm sadder than sad and pressed down beyond anything. Enduring the ups and downs of my anxiety, plus the fact I'm a widow, made my pity party one of disappointment and unhappiness. One of regret and shame. My chest heaved as if a hundred drums boomed inside my heart.

I wiped a tear from my face, pressing the brake, slowing down. "No! What a stupid driver! He pulled onto 7th Street in front of that green Ford." I stopped, looking both ways. "Are those sirens?"

Sitting at the intersection, I watched the camera crew on my left with their cameras, and they moved closer. Then I saw the crowd of people watching the filming from across the road. A man wearing an apron hung out beside an old store, waving his arms as if he acted a part in the show. "Oh, my goodness. They're right here. They're doing a chase scene. No wonder I couldn't find them in Hooks."

A black police car with flashing red lights chased the first car, whipping around the Model-T. I took in the action. "That was Mr. Pierce driving, in the black police hat. Those other two faces, they're famous actors. Willie was right, Mr. Pierce is playing a role in his own movie."

Pulling behind the cars, I followed them—staying a good bit behind, so as to not interfere. I found myself on a dusty road as the first patrol car left the trail, taking out bushes, with cameras filming the entire chaotic chase. I inched at a snail's pace to take it in myself.

I then parked on the side of the dirt road, stepped from my car, and watched the scene come together. I scanned the field like my eyes were cameras filming the action. A small group of people watched the filming too, positioned on the other side of a barbed wire fence—safely out of the way.

I realized, I ended smack dab in front of the cameras, and I worried the scene was ruined because of me. I wiped the dirt from my face, noticing a small child with his mother across the way. "Is that her? Could she be here?" The toddler's hair shone like a sunray calling to me.

Running across the set, I hoped to cut across the pasture, to get to her, to move quickly, to not cause any more problems. My jog sent me in front of Mr. Pierce's car as he'd turned around from circling a tree. I dove to the side, which caused him to weave, and the patrol car flew right into the pond. "Oh my! I'm in trouble now."

The camera man applauded, "That was great! Best part of this chase scene! And we got it on film!"

I charged to the pond as Mr. Pierce pushed the door open, the water inches deep, which kept them from drowning. "Are you hurt?"

He held his hat. "Not much! But wow! We got a true action-packed moment. I couldn't have planned that better myself."

"I'm so sorry. I didn't mean to get in the way. I surely didn't mean to cause this."

He rubbed his forehead, stumbling, and leaned on the crunched car. "I'm fine. You almost ruined our scene. I'll edit you out but splashing in the murky water will make the scene seem real."

The strong-man close by announced. "Real ... and deadly." He glared at me, as if his patience ran thin.

Mr. Pierce slopped through the water, coming my way. "I recommend you join the rest of the spectators. I'm not sure why you keep crossing my path. But today you created a masterpiece in my movie. Thank you so much." He pointed to the faces absorbing the history-making scene, those who traced the lives of friends of long ago with these reenactments.

"I'm glad it worked out for you. And I'm glad you're not hurt." I wiped my eyes, the sweltering heat beating like a giant heater.

I scooted to the fence row, darting from behind the men with cameras, and those who brought towels to the wet actors. I noticed Junior hurried to his daddy's side, jumping up and down. "That was wild. I love how you wrecked the police into the water. I didn't know you were going to have a crash."

Mr. Pierce rustled his son's hair. "It came as a surprise for me, too."

I inched away, torn between asking Junior some questions and seeking out Callie. Glancing to the people by the fence, four men in overalls appeared captivated by the movie crew. Three women in sundresses applauded with teeny claps, and two boys standing next to their bicycles hung close to the action.

"Where is Callie? She's no longer at the fence." Her absence made my decision easy, and I galloped up behind Junior, waiting for him to move away from his dad.

I skirted behind the patch of trees, while Mr. Pierce and the crew worked on details up the trail. Junior picked up a small limb, using it as a walking stick. He came to a stump, pulled out an apple and chomped down, beating the stump with the stick.

"Hi, can I talk to you for a minute?"

He twirled around. "My dad told me to keep quiet and to stay out of the way."

"But this will help my case. I'm trying to piece together the details of Ms. Clara's note. Can you tell me again how she gave it to you? And how it all came together?"

"I told you. She gave it to me one Wednesday night after I came out of youth group."

"Wait, you said she gave it to you on a Sunday morning after class. That she handed it to you personally—after Sunday school."

"Maybe, it was during the week. Or a Sunday morning. I don't remember now."

I touched his shoulder, his body shook. "Is there something you're hiding? You can tell me."

"I can't tell you. When I chopped up the clues into separate notes, I figured it would be fun, like writing a movie script. I didn't know Ms. Clara might die." He dropped his apple, kicking the core with his tennis shoe.

I knelt in front of him. "I'm your friend. I want to help. I need to solve this murder."

"But if I tell you who gave me the note ..." Junior charged off, heading up the dirt road, but stopped some twenty feet from me, twirled around and called, "It's someone who teaches at the college. He told me Ms. Clara wrote the note. He said she gave it to him. To give to me. To give to you. But I'm not to tell anyone of his involvement in the envelope or I'd regret it."

"Are you serious? It wasn't Clara? What's his name?"

Junior jogged ahead, and I vaulted to him, pulling on his sleeve. "Please, tell me. It will be a way for you to change a life. To save others. To make a difference. This isn't a movie. Or a script. We're talking about a real person. Like Ms. Clara, your Sunday School teacher. My co-worker and friend. She was in love with Gilbert. She had a life—and now she's gone. They're both gone, too." My temper rose, my voice cracked, and Mr. Pierce stormed my way.

Junior whispered, "If I tell you, will you leave me alone? Will you keep me safe? Can you promise me?"

"If we can catch him we'll all be safe. We need to see if maybe he's involved in the murders. But as long as you keep this secret, he's loose to prowl and hurt someone else."

"My daddy thinks it's a copycat murder to mimic the Phantom Killer since he's filming this movie. So, I can't tell you."

"You must." I held both of his shoulders tighter than I should have, and considering I was on the list of no-return with Mr. Pierce, I pushed the limit. "Please," the tears flooding my eyes. "Please, this isn't a burden a small boy should hold inside. Let me help."

Mr. Pierce marched closer, calling to his son. "Go get in the bus. And Ms. Raike, that's your name, isn't it?"

He didn't wait for me to answer, and I didn't let go of Junior's shirt. I held the fabric tighter, a death grip with a longing for a name.

Mr. Pierce touched my hand. "This must stop. You're interfering with my movie! And now, you're bothering my son again."

"It's important. He's lying about who gave him the note. He said Ms. Clara handed the envelope to him, but he's confessed to me that it's someone else."

Junior whined, "Daddy, if I tell her she'll leave me alone. But if I don't tell her, the man …"

"The man? It was a man? Not Clara?" Mr. Pierce drilled his son.

I chimed in. "Please tell me his name."

186

Mr. Pierce hovered over his son, peeling my fingers from his boy's shirt. "This has gotten out of hand. You can't keep doing this."

"But your son knows more. He can change a life. He can tell me what he knows. I could have helped the police when I was a kid, but I didn't. Let your son do what I didn't do. I never spoke a word. I never gave the families peace or answers. I hid the truth." I found myself blurting out everything I'd done wrong after witnessing attacks and murders.

Junior cried, "Daddy, I have to tell her."

Mr. Pierce held his son's chin up. "So, you do know something? Tell me. What is it?"

The three of us faced each other, a moment when a lie became a truth. I leaned closer, ready to listen. "Please, tell me."

Junior nodded. "Mr. Day bumped into me by the front door of the church one Wednesday night. He held an envelope. He asked me if I could keep a secret. If I could play along. If I would give the paper to you if something happened to Clara."

"What? Are you saying it was Taddy?" I grimaced at saying my friend's name.

Junior echoed, "His first name is Thaddeus. He's that college teacher who wears those brown suits and ugly ties."

Mr. Pierce frowned. "Why did you tell her Clara gave you the note?"

"Because he told me, that if I told anyone it was him, it might get a friend in trouble."

I coughed. "I don't understand."

"I was scared." He hugged his daddy's waist. "Daddy, I didn't know what to do."

Mr. Pierce covered his mouth, wiping his chin. "No need to worry. We'll give this information to the police. We'll let them investigate it."

Thinking faster than my words could get together in my throat, I choked on my request. "Let me tell Officer Teacup since I'm involved, I'll catch him up and tell him what you've told me. I know you have a movie to film. I'll go now. My car's up the road. I'm so sorry. But," I twisted down, kissing Junior on the cheek, "thank you for sharing this. Maybe Mr. Day is scared himself. Maybe someone is threatening him." I assured Junior to calm his nerves, or maybe to calm mine.

Mr. Pierce agreed, "I'll let you tell the police. We do have work to do. And Son, you're safe with me. Stay near my side. You're going to do great things with your life."

Junior joined his daddy as they hurried to the crew, and I hiked to my car around the bend. Talking to myself, I processed what Junior had shared with me. Why would Taddy give the boy a note? And how is he connected to the murders?

As I reached my car, the engine hummed, with the keys inside, and I rushed to the idling Rambler. Who is that? Who's in my car? Is that Callie?

The Box Holds the Answer

I slithered over to the passenger window, standing like a guard, blocking the door, and spoke to Callie who sat in the front seat with the window down. "Will you turn my car off? I didn't know I left it running."

"Yes. But talk lower, please. Harper is asleep in the back seat. I turned the key as you came closer to blow some air through the car—but your air conditioner isn't cooling."

"I know, it's broken. Sorry." I peered inside. "He's out like a light. So, you've called my home and your husband, too? And he left those notes for me at the cemetery that were more like riddles? What's with all the hiding?"

"Yes, we regret our approach. He figured if we hired you, you could solve the case of the Phantom Killer once and for all. We never expected for Clara and Gilbert ..."

"Did you know them?"

"No, not so much. We only heard about them from Mr. Day since my husband works with him at the college."

"Your husband works with Taddy?"

"He does. Jon is a teacher there, too. They work across the hallway, and they're wrapping up some summer courses right now."

I took a deep breath, my fingers tingled, and my energy left me with each exhale. This chapter of my story meant I might uncover and discover horrible things I might regret. "So, why are you in my car?"

"It's time to make this right. I know we've had a little trouble making contact, so I waited for you." She wiped the sweat dripping on her temple, her blonde hair the color of the inside of an apple. "After you came to my home earlier today, I knew we must meet."

"How did you know I came by?"

"Dennis told me."

"I hope I didn't scare him. He seemed so nervous."

"He gets that way. After I left, I took a chance you'd come to the filming today—in case our paths might cross. And yes, you've rattled Dennis. He's afraid his past will determine how others see his future."

"I'm sorry. With my husband's death, and with your calls, and with the clues on Clara and Gilbert's case flying into my life, it's one horrible nightmare. And my friend, River, got shot in her shoulder—and life has reeled into a disaster of too much—too fast—with sadness and loss. And I'm not coping."

Callie opened the car door, treading up next to me. "Let me assure you, I only want to give you this information, so we can move on. The only part you can never share is who gave it to you and how you received it. It's time for you to heal, for all of us to heal. For it would seem, a distant relative committed those crimes."

"Where is this box with the answers? Dennis mentioned you moved it, hiding the box and getting it out of the house."

"Yes. My son found it." She glanced at her boy in the seat. "We were in the attic going through old trunks when he happened upon a heavy metal box. Dennis had tucked the lockbox inside one of the trunks. He also had the key inside a drawer in his room—from back when he first found it."

"I can't believe you've kept this a secret. It doesn't make sense."

"It does, because Dennis was falsely accused of hurting a young girl years ago. The newspaper ran the story before he was able to clear his name. He spent time in jail for a theft which he did do, stealing a car after drinking with his buddies.

But he never hurt that girl. She lied about the whole thing—because the person who beat her—was her stepdad."

"Oh my, that's terribly complicated. The newspaper stories build the hype and things grow into monster stories—and the ugly stories sell papers."

Callie sighed, "When Dennis discovered the box on the dining room table, he hollered at me—but he finally let me open it after admitting he had a key."

"What's inside? What is it that tells the whole truth?"

"Dennis shared this evidence with your boyfriend years ago. And he knew you, too. And he also knew your life was riddled with nightmares—and he figured this could solve everything. That is, until Crush told him to hide the box, to let it go. That your healing would come by not knowing. But I'm sure now he was wrong. Then Dennis went away to jail for five years before he was cleared. His past haunts him, as does yours. He's not confident around others."

"I understand how the past can haunt someone, even in the present."

"The box will give you enough evidence to settle the case."

"Can we go to the box? Where is it?"

"Let me get my son. Our car is by the fence post by the main road. Will you give me a ride?"

"Sure, I'll be happy to." I marched around the car, opened the door and got inside, while Callie slipped into the passenger seat. Her blue-dotted cotton dress fresh and clean, except for the sweat stains beneath her arms. She sighed, "I can't wait to get this out in the open. To see this case solved." She cupped her hands, like she might pray.

"I hope I can help. If what you say is true, could it be this person lives here—lurking even now?"

A whine from the back seat took Callie's attention, sending her gaze to the boy wiggling in the seat. She petted his back. "Quiet now. We'll be home soon."

I backed my car up, turning the wheel hard, and drove to the fence row. I reminded Callie of my question which had dropped into the dusty road before I moved the car. "Is the killer alive?"

"Let me show you what I know. And you can decide."

Callie cradled her son, carrying him to her Pinto hatchback. After she set him in the seat, she called to me before getting in the driver's seat. "Follow me. You'll need to stay back some. I don't want to make a show. Seems you're pretty known by your lifestyle and the events in your life. I can't be connected to this day. I'm not here with you. Remember that."

I seized the steering wheel. "Can you tell me where we're going?"

"Yes, it's at a place less traveled, less activity—and not a spot anyone would care to look or think of searching."

"Now you're using your riddles on me."

"I'm sorry. I'm protecting my family. It's something I must do at all costs."

"Fine, I'll follow you. But, don't go too fast. I don't want to lose you."

As we drove down 7th Street, Callie cut through side streets as if to stay out of sight. We made our turns between the library, took the viaduct bridge, and made a U-turn. With my windows opened, the hot breeze added to my internal temperature—as if Callie took me on a tour of Texarkana.

Maybe she's not telling me the truth? Maybe this is all a part of something I don't understand—maybe, I should tell Officer Teacup everything I know before this gets worse.

Maybe her brake lights mean we're stopping our cars. And why are we at the pool hall? We're at the Royal Order of Moose Lodge on Broad Street next door to Alcoholics Anonymous where they try to dry people out.

Pulling to the curb behind Callie, I turned the car off, and jumped from my seat. We found ourselves standing outside the double doors leading to the bar and pool hall. I quizzed her. "What are we doing here?"

Callie pointed to her son who wiggled his head through the opened window. "I'll stay outside with Harper. This isn't a place for little ones. Nor for women. Inside, you'll find Dennis. He works here in the afternoon and evenings. Tell him I sent you. Tell him I'm outside. Tell him to bring you the box and not to forget the key."

"Your brother-in-law works here?" I glanced upward at the two-story brick building. "I'm pretty sure this is where Lester comes to drink away his life."

"Dennis should be at the bar serving drinks. His life is pretty much wasted inside this building."

Like an obedient child, I marched inside, taking in the shadows of low lights and the smoke-filled corners where men hung out who should be working. The mirror behind the bar in the back brought me to a slick brown counter with high stools where Dennis rubbed a small glass as if polishing the glass made it less dirty—less apt to cause trouble for a weak person who ordered whiskey or vodka. I slapped the bar with my hand. "Sir, can I have an iced tea?"

Dennis glanced over his shoulder, his face losing its color and turning ashy like the smoke fog in the room. "What are you doing here?" He inched to face me across the bar. "I don't serve tea in here."

"Serve me up a key and a metal box. Callie's outside on the sidewalk and she brought me here, so I could get the secrets to answering the cold case of the Phantom Killer—to help me solve the murders." I leaned forward with both hands on the counter. "She said you have it."

"I do have the box. But it's not like I'm hiding it beneath this bar. It's upstairs in the pool hall. In a closet. Come with me."

Tapping Dennis on the shoulder, his overweight body mushy with extra pounds, he spun around. "Don't get so close. I'm not good with people who get in my space."

"But, I have a question." I spotted the phone on the wall by the liquor bottles. "Did you work the night Lester came searching for my husband? Lester was here first, drinking—then he left drunk."

Dennis pushed me back with a shove. "I work most nights. As for Lester, I have his bullets. Still do. I emptied his gun myself." His voice raised, cracking as if he defended a friend who struggled to live sober—and with truth.

"So, you were here. You were ..."

"Like I said, I work most nights. Someone phoned Lester, or so I heard. He's trying to figure out who it was, but no one remembers the phone ringing."

I tailed Dennis up the twisty stairs to the left, to the top floor where streaks of light shot in from the oversized windows. Three men surrounded one pool table, arguing, debating and rubbing chalk on the cue sticks.

I shadowed Dennis, who lived a mere four blocks from me, and I'd never met him. Who had his own past. Who lived in a bar to hide from the life he could have, like this bar was his tree to escape. It reminded me of how I lived in the top of a tree to hide from my own truths.

Dennis pushed a swinging door. "Come in here. The closet's in here."

For a second, I halted, unsure to follow or to run. Inside the storage room, Dennis grabbed my arm, squeezing tighter than I wanted—his words ordering me to keep silent. "Don't scream. I'm not going to hurt you. But you must know, there's something wrong with Callie. Since Clara and Gilbert died, she's panicky and anxious. I'm not sure if she's been threatened or something. She's worrying too much. And this box has her fretting more than ever."

"I've not been myself either. The town's on edge, and I'm on edge. I can't sleep." The tears fell. "I don't know how to live without my husband. He's always solved everything for me. He was my guide in life."

"I'm sorry about that part, ma'am. But we need to rid our family of this curse. I think Callie believes our family will become murderers if we don't get the box out of our possession. But you can't disclose how you received it. We can't be attached to the equation because of my record. I'm trying to start fresh, but it's hard to overcome your past."

I pulled free. "Don't squeeze me like that again. Hurting me and warning me are two different things. Let me get the box and I'll leave for good."

"Sorry, it's a part of me that scares me, too. I overreact when I get stressed." Dennis opened the door to the closet, fidgeted around with some items on the top shelf and turned to me, holding a rusty, metal box. "The truth you seek is inside. I'm sure the truth will show you a name too. We want to live in peace at our home. Don't let anyone know how you came to have it."

Wrapping my arms around the box, I stumbled, the metal container heavier than I'd counted on. "Can I carry this downstairs and through the bar? Will anyone care?"

"No one will even notice. They come to play pool, to gamble away a few dollars or make a few, and to swallow away the day with drinks to hide their lost steps."

"I'm sorry this place is here. I'd close it down and make it into a place where children could perform plays and sing and make music." I found myself describing a theatre of drama, unsure how or why that popped out. "My high school teacher in Jefferson once told me I could be an actress since I loved drama so much."

Dennis bolted ahead of me on the stairs as the jingle of a bell from downstairs drifted its ring to us. "I've got customers. Please leave, and don't come back."

At the bottom of the stairs, across the room, a man who helped me color my hair brown glared at me. "So, what brings you to a bar in the afternoon, Annie Grace?"

"Taddy? I could ask you the same thing." I moved closer, clutching the box beneath my arm. "And who is with you?"

"This is Callie's husband, Jon. We're stopping by for a drink to celebrate. We've heard Officer Teacup made an arrest. He knows who shot Crush. And most likely, who shot Clara and Gilbert. And you're not going to believe it. It was Lester all the time."

"What? That's not true."

Taddy ignored me and skidded to the bar where Dennis poured him a drink over ice. I marched to Taddy. "You don't drink, what's gotten into you."

Dennis answered, his double chin wiggled beneath the unkempt whiskers. "I serve sun tea with lots of sugar. Sometimes the ants get into the jug out back when it's steeping, but I strain them little fellers out. Taddy loves my tea."

196

Jon, in his starched and pressed and near-perfect suit marched alongside Taddy. "I'd like a tall glass myself." He pulled his jacket off, placing it across the bar to his side.

I slammed the box on the bar. "Dennis, don't you just serve liquor here?"

"Well, for our friends who don't drink the booze, we have iced tea." His grin showed his yellow teeth, his eyes spoke of having put one over on me.

Taddy touched the box. "So, what's in there?"

"It's nothing that concerns you." I found my tone crisp, my heart judging and my mind wishing to know the truth.

"It's time for me to help you with your investigation."

"No, your timing is way off. My brother and sister are leaving tomorrow. I'll be saying my goodbyes to them." I tossed out excuses to keep Taddy away, not sure of what his intentions included. The longer I stay around anyone, the more suspecting I become of them. I needed to go. I needed to clear my head.

Jon slid to my side. "I suggest you leave with the box before Pandora's secrets launch questions you aren't ready to hear."

I cradled the box, offering my final words for the moment. "And by the way, Lester didn't shoot my husband. I have no idea what is going on, remember, his gun didn't have any bullets. They've cleared him."

Taddy barreled in front me, meeting me at the door. "You need to leave this up to the police. Everyone's saying he confessed."

"You need to get out of my way."

"Sure. You can do this alone or with friends. We're here if you need us."

"I'll let you know." As I made my way outside, Callie's car sped off—like she completed her task. But my task is deeper and muddier than ever, so what am I to do with this confession from Lester? Is it true? What is happening and what is real? And am I holding the answers I've longed for regarding the Phantom Killer?

The Key Isn't the Key

The orange glow from the lamp shone on the metal, and the lockbox almost begged to disclose its contents. Rusty, solid, and heavy, the box held secrets of Texarkana's past—in plain sight on the coffee table. Not too plain since we can't get the blasted box open. I longed to learn the truth but worried what that might look like since I've carried the burden and worry for years.

Leaning forward, I sat on the sofa, my elbows on my knees, my mind unable to understand why the box lay hidden for so long. But if your family has a secret, sometimes ignoring it—makes you think it's gone. But the horror never leaves until the truth comes out, but by then a killer might get away with his horrible crimes.

I learned from my conversation on the phone with Officer Teacup, Lester hadn't confessed to a crime—that it's another rumor floating around town. But as for this old case, I have evidence. It's right inside this box.

I'm at a loss for what's happening or why. On why life deals the cards which make you feel like you're losing at life. Or why you fold and shuffle circumstances until you've lost the ability to play the game.

Some investigator I am. I'm more mixed up now than before. One second, Taddy is my suspect. The next minute, I think Lester might be the one. I've riddled my brain with clues and information, and yet, I'm thinking fuzzy with too many facts and too many unknowns. All I can think of is not hearing Crush call to me with orders to come down from my tree. I'd give anything to hear him holler at me for using up all the hot water.

Willie broke the silence, kneeling on the other side of the table. "I can't believe you forgot to get the key. I've jimmied the hole with a screwdriver and tossed that box on the sidewalk and hammered the lock, but I can't get it open. If I mess up the keyhole, we might not ever get into the box. It's sealed shut—made to keep others out, that's for sure."

"I'll run over to the pool hall. Dennis is at work, and I'll get it."

Lizzy Beth cuddled close to me, trying to make up for her phone call with Maxwell, and she nudged me. "No, you aren't going. You don't need to hang out in a bar."

"I'm not going there to stay. I'm going there for a key. Plain and simple."

Willie popped to his feet. "I'll go for you."

I argued, "No, he won't give it to you. The key is for me."

Willie marched to the front door, peering through the glass into the darkness. "I don't think we should leave on the train tomorrow. It's too early to leave you alone. This box is added trauma and who knows how you'll react."

"I'll react fine. I've got this. Stop worrying."

"Stop worrying? I have no idea what that means in your world, but in mine, it's like you're a time bomb. I have no way of knowing how you'll respond to added stress."

I screamed, wishing I had sounded less like myself. "You and Lizzy Beth need to take care of your own families. I understand how you both want me happy and safe. But this is my home. I'm staying put for now. But you must go home—for me to move on."

Lizzy Beth hugged my neck. "I only want you whole. You've been broken for so long." She nestled her warm hug around me like a blanket of love.

"I need some quiet time to think and sort things out. Once I see what's in the box, I'm sure it'll change my nightmares into dreams."

Willie turned toward me. "So, are you sure that River plans to stay with you? I so wanted you to go with us." He rustled his hair. "You never intended to go, did you?"

"No, I was only trying to get you both to leave me alone. I planned to sneak off or to change my mind—once you were on the train."

"As much as I desire you to sit by me in the seat tomorrow, I'm trying to understand."

"River's coming in the morning and has Ed watching her camp. She'll move in for as long as I need her. It's not like I don't have plenty of room."

"Annie Grace, do you promise to check in with us? Please, keep us posted on the case with Crush and whatever you discover inside that box."

"Sure. There's no need to worry, Willie. River's a tough one. She can help me make peace with my new walk and she'll know how to pray for me. She constantly talks to God at the creek. She is helping me believe no weapon formed against me shall prosper."

Willie moved to the recliner, falling into the cushion like a rag doll. "It's late, I think I'll turn in. Can the box wait?"

Lizzy Beth touched the box, keeping one arm around my shoulder. "This may not be what you need right now. The clues inside aren't going anywhere. They aren't the answer to your living with hope, don't you know that?"

"I know. But since I have the box, it won't hurt to see inside. I've studied this case for so long—I need to see inside." My fingers itched and my desire to end the nightmare circled my head with a darkness, as if sleep might find its way to my pillow tonight. I knelt next to Willie. "Maybe you could go with me to get the key. It's Friday night, the partiers are out at the pool hall. I'll be safer with you by my side. Please?"

He shifted the recliner, putting his feet on the floor. "I'm exhausted. It can't wait?"

"No. This won't take long."

"I don't know if I'm able to go home. Maybe I should stay on. You could use a man around here."

I sighed, "No, you should go home."

"I think I'll stay. You need me."

"I need peace. Not a watchman."

"You need a brother who hasn't always been there for you."

"I haven't made it easy for you to stand by me."

Willie sat up. "This is true. But I am your brother. The time is at hand. I can be your strength." He rubbed his hands through his hair, yawning. "But could I get some sleep tonight? No more arguing, I'm staying here with you. Lizzy Beth and Archie will take the train home. I'm not leaving your side. But we'll get the key tomorrow, I promise."

Knock. Knock. Knock.

I stumbled to the door. "Who is here at this hour?" I stopped in my tracks. "Lizzy Beth, put the box over behind the piano out of sight."

Willie rushed around me. "Let me get the door. You have no idea who might be knocking. We've had too much sadness, and you've lost ..." His voice cracked, and he slid across the hardwood floor without saying another word, opening the door and yelling, "Oh my! What in the world do we have now?"

I charged to Willie's side, the stormy weather resumed with a summer rain soaking the parched streets. "River? What is it? You're drenched!" Her hair hung like string, dripping water, and her clothes clung like Saran Wrap to her skin. "Get in this house. What is going on?"

Lizzy Beth shuffled up behind me. "Let me get a towel. What's with all those sheets of paper?"

River announced. "That's why I'm here. I retrieved them by my camp. A stranger snuck into the woods tonight, and I could see him in the shadows. Flashlight barked and growled at him, and broke from my grasp—chasing the man."

I pulled a page from her grasp. "What papers? What's on them? What was the man doing?"

"He was throwing them in the river. The water's rising fast with these storms, but I got most of the papers. As I got to your porch, the bottom fell out and the wind picked up. I've kept most of them dry under my shirt. I couldn't figure out why that man wanted to toss them—they must be valuable to someone. No one comes out there to throw away words."

I straightened one of the damp sheets and placed it on the piano, laying it out to read. "Look at this. It's Clara's manuscript."

"My shoulder sure aches. I hope I didn't rip open my stitches."

I turned to River. "I'm sorry you've gotten involved in my mess. I never wanted you to get hurt."

"I'm fine. I'm trying to get as many scars as you have."

Hugging her neck, I kissed her cheek. "I'm thankful you're doing so good."

"Me, too."

I snatched the papers, reading the words out loud. "I know I've disappointed my father, he's always wanted me to marry into money. He dressed me in frills, giving me a canopy bed as a child and the prettiest dresses. He bought my love with presents, when I wanted his love. I've searched for love from men. Sometimes from the wrong men. And this leads to my secret life which is riddled with lies and secrets—those I plan to tell in my story. I want to help someone else walk in victory, to see that trusting in man for your worth is never the answer. My worth comes from God."

Grabbing more sheets of paper from River's hands, I searched for the next page, as Lizzy Beth draped a towel around River's shoulders. She turned to my sister. "Thank you, Ms. Lizzy."

Lizzy Beth responded with a grin. "Miss Lizzy? I like it. Has a nice ring. I may shorten my name. I do call Annie Grace, just Annie. Maybe it's time for a change."

I interrupted their name-changing exchange. "Both of you help me."

Willie moved in to help. "You're going to need the floor and the kitchen table, the hallway and the library floor."

I handed him a stack. "They're not all wet. Some are soaked, but you can still read most of the words. We've got to sort this out and see what it says."

River wrapped her hair in the towel. "Flashlight lunged across the creek at the man, and he screamed like a baby, scattering the words on the trail."

"That's great. We can see …" I held a sheet in my hand, and the title page was formatted like I do mine. "Oh my! This can't be her story." I plopped to my knees, next to a dozen sheets of typed words drying on my floor. "I'm not sure how this came up missing from upstairs! But the person who stole her manuscript was throwing it away!"

Lizzy Beth yanked the page from my fingers. "No way! Are you sure?"

"Of course, I'm sure. Her typewriter is my old one from ten years ago—and the letter *N* sticks. I noticed it the other day when I first found the manuscript, *From Nobody to*

Somebody." I pointed to the *N* in her title. "Why would someone steal it, and throw the papers away?"

River and Lizzy Beth shuffled papers, layering the downstairs with paper after paper. Willie slid the recliner off to the side between the piano and sofa and pushed the coffee table next to the fireplace.

I crawled to each sheet, hoping to find the one that followed behind the page that left me wanting more. "Are you sure you're putting these in order?"

Lizzy Beth scowled, "We're doing the best we can. And yes, we know how to count."

River gave her a high five as if they were ganging up on me. "Hey, Ms. Annie," River cackled, holding her laugh in. "Sorry, I thought I'd shorten your name, but it's not catchy enough for me."

I nudged her and loved hearing laughter for a change. I quizzed her, "What were you going to say before you mocked me?"

She scooted on her knees to place more sheets on the floor. "I was going to tell you how I watched the man and tried to see his face, but the shadows concealed his identity. He's a round sort of man—with whiskers longer than a day old— maybe a week's growth. And he wore a flannel shirt, but the streaks of gray light shot between the trees, and he appeared more like a ghost at the water's edge."

I repeated her words. "Flannel shirt? Whiskers?" I danced on my toes around the papers to Willie. "I know someone like that—who fits the description."

Willie reeled me in. "Lots of men are heavy. Flannel shirts in the summer not so much though. And whiskers. It's pretty common in this neck of the woods. Don't make a case on those three items."

Lizzy Beth shouted with a squeal. "What is that under the foot of the sofa?" She reached behind River who sat next to her. "It's ... it's the locket I lost earlier this morning!"

A Photo Tells All

I rocked on the balcony porch, sitting alone, with the night slipping into the wee hours—opening the silver squirrel locket with the teeny brass acorn. Shaking my head. Talking to myself. Speaking to Clara's photo on one side of the locket, I asked questions. "Who is the baby? Where did he go? Or is the baby a girl? What's his name? Or hers? And how did you get this picture?"

The squeaking of my chair spoke to my heart, like the squawking sound I remembered the day I stepped on that baby toy when Clara came to work for me. On the day she rammed my station wagon, when she seemed distracted. She was less mouthy, more subdued, and sad. Not at all like herself. She stammered in the street. She almost cried. She rambled on about her daddy's wallet not coming to her assistance anymore. Her erratic behavior reminded me of my crazy ways.

So, I offered her the job, hoping to gain clients, because Crush encouraged me to mend our relationship—hers and mine—by our spending time together.

The day I stepped on the squeaky baby toy, Clara yelled at me. "Give me that. It's not yours."

"Well, of course it's not. I have no children. Even though Crush would love to have a house full." I had tossed her the yellow rattle with the handle, unsure why she carried a baby toy when she had no siblings or babies in her family. But with time, the rattle never showed up again.

I peeked inside the locket again, the photo on the left shouted of a life lost at the hands of a killer. While the other one—left silent question marks on my heart. Clara's photo was one of perfection and beauty. Yet, she hid behind the locket of her broken life. Despite her rich and materialist world of big houses, plenty of clothes, and extravagant food, she longed for happiness—even though my world as a child spoke of boxcars, mission food, and sleeping in the woods or in alleys. Of dirty clothes. And an empty belly. But the bottom line, we both longed for peace and joy.

I longed for all she possessed, while she longed for the meaning to life. She longed for love—as did I—which was something we had in common. I stared at the photo of the baby, wondering who, wondering where, and wondering if I'd find out the answer to whose baby affected Clara with such an attachment she kept the photograph inside the locket.

Pulling the screen open, I slipped down the hallway and glanced into my bedroom where River snored, where her scruffy brown dog slept—after she came scratching on the front door. Now I have muddy footprints from a dog who saved Clara's words. I'll forgive her for that, but not right this second. Maybe tomorrow, I will.

In the next room, Lizzy Beth slept, her last night in my house. She's longing to sell my home, while I'm longing to stay put—to not run away anymore. To find my roots and plant them deep so the storms of life don't blow me around like leaves tossed in the wind.

I eased my way downstairs and peeked into the library where Willie slept on a sofa, with his arm cradled around Hank, the kitty who scatted at Flashlight when she bounded into the house scattering the papers to the manuscript into an unorganized mess.

Scooting downstairs and to the front room, I placed the locket around my neck, crossing my legs, and sat on the floor with all the papers. I whispered to no one. "The answer to the baby-gone part of Clara's clues might not even be her own clues, but maybe I can learn her story by reading the manuscript. But what if the page I need floated away in the creek tonight? What if the answers don't change a thing? What if I should sleep and not worry myself with this case? What if I should let Officer Teacup solve this one? And why would Taddy give Junior those clues in the first place?"

I slapped my noggin. "That's it, I must talk to Taddy after Lizzy Beth and Archie leave on the train. I must go to his house. I must see him in person. I know when he's telling the truth. I can tell from his eyes—or I used to could tell."

I gathered the papers, stacking them in order—one by one. I'm going to learn about my friend who never became my friend—and I'll help her life matter by publishing her book.

After an hour of stacking pages, I haven't even read one word. I'll rest on the sofa, and sleep for a while—because the rattling in my head is one of sheer exhaustion, too. I can't consume another piece of information tonight.

Cradling the cushion, I pulled my knees up, and clutched the locket. I popped up, talking to myself. "Could this picture be Clara's baby?" Answering myself, I shouted. "Nonsense. Clara didn't have a baby. Or I would have heard about it— except maybe I wouldn't since I don't have any friends, except for one. I have River."

I looked up as if I stared at God through the ceiling. "Dear Lord, did Clara give up a baby? Could it be she had a baby girl or was it a boy?"

I waited in silence but instead River startled me. "I can't sleep. I heard you talking to God. You should do that more often." She sat on my feet at the end of the sofa. "I remember hearing a rumor about Clara and Gilbert several years ago, but I shrugged it off—mostly."

She had my attention, and I faced her. "A rumor? When?"

"It would have been about three years ago now. But people talk, and I tossed the conversation aside. Rumors can be rumors."

"Or they can be true. What did you hear? Clara and Gilbert were in love, remember?"

"Well, I heard they liked each other. And I heard Lester got jealous. And I heard Clara decided to have nothing to do with either of them—since they were acting like childish boys."

"And that's it?" I rubbed my fingers on the locket, like I wished to learn more about Clara. I wanted to know her for real. Only now, it's too late.

River moved to the floor, the lamp on the corner stand shining a spotlight on the floor. "Well, the next thing I heard included a man who lived on Hickory and she got involved with him even though he'd gone to jail."

"What? She dated a criminal?"

"It's a rumor. Maybe."

"Why didn't you tell me?"

"It's a rumor. I don't repeat rumors."

"But she's gone. This might be important."

"That's why I'm telling you now." River held my shoulders. "Listen, I'm your friend. Not your enemy."

"I know, I'm sorry." I hugged River. "I know Clara went to Dallas a few years ago. Maybe she had planned to move away. Or … do you think she got pregnant?" I touched the locket. My mind raced with answers, those undoubtedly without merit or maybe they held some truth.

"I heard her pa sent her away. I heard it with my own ears. I heard it from Gilbert and he was heartbroken."

"No! Are you serious? That's not a rumor, and you never told me."

"I didn't know it mattered, back then it didn't so much. And I'm as serious as a cat being chased by a dog." River picked up a sheet of paper. "Hey, what page were you looking for earlier?"

"Page 83, to see what happened in her story about her wrong choices." I slid to the floor next to River. "Is that it?"

She nodded. "The rumors I spoke may be the truth." She handed me the page. "Read this."

I read the story of sadness and wept like a baby with each sentence. *"Until ... my daddy sent me away with a precious life inside me, I never knew how sad I could get. I carried a baby who was a part of me and a part of a man who'd never get to meet his child. I told the baby's daddy, and he's excited, but now I'll not have his child—and he won't have his child. Then while arguing and crying in the grocery store at Piggly Wiggly with my pa, I picked up this baby rattler at the front register—begging my daddy to let me have my baby."*

River snatched the paper from me. "Let me read it." She paused, then shared the words from the page:

"Daddy scolded me, 'Act like a grown up. Show some class.'"

"But Daddy, this is your grandbaby."

"We'll take care of this. We'll send you to a place to end this pregnancy. To end your embarrassing our family name. You will not have this baby." His tone matter-of-fact and without emotion.

A slender and kind woman came up to me. "I've prayed about adopting a baby. I can't seem to get pregnant. My husband works at the college and I sew for our neighbors. I would love—to love your baby. I heard you talking with your father. He is your father, right?"

"Yes, he won't let me have my baby."

"I believe God sent me here today to find you. Do you believe in miracles?"

"Yes, I can give my baby to you. My baby can live happy and whole with you. You will love my baby, won't you?"

"As my own ..."

And so, my daddy sent me to Dallas, to hide my belly, to hide my sin, to hide me from this town, and to keep his image intact.

When the baby boy came into the world, I wept with joy and the baby cried, too. I think he knew he was leaving me for another mama. But I loved him enough to give him life. I loved him enough to buy him a toy, but I never got to hand it to him. I never kissed his face except once. Then the adopted mama and daddy took him home. She sent me his photo and now I carry him with me inside my locket.

I'm sure he lives nearby since I met her in my hometown. But since I don't know where they live, I don't know where to look. I've tried shopping in the grocery store almost every day, but so far, I haven't see my baby or the mama.

I signed my rights over—so I must let him grow and be loved and find his own life. He's a miracle. And God sent his real mama to me that day in the store, at the right time when my own father walked to the produce section to buy some bananas and tomatoes—when we were acting as if we were normal and nothing secret happens in our family.

But I have news for everyone. I have a secret. I love my little boy. And his name is Harper. Because I finally found him while peeking through the window of the store one day—while gazing down the bread aisle. I recognized his mama—and she held him on her side. And all I could do—was watch him and cry!

I sobbed, curling into a ball in the floor, wallowing in the sheets of paper as if I floundered in a bed of regret and disappointment. River stroked my hair and simply held me. I couldn't believe Clara's little boy, the baby-gone from her sight lived a few blocks away and Harper never met his birth mother. Or knew his daddy. Or did he?

River whispered, "Do you have any idea where her baby is?" I cocked my head, convinced she read my mind.

I sniffled. "Yes, it's Jon and Callie's little boy. His name is Harper. I met him today." I sat straight up, holding River's calloused hand. "I'm troubled, because Callie told me she didn't know Clara. I suppose she said that because—she adopted Clara's son."

River wiped her nose. "So, the picture in the locket is Harper. And he lives in Texarkana? And his mama found him in the grocery store aisle before he was born?"

"I suppose so. It appears God sent Callie shopping at the right time to change the course of a baby's life. Now, that is a miracle."

River touched the locket on my neck. "Why did Clara's note point to Lester as a killer? That part doesn't make sense."

"I don't know. Tomorrow I'm talking to Taddy before he leaves his house. Before he has time to get to the college since I know he pulls some Saturday classes. Before the rooster crows three times. I'm tired of the lies. I'm getting to the truth—no matter the cost."

Pam Kumpe

When Taddy Loves Another More

I pushed the door open to the apartment building, the two-story brick held a handful of rooms. The tree Taddy climbed the first time we met intersected with my tree on the side of the building. We used to talk late at night about the dreams we dared to consider. Until my grandma Elsie stood on the small balcony to usher me inside—she loved reminding me of my unfinished chores. But I loved her for it, because I loved being with her and would do anything for her.

Memories from arguing and playing and learning and discovering life came with having Taddy for my first best friend. But after Oklahoma, and after his kidnapping, even though I rescued him with Tin Can Mahlee, Taddy never quite forgave me or found his way to having great dreams again.

He disguised his loneliness with goals and high achievements in school. While I disguised mine with long walks, fishing, and tree climbing.

Upstairs, I paused, afraid to knock, but as I reached to tap Taddy's door—it swung open. "Hello. Anyone home?" I peeked inside, to see Colleen sitting across from Taddy at a two-chair table, their eyes locked on each other.

I froze in place, taking in the private moment, realizing the rest of my life without Crush meant no more locked-eyes and no more mornings together. Or nights. Or cuddling. Or his snoring. Or his cold feet in the winter. Or his way of humming at the crack of dawn. Of his way of turning the radio to country music. Or his way of kissing my nose when I least deserved his kindness or sweetness.

Creak.

I leaned on the door, tumbling into the apartment, wiping the tears from my face.

Taddy jumped from his chair, holding his coffee cup in his hand. "Annie Grace? What about knocking? And what are you doing here?"

"I reached to knock, but the door was open, and I lost my footing, flying into the apartment. I'm sorry. I hoped to talk to you. I need to share some things about—"

Colleen rose, her eyes glued on me, as if she questioned my stopping by so early in the morning. She motioned for me to come inside. "Come have some coffee. How do you drink yours?"

"Thank you. I like cream in mine. Like Taddy drinks his."

She countered, "Taddy drinks his with cream and sugar. That's how I drink mine, too." Colleen shuffled to the counter in the kitchen, in the all-one-room apartment, and poured me a cup.

I marched up beside her. "I can leave and come back. I didn't mean to interrupt."

"It's fine. I have to get to the library. Work calls. I stopped by for breakfast on my way." She handed me my cup, pointed to the cream on the table, and kissed Taddy on the cheek. "I'll see you this evening, honey."

Taddy walked with her to the door. "I'll pick you up. We'll go get a burger after work. Or maybe a root beer float."

"I could use both. See you at five." Colleen scuttled from the apartment in her yellow skirt and white top, her wavy hair like ripples of butter. She nearly danced from the room.

Taddy's countenance changed, his smile evaporated as if the reason for his hope left the room. "So, what's with your visit?"

I sipped my coffee and swallowed the brew in a big gulp, burning my throat. "Hot! Too hot!" I licked my lips, placing my cup on the table. "I had some news about Clara's note. I'm not sure you've told me the entire truth."

"What have I not told you?" Taddy scowled, his neck turning red. I came to your assistance that night, and of course, with Crush—"

"With Crush dying, it changed our chance to investigate crimes."

Taddy echoed, "Your world is different. Mine, too."

"My life will go on, but I lost what you found in Colleen. I lost my true love."

Taddy nodded. "I'm sorry. I'm not great at showing compassion. After the shooting, I knew to stay away. My timing was all wrong. You needed time to grieve." Taddy sat at his table, pointing to the chair across from his.

I sat down, moving my cup closer, blowing on the coffee. "I hate to be this bold, but there's only one way to say what I need to say—and that's to say it. I'm concerned you are a clue to solving their murders."

Taddy pushed his cereal bowl with the soggy pieces of cereal to the side. "What are you saying?"

"It's what you haven't said to me."

"What? I have no idea what you're trying to say without cutting to the chase."

"Junior told me Ms. Clara gave him the note, and he cut them into clues to create his own mystery scenes. But I've learned someone gave the envelope to him, and it wasn't her." I leaned on my elbows, putting my folded hands under my chin. "So, do you have any idea who that was?"

"No, I don't know—" Taddy choked on his words.

"Taddy, it's me you're talking to about this. I have to know what you know. You can't hide in your apartment forever."

"You're a fine one to toss stones at me. You've lost yourself in that silly tree across the street. Don't remind me what I've lost. You've lost at life." Taddy put his hand to his mouth, like his words slipped from somewhere deep, like his wounds were not healed, like I brought out the worst in him.

"I'm leaving. This was a bad idea." I rose, sighing. "I'm sorry. I hoped to find strength from you. Why can't you be strong for me or better yet, for yourself?"

Taddy ordered me. "Stay right there. I have something to show you. And I'm sorry. I had no right to speak to you that way."

"What is it?" I gazed at Taddy as he slipped to the closet, the one by the front door, and he marched back to me with a shoebox, placing it between our coffee cups on the table. "Look inside. Tell me what you see."

I lifted the lid, picking up photographs of Colleen, one after another. "Who took these? She's at the library. At the park. At Guy's. At Belk Jones. At the gas station. At church."

"She has a stalker, and he's threatened to hurt her. He leaves photos on my windshield at work. It started weeks ago." Taddy pulled an envelope from the bottom of the box.

I grabbed it, opening the flap. "So, he left you a note? He glued letters on it, like cutouts from magazines."

"Yes, he wrote for me to stay away from you. And if I told you who gave me the note at church, I was to say Ms. Clara gave Junior the note, or I would lose Colleen."

The room spun. "Taddy, I had no idea!"

"It's hard to think someone might hurt my Colleen."

"Why haven't you told the police? You should go to them."

"And put her in danger? I need to keep quiet for now. And stay out of the news. If Ernie heard about this, I'd get plastered on the front page of the paper."

"So, what are you going to do with these photos and the note?"

"I'm going to put them in the closet, and act like you were never here."

I stormed across the room. "Are you serious? How can you be content with knowing someone killed my husband and two other people? Are you going to sit on this like it's not happening? That's how you've always handled life. You hide and act like nothing's real. But this is real. I've lost my husband!" I collapsed on the sofa by the window, sobbing my last tears—for they must be almost gone by now.

Taddy touched my arm. "I'm sorry. I am."

I sat up. "You're sorry all right. This is your chance to help solve a crime and you turn coward on me."

"I'm not a coward. I love Colleen."

"And I loved Crush!" I slapped Taddy as if hitting him might stop the madness.

He grabbed my shoulders. "Slapping me won't solve your sadness. Or bring Crush back. I process my problems differently than you. I'm hoping this will go away. I can't imagine losing my Colleen, and watching you suffer is horrible. I'm truly sorry."

I wiped my nose on the back of my hand. "I have to do this. I have to solve his murder."

Taddy paced. "I know someone who can help you though. Go see Jon, Callie's husband. He knows more than he's letting on. He gave me the note outside my classroom one day and told me to tell Junior that it was from Ms. Clara!"

Taddy blurted out an answer I longed for, and I charged to the door. I shouted at him. "I'll go see Jon. I'm sorry I ever came here. I cause you so much distress whenever I'm around you." I had blasted Taddy with my hate, realizing I finally held yet, a real clue—and talking to Jon might move me one step closer to finding out who killed Clara and Gilbert. And to the person who might have shot my husband!

I raced from Taddy's apartment, down the stairs, and tripped on my shoelace at the bottom, landing with my shoulder against the wall. I twisted the knob to the double doors with the small windowpanes and stepped outside. I was unable to stop the flood of pain rushing through my mind. The emptiness of not having Crush in my life sent shivers up my spine, leaving me unable to make sense of life. Had I woken up in someone else's nightmare? Or was it mine?

But I knew I'd left my heart at the grave when I said goodbye to my husband. And now, I'm missing him more as every step and each breath brings a reminder of his absence. He was my other half. I'm a broken piece, crumbling with each day and each new clue. Nothing is clear. I'm walking in a fog of confusion. And I want to go back to the way life was—when Crush lived with me and ate breakfast with me. When he cared for me. And held me.

I ran to the tracks, not wanting to go home—not wanting to say goodbye to Lizzy Beth or Archie. Not wanting to hug Willie goodbye, either. But I need them to leave. Or do I?

I don't know what I want, except facing another sunrise and sunset is like a horror movie. And I'm the main character. I don't want to make any decisions. Or face change. Or move on. At least not right now. But that changes like the wind. I'm fickle. I'm stuck. And I'm a wreck.

I fizzled, after walking a hundred steps to the tracks, and the rumble of a train rounded the bend—along with the call of *running away* which rushed through me. Something I used to do.

I touched the track, the pulse from the clacking wheels sent my heart racing—a reminder of yelling *Geronimo* when I used to hop those boxcars so long ago. Jumping back, the train whizzed by, but not before I saw the shadow across the way in the woods, like a shadow from my past glaring at me. The eyes were the same, the body older, and fuller. "Daddy? Is that you?"

My hair whipped across my face as the roar of the boxcars rumbled with a cadence of stories untold—or better yet, stories lost along the rail when my daddy shattered my dreams. The clunking boom-boom of a train rolling into town kept me from seeing who stood across from me.

"Daddy?" I trembled, knowing the fog and mist of my broken childhood tried to remain in my present life. And I screamed goodbye to the rail—for I knew my home on Laurel Street held my future. "I'm staying. I'm not running from my past anymore!"

I charged across the tracks behind the caboose unable to find the shadow and listened for steps behind the trees. My mind went back to how great it was to see my daddy after long nights where he disappeared—back during those five long years on the rail—from five through ten. I always longed to snuggle with him, hoping he'd never leave me at night by myself again. But he did.

Then I met Tin Can Mahlee, who taught me to read, who kept me safe from men who drank too much and slobbered like rabid dogs. She loved me as best she could—she gave me herself when my daddy couldn't do his part. And somehow, I miss them both—terribly.

I've found myself in boxcars with laughter and boxcars with sadness. I've slept and cried. I've taken in the countryside. Yes, I rode the rail—and survived the rail—and I once loved the rail. But now, I love Texarkana because it's the place I call home! The place I believe I must stay—and I pray I can stick it out.

The rumble faded, and the passenger train stopped. And for a second, my heart did the same, until I remembered how Crush made my pulse race and my smile grow and my life perfect. I remembered how he winked at me for no reason—just because he could. And yet, I never let him know how special and important his love made me feel—better than snuggling with my daddy or Tin Can Mahlee—any ole day!

In the past, Crush came for me—but now I must remain here and gain my life back. I must fight and win and find my roar and soar. I must write my poems. And write my books. Maybe I'll serve at church. Or love on others. I can become the woman God called me to be. I'll make my husband proud—and shine for him. I'll let others see God in me, instead of me questioning what I've lost. I need to see how God can use me. Crush would want me to change for good—on purpose.

I'll need strength beyond myself for such moments. I'll need faith to walk this road. I'll need the hope of Christ that I've tucked away. I'll need to remember who I am. And where I've come from. And how my grandma told me again and again, "You're a messenger of hope."

I called to the blue sky and the silent trees. "It's time for me to wear those shoes! It's time for me to take those clues! And time for me to follow through!"

I charged toward home, knowing Willie and Lizzy Beth would wonder where I'd gone—and for a brief second, I knew my name and what to do next. And I knew I still needed to retrieve that key!

Encounter with Myself

At the front door, Willie and Archie waited on the porch, with Archie holding my kitty. He kissed Hank's ear. "We're ready to catch the train, but with you missing again, well, Lizzy Beth's having herself a cry inside."

I strolled to the porch steps, moving with an ease and confidence I'd lost of late—but found this morning near the tracks. A renewed sense of who I am grabbed my entire being. "I simply took a walk. I disappeared into the beauty of the morning sunrise."

Willie squinted his eyes. "You see beauty in today?"

I nodded. "I sure do. It's a new day. Crush would think this is a perfect day to make a difference in someone's life. So I'm trusting that as my new motto."

"You have a motto, too?"

"Can't a girl have a new outlook on life?"

"You have an outlook that's positive?"

"Yes, you act as if I'm crazier now with a good attitude."

"It's new to us. We're used to your crankiness. Your self-defeating, life's over and too hard attitude." Willie hugged me. "But I do love this new you. Where did she come from?"

"She came from inside me, deep within a place God tucked away for such a time as this one. When I needed to stand on my own with a trust in Him."

Archie shook like a dancer ready to square dance. "That's the best news I've heard from you in years. I pray the cloud of despair has lifted and your eyes see how God is with you and holding you through life."

I embraced Archie from the side. "Let's get you, and Willie and Lizzy Beth to the train station. Hey, where's River?"

"She's not with you?" Willie quizzed, pursing his lips. "Her dog's not here, either."

Squeak. Creak.

Lizzy Beth stuck her head into view from behind the screen. "Where have you been? You can't keep disappearing and running away and going off and wandering the streets."

I placed my fingers over her lips. "I took a walk. I'm right here. I'm fine. I am. I will be—honestly, it's time for me to wear my own grown-up shoes and live my life. I can serve God with my mustard seed faith."

Lizzy Beth moved my hand. "You're not leaving or hiding or running away? Or going to come up missing?"

Willie stepped beside his sister. "Enough with your rambling. She's entitled to a walk."

"I love that you both love me so much to come all this way. But, Willie, you should go home, too. I'm ready to face my life. To hold onto my memories with Crush. And to get to my writing. I have so much to say. Life's filled with death and life. I need to live. I need to find my joy. I need to do what I've been placed here to do, which is to encourage someone with my words, with the lessons I've learned. To help someone win at life, too."

Archie agreed, passing my kitty to me. His words echoed mine. "Crush would be so proud of your new stance. It's like you've had an awakening."

"The roar of the train reminded me of what I've survived. Of where I've come from. How I rode into town after town and found my way here. I know Crush would be proud to see me conquer my sorrow. I'll see him again, someday in heaven. And I can't wait, but for now, when I don't know what to say or do, I'll hear him speaking to my heart. I'll hear him sharing his favorite verses from Psalm 51 where he tells me about the mercy of Jesus."

Lizzy Beth sat on the steps, and I joined her, while Hank scampered into the yard to piddle. Lizzy Beth asked, "Tell me about him. I didn't know him like I should have."

"He loved to remind me of my worth in Christ. Of the generous love God offers each of us. Of amazing grace that's poured into our hearts with mercy. Sure, he was firm with me. But soft. He was kind and gentle. He expected more from me than I gave, but he knew me like no one else. His commitment to me lasted through our hardest days and our not having children. Of my near insane chaos, too."

Willie sat next to me on the other side. "When we were small, you shared verses with Lizzy Beth and me after we moved in with Mr. Boyd and Ms. Susan. And you often shouted when praying to God."

"God gave me a brother and a sister. And I've never been the same. I am the happiest woman alive!"

Together Lizzy Beth and Willie bellowed, "We've never been the same. We're the ones who are happy you are our sister."

I laughed, "That's what you both would say when I thanked God for you."

Lizzy Beth kissed my cheek. "Please know you're my sister through everything. Good or bad. Sad or glad."

Willie nudged. "Count me in, Sis. We're family. No matter what we face. You're welcome anytime at my home."

Lizzy Beth echoed, "And at mine."

Archie marched to the side of our family reunion. "If we're going to catch the train, we've got to leave now. So, Willie, are you staying or leaving?"

I answered for him. "He's leaving. River will take care of me. And I'll take care of her. I'll get the key from Dennis and open the box and turn the evidence over to Officer Teacup. I'll let them do their job in solving the murders of Gilbert and Clara, and of my sweet Crush."

I sighed, wondering where River might be, and somehow knowing I'd do my best to let the police investigate. But I might need to ask Jon a few questions to ease my mind. Rubbing my fingers across the locket, I couldn't help but think how Callie was a miracle for Harper and how she might also be a miracle in solving the case of the Phantom Killer.

Willie jumped to his feet. "Annie Grace, will you please lock your doors and stay inside at night. Will you promise to let me know if I need to come back. I can be here in no time."

"Yes, I'll lock the doors. And I'll call you if you're needed. I can reach Pastor Toby too, he's right around the corner."

Willie jumped to his feet. "Let me pack. I haven't many clothes."

**

Chug-a-lug. Chug-a-lug.

The train slugged from Union Station with the twins inside, with Archie at their side. I had hugged them over and over, crying on each of their shoulders until Archie broke our embraces by peeling us apart.

Now I stood inside the monster-sized train station, a maze of activity, of passengers arriving, of people finding their families or friends, as beams of light cut through the building from the giant second-story windows. I absorbed the noise. The laughter. The movement. The authenticity of life.

I marked each step I made with a cadence as if I marched a new path, one less traveled as I entered a new chapter in my life. As if the old me rode the train out of Texarkana. As if the hope in me was exploding into my future beyond my failures, beyond my nightmares. Beyond the regret and the worry and the fear.

Outside, I dug for my keys in my pocket, dropping them to the ground with a jingle. I bent over to retrieve them, and a manicured hand reached for the keys, grabbing them, and the woman placed her hand behind her back.

I shouted at Colleen. "Hey, give those to me."

"We need to talk. I slipped out from work for a break and took myself a walk. And look who I find. I haven't gotten you out of my mind—you're running around in my head like a ping pong ball. What made you show up at Taddy's apartment this morning? You interrupted our breakfast. I go there nearly each morning to greet him with me—with myself. And you come by his place. Tell me what that was all about?"

"It's not what you think. I'm investigating Clara and Gilbert's murders. And my husband's murder. I had a lead on something Taddy might know some details on." I scratched my face. "It's hot out here. Please give me the keys. We can drive to my house and have some iced tea." I used normal woman-like phrases, saying a friendly not-so-natural thing, like inviting Colleen for tea.

"I don't think so. You're in his head. And now, you're in mine. Taddy's caught somewhere around 1946 when you two became tangled in the Phantom Killer mess and the present. He's restless. He feels uneasy. He believes he should have done something to help those families. I don't know how to help him with his past."

I coughed. "I know how he feels. I struggle with wondering if I could have changed something. Or done something to catch the killer. That's why I can't seem to let Clara and Gilbert's deaths go, nor my husband's death." I wiped a tear that snuck from my eyes.

Colleen placed the keys in my palm, squeezing my hand. "I'm sorry. I've judged you. Please, forgive me. I care so much for Taddy, and he's so fragile."

I could tell she loved him, that sparkle in her eyes reflected the same sparkle I had for Crush when we married. I encouraged Colleen. "He's much stronger than you know. He's a soft-hearted man. But he'll never leave your side. He'll come through for you when you least expect it. You'll be blessed to have him as your husband."

Colleen sighed, "Thank you for being you. You're authentic and real. We need more people like you."

"Thank you. That's the first kind thing anyone has said to me in a long time." I collapsed on the hood of my car, my sorrow and loss overwhelming me. I couldn't believe I had a conversation without hurting someone. And it made me hopeful, as if the Lord sent Colleen to be my friend as I lingered in loneliness and unsure steps.

She touched my shoulder. "Should I drive you home?"

"Would you mind?"

"I don't mind at all."

I climbed into the passenger seat, and Colleen, with her beauty and pink cheeks grasped the steering wheel. "I understand you once colored the big oak at the elementary school with crayons after you got embarrassed when the kids laughed at you."

"I did color a tree, along with plenty of other escapades."

She backed up the car. "Taddy told me it was because you didn't know what a candy cane was on the coloring page—and you ran from the classroom."

"Taddy remembered that?"

"Yes, he tells me a lot of your tales and how fun you were, and a little wild, too. That you never stop to think of consequences."

"I still struggle with the thinking part. And the wild part."

"I tend to think too much and not react." Colleen steered the car toward the Arkansas side, but when she came to Laurel Street, she kept driving. "I'm taking you for a drive. We're going to take a walk through a field where a chicken hawk swooped on you, and he's been swooping ever since. I want to show you that he's not there, and that you can rise and be whole."

"What? Where are we going? You didn't happen upon me, did you?"

"Not exactly. Taddy phoned me at the library. He knew of a place that might restore you beyond your loss. He asked me to take you."

"Taddy sent you?"

"Yes, he's a good man. With a great big heart. He knows you're suffering."

I wiped sweat from my temple. "I am suffering, but I feel a breeze. The wind of summer is changing."

"Well, this evening they're filming at the Stamps Farm. But it's not the actors we hope to see—it's someone who knows you from your past." She nodded to herself. "I have a feeling the healing rain of a summer day is what we need. I could use a friend. I'm not one to fit in with others."

I pulled up my ankle sock, which had slid into my Ked. "I'm not great at fitting in, either."

"Maybe we'll get together for iced tea on another day, too. But for now, we're taking a small trip to Highway 67 to where you lost your kitten—to where you lost so much of you, to where you lost a part of your life and forgot to live."

I nodded, unsure how or why she knew so much about me, but I figured Taddy told her about the farm. But I had no idea how seeing an old house from 1946 might heal my heart—until we drove up.

Plenty of Precious

Colleen parked the car beside the run-down house where a woman in a beige sundress sat on the porch, her feet barefooted, her brown hair tangled, but somehow perfect. I pointed. "Who is she?"

"You'll see. I've heard she's a ghost from Memphis, only thing, she's real. Like strawberries. And sunflowers. And hope."

"I know her?"

"You knew her when she was girl, she was around five. You were twelve, if I'm correct." Colleen nodded. "At least, that's what Taddy told me on the phone."

"I don't understand. How does Taddy know about her?"

"Because Taddy has a photographic memory. He remembers everything about everyone."

"He does remember details. No doubt. Does she have a name?"

"Yes, it's Precious. Actually, it's her nickname." Colleen patted my leg. "I'll go over there and wait in the shade of those trees. There's a bench by the trash barrel. Go say hi to her."

"But I don't see the film crew. You said they're coming."

"They're supposed to gather ideas for the filming at sunset. I'm sure some of them will arrive soon."

I turned to her. "And how do you know this?"

"Well, if you must know, I'm a movie buff. I love stories and movies and acting. I can't get enough. I love reading Ernie's take on each location and what the crew does, and keeping up with Mr. Pierce and his antics, too."

"You love stories?"

"Yes, I'm a songwriter, too. I play instruments and love to write bluesy-folk music. I've written a song called Playground Promises. Maybe, I'll sing it for you sometime."

"That would be great. Maybe over tea?"

"Sure, but here comes Precious. She probably wonders why we're sitting in the car."

I stepped from the passenger seat, while Colleen slipped to the side of the driveway. Precious stirred up dust from the loose dirt with her shuffles, and she called to me. "Are you the girl who stopped the black market adoptions?"

"I did. I'm Annie Grace Raike. As a child, everyone called me Shoelace."

She reached for my hair. "Your hair's golden, but it was much longer when we were kids."

"Actually, I recently cut it. But I've decided longer suits me." I shut the car door. "So, how did we meet each other—exactly?"

"Come sit on the steps with me."

I followed her, taking in the sagging roof, the holes in the porch, and the ripped curtains in the front windows. "Do you live here?"

"I do. With my ma and my granny. Granny's napping next to the window fan inside. Mama's in the living room." Precious touched my arm. "Thank you for coming."

"You're welcome. I didn't know I was coming though, but it must be the right time since I'm here. So how old are you now?"

"I'm 35, and I've never married. But I have my family."

"Colleen told me how we met when I was a girl, when you were at the orphanage in Memphis."

"Your friend asked me to share my story with you."

I fell to the porch, sitting with a thud. "Yes, tell me how we met and what took place."

Precious snuggled up next to me as if touching me might make all things new. "I'm the little girl who came to the kitchen the night you stormed inside Georgia Tann's home. The night when the house went dark forever. The night a detective died. But it was the night dozens and dozens of girls were rescued from that horrible-place orphanage—thanks to you!"

"I don't remember." I folded my hands, and she took my fingers, holding them with hers. "I don't remember much about that night. I tend to block out portions of my life. I'm sorry I don't remember you."

"I don't mind that you forgot me. What matters is I have never forgotten you. With your coming to Memphis, you changed my life. Ms. Tann's people snatched me from my own front yard, telling me my ma might die, so they were keeping me until she got well. I was too young to know what happened, but I knew one thing—I missed my ma and cried every night."

"I'm so sorry. You were kidnapped?"

"Yes, it was the worst day of my life."

"I was kidnapped by my daddy when I was five. He was going to sell me to Georgia Tann's clan, but he had a change of heart."

"So, you had a good daddy?"

"He had good days, some not so good." I wept at the memory of my daddy's broken love for me. I asked more questions. "So, when they rescued the children at the orphanage, you were reunited with your ma?"

"Yes, and she wasn't ever sick. They lied to me. But you," she embraced me with her thin arms, "you saved me. And so many other girls and boys."

I swallowed, my saliva turning into a knot in my throat. "I saved you?"

"Yes, you are the reason I have this beautiful home. My ma came to Texarkana to find her cousins. And they bought this house since no one wanted it." She pounced to the porch. "It's a great house."

I rose. "It's in need of paint. And a new roof. And this porch is going to fall through to the dirt soon." I listed the needed repairs as if my explaining the faults of her house mattered, but she couldn't have cared one bit.

"No, you don't get it. I'm free. I'm alive. I have my family. And my ma! And Granny! Our cousins live in the house beyond the tree over there. This is heaven on earth."

My tears fell like a summer rain. "Can I meet your ma?"

"Sure, come inside. She's probably asleep in the rocker."

Precious swung the rickety screen open, and we stepped into the living room where blood stains once covered the floor that summer I ran off, when the Phantom Killer shot Mr. Stamps through the window of this very house.

I glanced at the floor, frozen in place, staring at a rug.

"The stains are still there. But they don't bother us. We're alive. And that's all we care about. We know what happened here, but it's our job to thrive in spite of it."

I shrugged a shiver. "Is that your ma by the window?"

"Yes, she's napping like my granny, but we'll wake her."

"No, don't bother her."

"She will want to meet the woman who saved my life. I have to wake her up." Precious ran her fingers across her ma's forehead. "We have company. This is someone you should meet. She's the reason we have each other."

The woman with the long stringy hair and dark circles beneath her eyes, squinted and blinked. "Who's here with you? Bring her close, let me touch her face."

"It's Annie Grace. Remember, she's the one who helped close the crooked adoption ring in Memphis. She's come to visit us."

"Hello, it's nice to meet you." I reached out to shake the woman's hand, but the woman didn't respond.

Precious said, "My ma's lost her eyesight this past year, but she knows every inch of this house. She gets around better than I do."

"I'm sorry."

Her ma put out both hands. "Let me touch your face. A face of a beautiful soul must be in my house. I've always longed for the day to thank you for returning my baby to my arms. She gave me a reason to live. And you gave her a reason to play and sing." Her mama ran her fingers over my eyes, my nose, and even my lips. "You're the prettiest thing since those watermelons we had in the garden."

I giggled. "No one has compared me to a watermelon before."

Precious added, "Be glad she didn't call you a bean stalk."

"I'm so thankful to meet you both. You have no idea what this has done for my spirit. My husband would have loved to have met you."

Ma nodded. "I'm sure we'll have plenty of time to get to know him."

I sighed. "He died, recently."

"Then we'll meet him in heaven one day, which will be even better—and I'll be able to see in heaven."

Precious tugged on my arm. "I told her about your loss before you got here. But she tends to forget things."

Ma replied, "I can still hear you, Bean Stalk."

Precious grinned. "That's true, Ma." She motioned for me to follow. "I want you to see my room." She led me to the first door on the left, pushing the door open, flipping the light switch. "Take a look at the walls. I have photos of the children you saved."

The room displayed a photo album with picture after picture on all four walls. Every inch held a photograph of a child or a baby's face. I ran my fingers across a group of images and I touched the face of a photo of a small boy. "That's my brother, Willie. I saved him, didn't I?"

"You did. You were born to change lives in spite of how hard your own life may have seemed at times."

"How did you get these? There's dozens and dozens and dozens."

"Mr. Archie Gabs made copies for me a few years ago from the archives. I begged him until he finally gave in. I had to see them. I needed to remember."

"Good old Archie."

"Somehow I believe you needed to see the faces of the lives you saved, too—children who were returned to their parents. You need to remember."

I hugged Precious. "Thank you. Thank you so much."

"No, thank you. I have my ma because of you! Now, with the days you have left—capture a few more photographs of people who need the hope you gave me."

"I will. I plan to take more photos."

"Make memories with your loved ones. Time is short. Tomorrow isn't promised to anyone."

"I agree. I've lived in the past too long. The last few weeks fell in on me, but the Lord's opening my eyes to life. I'm seeing with new eyes."

Ma called from the living room. "There's a commotion outside. Must be them folks from the movie."

Precious led me from her bedroom, and we marched to the porch, meeting Colleen in the yard. She motioned with her hand. "Hi, Precious. I've got to get back to the library. The actors and crew are piling into your backyard. We'll be going now."

I held onto Precious as if she might deposit home inside my heart. "I'll come see you, again. I promise."

"That would be great. Maybe we could fix supper for you and you could stay awhile. We could have some watermelon too!"

"I'd love to come, and I would love to get to know you."

Colleen scuttled to the car, moving to the passenger side. "You can drive now. I have a feeling you're much better."

"I am. And thank you for bringing me here. Tell Taddy, he's saved the day."

As I backed the car into the highway, the warm air dusting across my face, Precious came running around the bus and the slew of cars. She waved her arms with a frantic wild motion. "Ma answered the phone. Something's happened at your house. You best hurry. It has something to do with a fire."

Photos Don't Lie

"River, why were you burning trash in the backyard? If you haven't noticed, the grass is browner than dirt, dead from this heat. You could have burned down the entire neighborhood." I scolded her as if her smoke signals meant the neighbors would have a new topic for their Sunday morning glares when I came inside the church next week.

She spun away from me, storming toward the water faucet, turning the nozzle off. "The barrel sent those flames higher than I planned, and those lower limbs caught fire. It's not like I wanted the fire fighters to practice their skills over here. I figured it was safe since it rained last night."

I stormed to her side. "What were you burning anyway?"

"It was ... you might not need to know." She tossed the end of the hose down, and Hank licked the dripping water coming from the end.

"What do you mean?"

"I found some papers on a shelf in your office upstairs and knocked off some photographs stacked behind the encyclopedias."

"What were you doing in my office? And where were you this morning?" I drilled her with questions, forgetting she was my last remaining friend, one who puts up with my utter chaos.

"I went to the camps and checked on things. Ed told me he'd watch my site, and I packed my items inside my tent, did too much, and my stitches in my shoulder bled through my shirt. I searched for gauze in your bathroom by the downstairs hall and then went digging in the upstairs bathroom."

"I see blood on your shirt. Do we need to have you looked at by a doctor?"

"No, I'm fine. I never found one blasted Band-Aid though, but I found those pictures. And you didn't need to see them."

"What are you saying? So, you got nosey while looking for gauze?"

"I may have touched a few things."

"But how could you destroy photographs which I snapped with my own camera? It's not like I keep gauze in my office." My words flew from my lips with accusations. "Were you snooping?"

"I took a tour. It's a grand house. Did you know you have a bedroom with a baby crib? With ruffles? With a rocker? And the cutest little bouncy horse?"

I snapped. "You're not allowed in there. Crush decorated the baby's room the second year we were married. He so wanted to become a father." I picked Hank up, his paws gray with ash and soot and mud. "Dirty little kitties get in trouble. And friends who snoop get in trouble, too."

"I'm sorry. In all those times we ate lunch, you never showed me your home. I grew up in foster care when my mama stopped coming home—when my brother and I spent too many nights without supper or running water. I love your place. It's perfect. Too big. But with all those antiques, the house is a showcase. You could show it off and charge people to know about its history."

"And I suppose you could run those tours?"

"I could do it. I'm organized. I love history. I also love telling stories." She danced around the smoking barrel.

"So now that you've distracted me from the photographs you burned, will you please tell me what you found?"

"If I tell you, will you promise me you'll leave it alone?"

"I can't promise something I'm not sure I can honor."

"I'm not going to tell you." She pounced to the porch with me on her heels, and we rounded the side to the front where the last fire truck drove off as we marched to the door. I jumped in front of her, cradling Hank to my chest. "Stop walking away from me."

"I can walk anywhere I want to, and I'm only protecting you. You've gone through too much lately. I didn't want to worry you."

"Worry me? Don't you see that now you have to tell me what you burned in my barrel? It's my property you destroyed." I blocked the screen door, not letting River scoot by me, shaking my head as if I wished I could read her mind.

River argued her stance. "Don't you get tired of all this chasing? You're always after the next big case or you meddle in the affairs of others, giving your opinion on things you have no business involved in."

"Where did that come from? You didn't even take a breath in your attack of me." I stepped to the side. "Go inside. I'm not sure we're going to have a civil talk right now."

River halted inside, twirling around. "Civil? Are you serious? I live in a camp. In a tent. By a creek. I take care of my own. I take care of me. I don't bother anyone. I don't make a spectacle of myself. I don't run away from life. I live life on my own terms. And I'm fine."

I yelled, "You have some nerve!" Hank scatted at me with a hiss, and I tossed him to his feet, to continue my argument with River. "I can't believe you're talking to me this way. It's like you resent me."

"I resent how you take your life for granted. How you never appreciate anyone or even your home."

I moved to the front steps, sitting down. "Maybe your moving in with me isn't the answer. I make you mad at every turn."

239

She plopped next to me. "What are you saying? Do you want me to leave?"

"I don't know. If we can't trust each other, how will we live together? Even as big as this house is, we need to tell each other the truth and communicate." I rubbed my eyes, tired of feeling worn down.

"I do trust you. But if you knew about those photographs, you knew something, which is anything but truthful. I simply burned up some of your ghosts."

I glanced into River's eyes. "Please, let's call a truce. Let's start over. I'll tell you the truth. But, will you?"

"Please, don't judge me. I only wanted what's best for you."

I touched her chin with my finger, as if she were a child. "I'm sorry. All the secrets of my life have trapped me, and I even make a mess at being your friend."

"Don't stop trying. Keep trying."

"I will. My frustration level is high right now. Come inside. Let's get some iced tea." We rose like robots. "Did you know Colleen might come for tea someday? She's Taddy's fiancé. She showed me a place today that calmed my heart."

"No! She's not allowed inside this house. Ever again!"

"What? How do you know her?"

"She runs me off from the library when I stay too long. I know her. She's stuffed like a turkey, full of corn bread."

"Stop it. You're my best friend. No need to be jealous."

"Jealous. You're the one who should be jealous. Those photographs tell the story."

"The ones you burned?"

"Maybe!"

**

I rested my back against the back of my chair, sitting at my desk, leaning on my elbows while glaring at River. She returned the stare, sitting at Clara's desk, holding her ground on letting me in on the photographs and what her secret might be in the equation.

I picked at the splintered wood on the top of my desk. She tapped her fingers in a rhythm across from me. I sighed. She huffed. I pounded the desk. She rocked in the chair, not made for rocking.

Our standoff inched toward an hour, after I knocked most of the books from the bookcase behind my desk in search for any more photos.

River shook her head. "I told you, there's no more. I'm not telling you anything that will cloud your view of Crush. He was a good husband. If I tell you, you will keep frowning—for years."

"I'm not smiling because you've decided to hide the truth from me. You're involved in my life, so you must be honest with me. You're my best friend." I scribbled with a pencil on the yellow pad.

River popped to her feet, running to my side. "I'm your best friend? So, no one will take my place?"

"Nobody could ever take your spot in my heart." I hugged her neck, unsure why her secret to keep the photos from me meant so much to her.

She scratched her ear. "I saved one."

"Saved one, what?"

"I saved one of the photographs."

"Why would you do that, if you didn't want me to see them?"

"Because, I wanted this one."

"Why would you want it?"

"Because it's the one I should keep."

"I don't understand. Why would you keep one lone photograph?"

"Because it's the one with the answer to—"

"To what?"

River leaned on the desk, folding her arms. "If I show it to you, will you promise to not go berserk?"

"I will try not to do anything out of character."

"That's not good enough."

"You must promise."

"Why? How bad could it be?"

"It's not necessarily bad, it's revealing."

"Revealing?"

"Very."

"Now you're playing with me." I jumped from my chair, marching between the two desks. "Where is it? Where did you hide it?"

"Sit down. Wait here. I hid it under the mattress in the baby's room."

"What in the world? You hid one photograph and yet, you set fire to the rest?" I charged from the office, into the hallway and toward the rear of the house, stopping with my hand on the doorknob to the room where hope dies, and dreams fly away.

River put her hand on mine. "Open the door. It's a beautiful room."

"I don't know if I can. I never go inside this room."

"You can go in there. You had a husband who loved you and would have doted on a baby."

"He would have been the best."

River twisted my hand, and we opened the door together. "Let me show you what I found."

We hovered at the crib, the brown polished wood a call to my heart of what could have been, but won't now. I shook with a sadness, my tummy aching with a ripple of sorrow almost more than I could bear. "I've got to sit down. I'm weak. This room is taking any strength I have left."

"That's why I burned the photographs."

"I don't understand. You've exhausted me with this entire escapade." I moved to the rocker by the window, sliding into the seat, folding my arms, disappearing to a place where the light stays on forever—and no one ever cries or dies.

River knelt at my feet, holding a photograph. "Here it is. Look and see what you may not speak of—to anyone."

True Loves Never Dies

I bent forward, clutching the lone photograph of a dozen years ago—of a time when fear and distrust rose up in my journey, with each step leading to the day I married Crush. I didn't understand all of the choices I made, let alone those Crush made in our steps and in our courtship. But the excuses and insecurity I carried sent me to a place with my camera where I followed him, where I snapped photographs from behind trees and across the street, through store windows and from inside my car.

Life's broken steps kept me from accepting the bouquet of marriage, arguing for years with Crush over an event, which caused me to spiral into one of my tantrums. I had captured photographs, stealing moments from his past, which played into why we married when I was thirty—and not one day sooner.

I realized how far the fruit fell from the tree in my life, rolling like a bad apple, and I sent Crush away to the arms of another woman—almost. My saying no to his every proposal took a toll on his heart and mine.

River tapped my leg. "Are you with me? You look like you saw a ghost."

"I did see a ghost in this photo. I first met her in Millerton, Oklahoma, at Wheelock Academy, the year after the Texarkana killings. I was eleven."

"Why were you there?"

"We were helping Taddy find his mama's sister, Margo. Which ended sadly, like many of my chapters in life. The woman in the photo was a girl then, a Choctaw orphan and she met her adoptive family who happened to live in Jefferson.

She walked with a limp, but the caretaker of the grounds who made coffins, fixed her shoes, padding the bottom for her on the short leg, so she could walk like the rest of the girls. Her name was Imogene."

"She grew up with you in Jefferson?"

"Yes, she went to school with me—but all through high school she hung out with girls like Clara—those with money and new clothes—you know, the pretty ones."

"So how did she come to kiss Crush in that picture?"

"One might ask, how did she walk arm in arm with him? Or to sit with him in church? Or to take walks with him at Spring Lake Park? Or to carry picnic lunches to the lake? Or to sit in the Saenger Theatre watching movies with her head on his shoulder?"

"So you did take those pictures?" River crossed her legs, whispering under her breath. "Burning those photos was the right thing to do."

"I took every one. I threw them up on that top shelf forever ago—after coming across them in an old trunk. Crush had come into my office and I didn't want to remind him of Imogene's accident—which happened the summer before our wedding. I couldn't let Crush see the photos. It was old news. Sad news."

"Accident?"

"It's a long story. And by the way, we need to go over and get that key from Dennis. I need to solve the case. I'm torn between resting and doing something productive. I can't sit in this rocker and tell you stories from my life—forever."

"But maybe, if you tell me the story of the other woman— you'll count your blessings and see the beauty of what you shared with Crush. I've never married, and don't think it's in the cards. But I would have loved to have had a husband like yours."

"He was so good for me. Strong and confident. And determined. As for Imogene, she worked as a waitress at Kings Row Inn. She floated across the floor like a butterfly, delicate and sweet."

"Butterfly?"

"Yes, remember I took pictures. She was everything I'm not. Her limp never kept her from living and enjoying life."

"You're like a butterfly, too. One with barbells for wings."

I slugged River. "Stop it. Don't make fun of me when I'm wallowing."

"Sorry, you're an easy target. But remember, comparing our lives with another person only leaves us wishing for something that's not ours. And who knows, that person might wish to be like us."

"Whatever. No one ever wished to be me."

"Are you kidding? You've seen parts of the country I've dreamed of going to, and you've met the most amazing people. You're braver than anyone I know. And wiser than most. And you have a keen eye for what's happening—except in your own life."

I rocked in the chair. "I'm blinded to my own surroundings and get stuck on certain topics—like murder and death and suffering."

"Me, too. I think we tend to lose sight when we spend time thinking on what we've lost. Or don't have."

"I have to say, that's the first time, I've agreed with you today." I ran my hands through my short hair, wishing I'd never cut it.

"It's nice to see you relaxing."

"Did you know that Imogene spent six months convincing Crush not to give up on me. Her motive included me as his spouse, nothing more. And the one time she kissed him, it was to tell him she'd never go out with him again—because she could see it in his eyes—that he loved me."

"Oh, how romantic."

"But the tragedy threw Crush into a depression, a horrible sadness. He struggled with her death."

"Her death? No! What happened?"

"She stepped from the motel after work one day to cross Stateline, headed to the store, when a couple of teenagers raced their trucks into her path. The truck took her last breath and the impact tossed her body to the bushes—right in front of the driveway at the motel." I put my hand to my face, a flash shot through my mind of me watching Crush collapse under the same driveway awning, replacing the image of Imogene.

River rose to her feet, putting her hands on the arm of the rocker. "What's wrong? You're stuck in mid-rock. Hello, Annie Grace, what's wrong?"

Unable to speak for a moment, the memory flashed inside my head of a whiskered man who stood behind the hedge. Who held a gun—which meant there were two guns—and the man who ran from the scene at Kings Row Inn the morning my husband was shot—could be the killer! "Oh my! It was Dennis!"

"Dennis? What are you talking about?"

"I remember now, with all the shouting and commotion and with the fighting; I forgot whose face hid behind the bushes off to the side. It was Dennis. He shot my husband. He held a pistol." I barreled from the chair, darting into the hallway, with River behind me.

She grabbed my arm, stopping me at the top of the stairs. "Where are you going?"

"I'm going to see Dennis. I'm after that key—and I'm looking for his gun. If I find the gun, I can prove he's the killer. If he killed my husband, he may have taken Clara and Gilbert out, too."

River bounded in front of me. "I'm going with you. Let me do the talking. You're too close to this to see clearly."

"Too close? I remember his face! I saw his gun! No one gets away with taking my husband from me."

"Annie Grace, we should call the police."

"We'll call the police when I have that gun!"

The Key to the Past

I swung my fist, ready to pound on the door, but River pulled me to the side, away from the porch screen. "No! Don't you hear them laughing? They have company for supper. We can't barge in there as if we know about Dennis. The end of a great day will blow up in our face like a fire from your past."

"I can't pretend I don't know. I have to address this and get my answers. There's a killer having a party inside. He shot my husband!"

"No, I'm begging you. Stop. You can't go in there and make accusations."

A tap on my shoulder from the other side came at the same time as River's eyes went big. I spun around, facing Dennis who partially stood behind the screen. "Come inside. We're having chicken and dumplings with Mr. Pierce, his wife, and their three children. I know you've come for the key to the lockbox."

I paused at the entrance to the front room. "If you'll get the key, we'll be on our way." I panicked, my heart raced, and I couldn't decide to stay or run.

Dennis pulled on my shirt. "You must come inside. We're sitting down to eat now. We have plenty. But don't let Callie know you forgot the key. She thinks we've handled the box of secrets."

"There may be other secrets your family has, those you're not telling anyone." I spouted off words I couldn't retrieve.

Dennis moved to the porch, letting the screen bounce shut. "What do you mean by that?" He glanced toward the laughter, through the mesh as the door to the front swung wide, and he reached inside, pulling the door closed. "What's going on here? Didn't you come for the key?"

River nestled between us, pushing me to the side. "We came for the key. Yes, we did. We need the key and if you'll get that for us, we'll be on our way."

Dennis shook his head. "Wait, I'm not so sure you're telling me all you know."

I peeked around River. "We know that you gave clues that pointed to Lester as a killer, and you gave them to Jon, who gave them to Taddy, who gave them to Junior. Why would you do such a thing?"

"What do you mean? Junior's inside the house now. I never gave him any clues."

I rattled on. "No, you gave them to Jon. Who gave them to Taddy. Who gave them to Junior."

River added her two cents. "What's your connection to Lester anyway?"

"My connection? He's a cousin. We're third-removed or second. I don't remember. We're family. I have no beef with Lester."

I stormed to his side. "Wait, you weren't at Gilbert's funeral. Family shows up for things like a funeral."

"How dare you call me out? I came to his funeral. I sat with his father on the second row. On the end. I didn't know I needed to report to you." He scowled. "Let me get the key for you and you can leave. I think we're running low on dumplings." Dennis marched inside, the door swinging wide, and I peered inside as if a glance might give me a clue to where Dennis might hide his gun.

Across the room, leading toward the large dining area, Junior giggled at the table, and as if in slow motion, he glanced my way, jumping from the chair. "Harper, come back here." Junior chased the toddler who ran from him, wobbling with each step.

At the front door, he picked Harper up, turning toward the porch. "Are you here for supper? Come inside. We're having a birthday party for Harper. He's two!"

Callie popped into view. "Well, hello. Come inside, Ms. Raike. We're having supper now, and we'll have cake soon. And who is that with you?" Her eyes squinted, her words strained, and she appeared puzzled by our presence.

I smiled. "Hi, this is River. We came by to—"

Dennis stormed from upstairs. "Take this key. Get out of our home."

Callie shuffled Junior off with Harper to the dining room. She turned to me, calling across the room. "I'm not sure what you're doing here, but this is not a good time."

"You don't understand." I reached for the key from Dennis. "Please call me. We need to talk and it's not about the lock box."

Dennis ushered us out almost before we were inside. "I suggest you tuck away what you think you know before you know more than what will keep you alive." He bent close to my ear to toss those words at me. "Three people are dead. What's one more?"

I shoved his flabby body away from me. "I plan to tell the police everything I know. You better not leave town."

River yanked on my sleeve. "Stop while you're ahead. We need to go. And now."

We charged from the porch, rounded the side of the house to the Rambler on the street—and out back, Junior chased Harper across the yard. He waved to me. "I'm going fishing after church tomorrow. Daddy's almost finished shooting the movie. See ya."

**

As we sat in the floor next to the coffee table, the lock box between us, I fumbled with the key. "Hey, let's make sure the house is locked up. It's dark and we don't need anyone stopping by and finding out what we're doing."

River nodded. "I've checked the doors. The blinds are pulled. We're home safe, and by the way, I told you that was a bad idea to go to Dennis acting like you knew he was a criminal. He's not happy with us. Even Callie was shaken by our presence."

"You're right. My head got me wound up, and I'm surprised he didn't hurt us right there."

"But how could he hurt us? We were surrounded by his family and their guests who came to the birthday party." I scratched my head. "I had no idea he was related to Lester and Gilbert. It's such a small world."

River grabbed the key, sliding the box around to face her. "I'll open this box. We need to see what clues are inside. Surely, it's nothing. Or what if it's everything?"

"Callie doesn't want anyone to know her family had it, and she wanted to deflect attention from Dennis. Maybe she's covering for him."

River argued, "Or maybe she believes he's rehabilitated. You said he went to jail."

"True. She's worried this box might put them in the spotlight—the wrong way."

Squeak-a-jig. Creak.

River lifted the lid, using both hands on the heavy metal. She reached inside, while I shuffled around, to see inside. I slammed the lid closed. "Maybe we should call Officer Teacup and Ernie, to show them as we look at the evidence. If we don't, they'll believe we tampered with it."

River shook her head. "Too late for that, it's already open."

I pushed the lid up, and caught myself shaking, as if touching the items might contaminate my own heart. I slammed the lid shut again.

"Stop doing that. You're acting childish. If you can't go through the box, I'll do it for you." She reached inside, pulling out a class photo. "It's a high school group from 1948. There's a circle around the tall boy in the back row." She placed the photograph on the floor.

I found myself picking up another item. "This is a ticket to a movie, *Spellbound,* by Alfred Hitchcock."

River gasped. "I watched that movie as a kid, scariest thing with a masked man in it. Oh my!" Her hand went to her neck. "A masked man like the Phantom Killer!"

I sighed, my breath shallow, my heart pounding. I found a folded piece of paper, written in blue ink. "Let's see what this says: It's late October, 1948. I've written notes in another lockbox which will be discovered, with my confession to the Phantom Killer murders. But when I take my life, the person reading this will have found the second box with the complete evidence to convict me if I had lived." I tossed the paper down.

River snatched it up. "Is that all it says?" She mumbled to herself.

I ripped the paper from her fingers. "If you're not going to read it out loud, let me see it." I mumbled, "River, this note tells us he planned his death for November 4th, 1948. He was going to kill himself."

River whispered, almost like she was afraid to speak up. "He confessed to the murders. He said he had eight things in the strongbox that revealed he was with each one, even the three who lived."

"Look at this. Name tags. It has Martha Long and Jack Hall's names with a title, *Three Strangers*, with a date, February 22, 1946. Is that a book?"

I slid closer to River. "I think it's the title of a movie. If I remember correctly, they went to a movie that night before they were attacked."

"And this tag has Reed Gordon and Patti Malvern. It also has a title, *Black Market Babies*. Another movie?"

"I bet it was. Does it have a date?" I took the tag from her hand. "Yes, right here in pen. April 13, 1946." I paused, wondering what it all meant. "Hey, do you see one for March in there?"

River dug in the box. "Here's another one. Yep, here is it, March 23, 1946, and another title, *Snafu*. And one more tag with Victor Stamps and Kacey Stamps written on it, with the date, May 3, 1946."

I placed each tag in order on the floor, taking in the boy in the high school photo and watching River put another photo down. "Here's a boy around the age of ten or so, holding a rifle. Do you think it's the same boy?"

"It could be, it's an older photograph, look at the paper."

River dug out some other items. "Here's a marble. A dime. And a poem—on a paper sack."

I seized the poem, reading it first silently, then reading aloud, I made Hank scat from the recliner across the room. "Oh, my word, River! This is my poem! I wrote it when I was ten!"

"What do you mean you wrote it? How could that be?"

"It's in my first novel. I have proof." I charged upstairs, darting into my office without turning on a light, racing back to River with a copy of my novel. "I wrote this poem when I was ten, and I stuck them inside a can in the oak tree at

Grandma Elsie's manor. I don't remember where the original ended up. But now, I know—it's right here!" I crumpled to my knees. "This person took my poem."

River looked at the stained and worn paper. "Tonight, I'm afraid to sleep. When I close my eyes, I see a shadow. Of a face in a boxcar. The skin melts and oozes like honey. And bumble bees fly right by. I run down the tracks. I fall from the bridge. And jerk awake on the floor."

I paced by the fireplace, not sure what to do, not sure what's next, but sure of one thing. The person who had these tags, took my poem, too. I marched to my kitty, caressing his ears, as if touching something soft made this hard spot easier to digest.

River interrupted my erratic patrolling. "Oh no, look at this tag. It has your name on it. Annie Grace Kree, April 13, 1946. Found her shoes at the park. Hoping she didn't see what happened."

"No! The night of the murders in Spring Lake Park, I slipped off with Tin Can Mahlee to retrieve my grandma's car keys. I had left her keys inside my PF Flyers by the water and wore my Oxfords when I snuck out. Then I left those shoes when I put my PF Flyers on. The next morning, the Oxfords were on the porch. He must have put them there."

"This can't be real. You're connected to the killer and he has information about you inside his box. What shall we do?"

"I'm calling Pastor Toby. This is more than I can process. I need his guidance tonight. I should have let Willie and Lizzy Beth stay. I should have let Archie stay. I am not this strong. We need someone else to handle this information. I'm not up for it."

"I agree. Do you want me to finish looking inside? I mean, these clues don't solve the murders. They only make them real for you right now—and fresh, piercing your heart."

I crawled up to her side on the floor. "I have to look inside. I need to for me." I moved around some envelopes, the ends stained, the paper crunched, pulling them one by one from the box. "There's five envelopes. Shall we open them?"

"Yes, do open them. Maybe we'll find something concrete that points to real evidence."

I flipped the envelope open, and inside were two pieces of fabric, frayed and rotted. "What's this?" I dug into the next envelope. The same thing. More swabs of fabric, each about an inch in size. By the time I opened the last envelope, I had eight pieces. I sat there staring at them, after placing the teeny cloths on each envelope.

River shouted, "Don't you see?"

"See what? I see some photos, a dime, a marble, those horrible tags, one for me, and these eight splotches of fabric." I stared at the contents sprawled on my floor. A lightbulb of questions jumped into my brain and I blurted them at River as if she had lost her hearing. "Do you think these pieces of fabric came from their clothes? Do you think he kept them as souvenirs?"

River nodded, not saying a word. She picked up the photograph with the small boy, turning it over. "Look on the back, someone wrote Doodie on the paper."

"I'm calling Pastor Toby. I'm turning this over to him, but first I'm getting my camera, so I can take some photographs of this stuff. In case it comes up missing." I charged up the stairs again, hurried for my camera, and realized I had run out of film. "I can't believe I haven't got one roll of film."

Back downstairs, I dialed the phone, waiting for Toby to answer. "Yes, it's me, Annie Grace. Can you come over and talk to us? We're in a bind and need your help." I hung up, moving back to the front room.

River stacked the items on the top of piano. She wept, turning to me. I rushed to her side. "What's wrong? Tell me why you're crying."

"I found another note in the box under an old sock and some ink pens. You better read it. It's not what you want to know, but it's what you need to know."

I took the note she held in her palm. I read it aloud, "I didn't act alone. My friend, who taught me to play cards, who went by Sidecar Ace, showed me how to drink whiskey and to sneak up on folks at night. I met him after I left work at the theatre and he trapped me into his world of lies, where we took part in heinous crimes. Lord, forgive us. For we deserve to die."

"Isn't that your pa's rail name?" River's hand went to her mouth, as did mine.

I stumbled backwards, unsure I'd read the words right, unable to get the picture of those eyes from jumping inside my head. Those I peered at from the boxcar on the dreadful night when I pulled the mask off his face and fell into the creek. With each blink, I remembered his hair, his nose, his lips, his ears, his neck—and I knew it. My daddy did horrible things! "River, they never found my daddy's body when he tumbled from the coal car in 1945, in Memphis."

"You've told me."

"My daddy's grave is empty at Rose Hill Cemetery. I was told they found his body in the Mississippi River in Memphis, but that's not true, either. I learned the grave at Elmwood Cemetery is empty, too. I'm not sure why he gets two graves when no one knows what happened to him."

River touched my arm. "What's this have to do with the Doodie person?"

"Well, I've always known my daddy was alive. A part of me sensed it, and I knew he deserted me. He ran away from his family. And his broken walk kept him stumbling. Sin ruins lives. Not only his. But others."

I rattled on, talking to her, speaking to the cat, and telling the photos on the mantle about our father, those of Lizzy Beth and Willie. "He's not a good man. He's involved in a terrible crime. Now, I know who the Phantom Killer is—it was my own father! And possibly the boy in the school photo!"

River called to me. "What in the world happened to your daddy, if that other guy killed himself?"

I withered like an angel held me in her arms, because the dark cold of night on a summer's night wrapped around my entire being. The reality of knowing my father ended up in the wrong place, doing repulsive things to other people—who never did him wrong—was more than any daughter could bear.

Sobbing, I curled into a ball beside the wall, rocking and shaking, and losing my ability to gather myself. I closed my eyes, wishing to fade into a land where little girls get the good daddies.

Knock. Knock. Knock.

I stood, holding onto the wall. "River, that's the pastor. Will you let him in?"

From the front door, I heard. "No, she's asleep. She's already in bed. You'll have to come back tomorrow. No! I told you, she's asleep!"

I peeked around the wall into the hallway, glancing at the front door and a man pushed his way inside. Dennis shouted, "I'm here to clear the air. To give you both some perspective." He pounded into the house, waving a handgun, stomping into the living room—while I snuck around the fireplace, to the hallway, and to the kitchen, hiding behind the door.

"I told you she's in bed. Leave now, or I'll call the police."

Slaham-puck.

Something hit hard in the other room, and then the silence riddled my heart—and I tiptoed to the backyard, to the alley, and to the street.

I turned to run inside for River, but knowing Dennis held a gun kept me from moving from behind the tree. A shadow marched toward me from the back of the house, it came with a sprint. "Run, Annie Grace. Run! I hit Dennis in the head with the metal box."

River and I charged toward the camps, charging like hunted deer—like human prey on the run, on a night when answers unfolded faster than having a key to a lockbox! When death knocked on our lives like the storm coming in from the west—and as the rain came, the lightning flashed in the sky! And we ran until the trees swallowed us whole!

The Confession

I rolled over, catching my arm on a wad of fabric. Rising to my knees, unable stand up all the way, I tried to figure out where I landed from last night's horror. I whispered, "River, are you close? I'm in your tent, right?" I pushed the taped canvas door to the side, peeking at the new day.

Shhh! River squatted next to me, inching from the other side of the tent. "We've slept too long, the sun's high in the sky. And he's waiting for us."

I put my lips near her ear. "Are you sure? We lost him last night. I'm sure of it."

"We did for awhile, but he's out on the trail. He's calling for you. I smelled his sour odor earlier; the wind of a hunter's scent strong with hate. I sense his desire to make sure we aren't alive tomorrow."

"So, you think he's the *killer*, too? Maybe I've taken the clues out of context. I've never solved a case before, not once in my life. What makes you think I am now?"

"You have the guts to ask questions, to push people to squirm and if they're guilty—they'll react. Like Dennis! Something's wrong with his life, or he wouldn't be after ours."

Pad. Pad. Pad. Pad.

Flashlight slipped into camp, carrying a bone, wiggling her tail and River called to her pup in a quiet voice. "Come here, girl. Come on."

The dog squirmed between us, dropping her bone, licking my face as I knelt on the ground. She swiped River's cheek with a slobbery tongue washing. And I tossed her bone out toward the trail to see if I could hear someone hiding in the brush.

Ska-tle-crunch. Ska-tle-crunch.

River pointed, whispering, "He's over there. Walking near the creek, behind us. The water's up from the rain last night, so if he's on the other side, we can head up the hill, to the bridge and head back toward town."

"It's time for us to go see Officer Teacup. After leaving like we did last night, I need to call Pastor Toby. He'll be worried."

Skat-tle-crunch.

"I hear you both talking. I know you're there."

I hid behind the thicket, staring at the outline of Dennis who weaved between trees on the other side of the rushing water. I responded to his call, unable to control myself. "Why did you kill them?"

"Kill who?" Dennis answered, using a mocking tone like a bird copying another's bird's song. "What makes you think I've hurt anyone?"

"Well, you did chase us and follow us and hide in these woods all night, hoping to find us. And you have a gun."

River pulled on my arm. "Get down. He'll see you."

I slid to my knees. "Let me get him rattled, and he'll blurt out everything. You'll see."

"Whatever, you're the one who is rattled."

"I am not."

"You are."

I pushed her away. "I am fine. I'm not rattled." I shouted at River, using my loudest voice, and a group of birds fluttered in the trees.

"I see how you are. You're ready to bolt. If the banks of that river were lower, you'd rush him—and get yourself shot."

"I would not. But there's some rocks up at the bend on the other side of the bridge near the tracks. I could get to him if I snuck up behind him from the east. I can't challenge him as long as he has a pistol, I need something of my own." I danced like a girl ready to fight a boy on the playground.

River cautioned me. "If he sees you, he could shoot you." She rummaged in the duffel bag next to her bedding inside the tent.

"Hey, you two. I'm coming for you. I'll make sure you never speak of me again—for your flight in life will come to an end. Those birds revealed your hiding place. I know where you are."

I tapped River. "What are you searching for?"

"I found it. It's my slingshot and my Bible."

"What are we going to do with a slingshot?"

"I'll shoot pebbles to distract him, so he has no idea who's around him. I'll make him think we have help."

"And the Bible?"

River tucked the pocket-sized Bible into my back pocket. "You're going to need this. Remember, God goes with you."

"When did you get spiritual on me?"

"I have my faith. Always have. I know where our help comes from, it's the God of this earth who delivers. I need Him to bring you through this, because I'm convinced you're going to do something against my way of thinking." She hugged my neck. "Now, get going. And be careful."

Flashlight tailed me. "Go back. Stay with River. She needs you. Get …"

River echoed my command. "Flashlight, come on. Sit. Stay here."

I climbed the side of the hill, to the bridge, running like a wild dog, ready to pounce on Dennis—or at least somehow knock his gun from his grasp. But I'd need to get behind him, in the woods, and dance like a ghost at midday. I tumbled down the embankment, charging up the trail, blazing a new path. I darted behind the trees as the burly man with the pistol stomped up my way, hurrying toward me, muttering—I held my breath and hovered behind a patch of tall brush.

I'm not sure why he headed the way I'd come from, so I tailed him, noticing he'd gone to the ridge, to the top of the hill where the train tracks headed over the twisty creek toward Union Station. He bellowed from the top of the bridge on the tracks like a gorilla on its war path. "I know you've got me circled, and I know you've brought in your friends. I heard them back there. They're pressing in around me, like wolves ready to attack."

I shrugged, unsure what to make of it, unless River's rock-throwing slingshot activities had slapped enough noise around in his head to cause him to turn scared. Either way, Dennis marched over the slats, balancing with wobbles, and stumbles.

Climbing up the slope toward the tracks, hiding and kneeling, and wondering what to do next, I kept looking over my shoulder, afraid I was being stalked. I've spent too many years caught in places with my back in a corner—without an escape.

A soft voice spoke to me. "Hello, Ms. Annie Grace."

Down below, beneath the spot where, as a girl, I'd fallen from that boxcar into the water, a boy sported his smile and a fishing pole. "I told you I planned to fish today. Pa let me take my pole to church so I could come straight to the creek. He warned me to stay clean and to watch out for rising water from all this rain—the water backs up down by the cemetery and gets deep fast. But these fish are biting, and I'm catching 'em as fast as these worms will let me put them on the hook."

I waved, not saying a word.

Junior waved. "Whatcha doing up there?"

Dennis spun around, nearly tumbling from the tracks. "There you are!" He pointed the gun at me. "Come here. We need to talk. And get Junior. I'm not leaving one witness behind."

I maneuvered the rest of the hill, stepping between the slats. A small rumble told me a train might interrupt our meeting on this bridge—and soon. "Hey Dennis, leave the boy out of this. We can solve this. It's some sort of misunderstanding. I'm known for my crazy antics, so no one will believe me anyway. I'm ready to let this whole thing go. I'm sorry I accused you of—"

"Of killing three people?" He waved the gun. "I had to, it's the only way I could live."

"What? The only way you could live?"

"They knew! And she left me out! Plus, Crush got in the way! He was going to turn me into the police."

I took a step toward Dennis, the water swirling with foam below us. I asked, "Who knew what? I don't understand."

"Three years ago. Clara had a secret."

"What are you saying?" I teetered between the cracks on the tracks, the boom-boom vibration beneath my shoes grew, and knew I should run for safety. "Hey, we should get off this bridge. There's a train coming."

"Sure, there is. Good try. You're like all the rest. Like Clara who gave me a wink, who flirted with me at Guy's Orange Stand. Who didn't like it when I kissed her. When I took her to—"

A small shadow stepped beside me. "Ms. Annie Grace, what's going on? Why does Dennis have a gun? Is this for real? Or a scene from the movie?" He glanced around, and along the tracks. "I don't see the crew. This is real."

I held his hand. "Junior, we'll be fine. You'll see."

Dennis shouted, "I was going to be a daddy, but Clara's pa sent her to Dallas to hide the baby, to give our little girl away."

I grimaced, realizing Dennis was unaware Harper was his son. "So, you're the reason she went away?"

"Not by choice. I would have married her. But she didn't love me. And now, I'm a father to a small girl. And I'll never see her. Then Clara goes and writes the story of her life in her book and leaves me out of it. Like I never existed. But she put Gilbert in the story, telling of their romantic picnics at Crystal Lake. Of their love." He hit his chest with the butt of the gun. "What about my love for her? She gave away our baby girl."

I stumbled for words, and Junior put his hand on the tracks, tugging on my arm with his free hand. "Ms. Annie Grace, there's a train coming. I can see it behind us."

Chug-a lug. Choo. Choo. Chug.

The roar of the engine barreled for us. "I know, we need to either go back or go across." I called to Dennis. "Hey, we need to get off this bridge."

"No! Stay right there." He backed up, moving himself with uneven steps toward his end of the bridge.

I yelled, "Let us come to you. We can talk some more."

"You know everything you need to know. I had a baby by Clara, and she was a tease. She never loved me."

"But how do you know you had a baby girl?"

"She wrote me from Dallas. Told me to stay out of her life—to never force her the way I had before. That she wouldn't tell anyone how I'd hurt her. But I didn't mean to hurt her—I wanted to love her. And then, she goes and gets the good life with Crush!"

"But why ... why my husband? What did he ever do to you?"

"He was going to turn me into the police, because Clara blabbed—so I took care of them!"

Junior launched his words into our mix. "I'm a witness. I've heard everything you've said, and I never forget a thing. I have the best memory."

Dennis pointed the gun at Junior. "Stop talking. You are pushing me."

Junior exploded with more words. "I've recorded your confession, too. I have it right here." He pulled a small cassette recorder from his pants pocket.

I grabbed the recorder. "That's right. We have everything we need. And you didn't have a baby girl. You have a baby boy. His name is Harper. Jon and Callie adopted him. Clara lied to you—so you wouldn't go searching for him." I choked on my unloading things I should have kept inside—like a train barreling on the tracks.

Junior screamed, "We can't get off in time! We'll have to jump into the water."

I shook my head. "But your recorder will get ruined." Junior snatched it from my hands, tossing the player to the bank below, and it rolled to the edge of the river.

Dennis charged at me, coming across the bridge. "I'll get that recorder." He pointed the pistol at my face, two feet from me, but Junior pulled me sideways with a quick jerk, and we tumbled from the bridge, hitting the water like two boulders.

I choked, and the current slapped me under, only to shoot me upward, and I swallowed water, losing my breath.

I lost sight of Junior, afraid of where he'd gone, but hearing Pastor Toby's words in my head calmed me, even though my ear throbbed with an ache. "God is our refuge and strength, a very present help in trouble. Therefore, we will not fear, though the earth gives way, though the mountains be moved into the heart of the sea, though its waters roar and foam, though the mountains tremble at its swelling."

Another boom on my head sent me swirling, causing darkness to set in, as I watched the train roar across the bridge, as my eyes closed, as a voice inside me sounded like God called my name. "Annie Grace, you're free. Be still and know that I am God."

I faded into the foam, sinking in the rumbling and rushing water, until a hand reached for mine. Was it God's hand to rescue me from death? To save me from my past? To plant my feet on a solid foundation where I could now inhale the beauty of my own life? Even with the scars, even as I faced my future—I'm choking on water. Will I fade to the boxcar of lost chances? And lost joy?

Pam Kumpe

River to the River

I sensed a shadow around me, and the light entered my soul, and the chatter seeped into both ears. Who talked? Who called to me? Who wept for me?

My nose caught a fragrance of hope as if I could see from the deep pit I'd fallen into—the abyss of unexpected sorrow. But despite the weeping, I rested—awake but asleep. I heard jabbering and pieces of conversations, but I couldn't speak.

I lay flat on my back, not able to sit up or respond. I longed to let someone know I'm alive, that I didn't drown. But now, I'm sinking again.

My fainted heart, my tainted hands longed to find freedom from the hurts and the lies and the loss. A song came from above me, or was it next to me? Someone sang *Blessed Assurance, Jesus Is Mine*, and yet, I couldn't sing with the angel. Or was the voice that of Willie singing in church? And not an angel? Where did I go after the fall? Am I in a coffin at my own funeral?

Wiggling inside my body, I sensed that my arms responded deep within, but with no outward motion. My legs longed to rise too, but the feeling beneath my skin raced from muscle to muscle, and nothing happened. Only the blood flowed through my body, along with my heart pumping. I believed if I could wiggle one finger—they'd know I was inside here—inside this ragged and bruised body.

I imagined a miniature me, traveling behind my eyes, through my neck, into my shoulder—like a speck of dust, too small to see, but big enough to make nerve endings wake up. My tissue squirmed, tightening around my veins, shooting life to my left hand, rushing to my fingers before the darkness covered me.

I jiggled the tip of my finger, waving to anyone, to any sound, to any person staring at me inside my coffin. I must let them know I'm not dead!

Oh God! Call to them. Speak to them. Yell, if you must. But let my family and friends know I'm not dry bones, I'm alive. I need to live. I know there's something else I must do. Let me follow through.

**

"She's better today, I'm sure of it. I need my big sister to get well."

"I think her color is better. Not so ashy. Willie, we'll see our sister whole again."

"Now you two, it's only been a week. The concussion bruised her brain. It will take time for the swelling to come down. When it does, she'll wake up. At least, I pray she does. Here, you two. I have extra handkerchiefs."

Their conversation swirled inside my head, like a new day, like a new dawn, like complete sentences. I'm not moving yet, but I'm alive. Your brother and sister don't talk about you getting better if they're burying you. And Archie, always with a hanky for someone.

I jerked my eyes glancing both ways. I did it so many times, they should have gotten stuck to one side.

"Her eyelids are moving. Lizzy Beth, she's responding to our talking about her."

"Annie, can you hear us?"

I sensed someone holding my hand, kissing my fingers.

"Oh, dear God, please give me my sister back. Willie and I need her."

I shot the imaginary me under the skin of my arm again, this time, wiggling my pinky finger—as if to say I'm coming back.

"Annie? Did you wiggle your finger?"

I answered her inside my head, and slipped away, to my world of no movement—the darkness turning into a river of lifelessness.

**

Where am I? My eyes opened, like my lids peeled an orange, and my eyes burned from the air. My legs slid to one side of the bed, and back to the middle. And I lifted one arm, and a small movement with the other. I tried to roll over, but the rest of me stayed behind, forcing me onto my back again.

This room. Where am I? I touched the squishing spot next to me. A mattress? I'm in a bed. But where?

I sensed a bandage, and reached up, touching the gauze wrapped around most of my head. The throbbing on my left ear grew with each movement I made, but I had to sit up. I had to call for help. I had to get out of this room. I had to find River. I must find Junior. And what about Dennis? And did anyone get the cassette tape?

Balancing myself, I leaned on my arm, too much wiggling, and I fell backwards, convinced of my weakness. How long had I been out?

Squeak.

A light behind the door let the world into my room, and a stranger scooted up to me. "Well, look who's awake. Can you hear me? You're weak from the accident. Do you remember what happened?"

I swallowed, the dryness in my throat, sending my words into a shallow hole, into a forced whisper. "I can hear fine, but where am I?"

"I'm your doctor. You're in the hospital. You've been unconscious for days. Your family will be so proud to see you're awake." The doctor took my pulse, smiling at me. "So, did you know you're famous?"

The pounding in my head sent a pain to my neck, and I jerked from the sensation. "Did I cut my head?"

"You sliced it wide open. I've stitched you up, but mostly your concussion worried me the most. I sure needed you to wake up."

I patted my ear. "Did you say I'm famous? For what?"

"You caught the Copycat Phantom who shot Ms. Clara and her boyfriend, Gilbert. Ernie wrote about you on the front page. Oh wait, I'm sorry—I didn't mean to show any disrespect. I know you lost your husband to Dennis, too. But thanks to little Chuck Pierce who knocked you off the bridge, and into the creek—you're alive."

"He could have drowned me. I can't swim."

"Well, someone pulled you from the water, and poor Chuck—he broke his leg in the fall and floated down river, unable to hold onto you."

"Is he home now?"

"Yes, he's doing great. He tells everyone you're the bravest woman he's ever met, that you stood up to the bad guy."

I wiped a tear. "What about Dennis? Did the train hit him?"

"No, he tumbled from the bridge, too, disappearing under the surge of the rain water. The officers found his body two days ago, washed up in some tall grass. He didn't make it."

"But if he's dead how did everyone come to believe he's guilty?"

"Well, that's where Chuck comes in; he recorded the confession and the police used it for evidence."

"Dennis caused so much heartache, so much loss." I toppled backwards, my head heavy. "When can I go home?"

"I'd say a couple more days of rest, and you'll get your strength back. But for now, get some sleep. The light of a new day is ahead, but let's take it slow. You have suffered loss yourself. I'll be by in the morning."

I closed my eyes, whispering to myself. I forgot to ask about River. I hope she's staying at the house. I stumbled to the floor, weaving like I'd had a drink of someone's whiskey, and opened the door to my room.

The doctor stood at the nurse station, holding a chart, explaining something to a nurse. "No, I didn't tell her about her friend. She's fragile and weak. Ms. Raike doesn't need to know River drowned in the river—to save her. Not right now."

I collapsed to the floor, yelling, "My friend? River's dead? No!"

Letting Others Help Me

I slipped in and out for days, struggling to let go, to live, to rise up, to fight, especially since hearing of River's death. My heart ached worse than my head, and I stopped listening to the doctor, and tried to shut everyone out. I mumbled and cried. I slept. And cried some more. Willie and Lizzy Beth came and sat with me, unable to get me to interact, but they never left my side.

One day the cards came, from Precious, from the family members of those who remembered the five who died from the Phantom Killer and they shared their loss with me. And they offered prayers and comfort and encouragement.

Even the three who were still alive sent personal notes and condolences to me. They shared the lost dreams and the emptiness, the fear and the rising again, of how they endured those unspeakable months. They knew my sting of sorrow and they reached out to me with their kindness—thanking me, for stopping at least, this killer of 1976.

Willie told me Colleen reached out to the families and told them my story—and I'm grateful for the support. Something I've struggled with for years—letting others help me—it's never easy.

I rode in the wheelchair to the car, as Willie and Lizzy Beth prepared to drive me home from the hospital, and a crowd gathered outside—cheering me on, rallying around me. I caught the eye of a small boy with yellow hair, and his mama held him—and Harper waved at me with his tiny fingers.

**

Now, my front room rattled with noise since I arrived home yesterday. I'm holding my kitty, petting him nonstop. I'm wearing faded jeans and a tank top, sitting barefoot on one end of my sofa. And I'm biting my fingernails in between stroking Hank.

Willie's sipping coffee. Lizzy Beth's sighing and pacing, and dusting, but not dusting, mostly she's pacing. Archie's tapping his fingers on his crossed legs in the recliner. Using one of his own handkerchiefs to wipe his nose.

Pastor Toby's glancing at me, turning his head when I catch him. He's prayed for me nonstop, whispering verses to remind me of belonging to God—no matter what this life offers.

Lester's here, too. He's made small talk, tried to crack a joke—a failed attempt to break away my shell of sadness. I so misjudged him. I will seek his forgiveness more than once—I'm sure.

Ernie stopped by, apologized for all he's done to irritate me over the years, and told me how he loved my grandma's cooking, and even hugged my neck.

Officer Teacup sent me flowers, which wilted from the heat right after he left. He gave me a wink, reminding me of my husband who winked at me almost every day—when he wasn't mad at me.

Callie and Jon sat across from me this morning, and she shared how she'd lied about knowing Clara, to keep Harper's secret adoption safe. Jon worried he missed the clues of having a brother with mental illness, who was capable of taking lives to conceal his sins. He apologized for giving the envelope to Taddy who gave it to Junior—after Dennis asked him to pass it on. He said he wished he'd read it before doing something so stupid. They also didn't know what to make of the lockbox, as far as knowing if the contents held lies or truth. But when they saw the part about me, they knew I had to see the contents.

They regretted keeping the box in their care for as long as they did though, and Callie worried her son Harper might be in jeopardy, so she played a game with the entire situation. They're saddened and broken by the entire journey and Jon was at a loss of what to say—mostly. He looked at the floor during their stay, biting his fingernails and wiping his tears.

Taddy and Colleen showed up, but they stayed for only a few minutes, because Coleen couldn't stop crying. I didn't cry since my tears were swallowed up in the river.

Precious drove to town in a neighbor's car, hitting Officer Teacup's police car when she parked on the street—and we learned she never has gotten a driver's license. But she told me she deserved any ticket he gave her, that it was worth the drive to come pray with me. He didn't write her up. But he did take her home. And Lester said he'd pay to fix her friend's car. A kindness I'd not seen in him before.

Willie and Lizzy Beth know about the lockbox, and I have it tucked away in the trunk in my bedroom. I'm not sure if now's the time to talk about the contents—because I'm numb, it's all I can do to process the hellos and the goodbyes. I'm pretty sure of what to do with the box. It's something I must do alone.

The loved ones who lost someone to the Phantom Killer faced my sadness, too—a fog of toxins that poison us. The overwhelming sense of the worst summer in my life burned at my soul, even though I'm breathing, and the smoke of death made my house seem like a giant coffin. With sprouts of life lurking beneath the slats—somewhere.

Knock. Knock. Knock.

Pastor Toby ushered in Chuck who limped as he held onto crutches. Whose daddy stood by the fireplace waiting and watching. Toby motioned. "Go sit by her."

Chuck folded his hands in his lap, after placing the crutches to the side, and he wiggled in the middle of the sofa. I noticed the cast on his leg held a slew of signatures. He turned toward me. "I'm sorry I knocked you from the tracks, but the train was coming. I knew we'd get hit, and I couldn't leave you there. You stood your ground even with a gun pointed at you." He brushed his bangs aside. "I didn't know about your friend River dying until yesterday. Pa said she saved you from drowning in the river." He rattled with a nervous twitch, like a boy who planned his words before he arrived.

I spoke for the first time in hours. "But she can swim, that's how she got away from some men who tried to hurt her on the rail. I don't understand how someone who can swim would drown. I can't swim and I'm here."

"My pa told me understanding life doesn't come in packages found in the store. Or in a script from a movie. That it comes in seasons of change, where things grow and die, but some survive." He glanced over at his daddy.

I nodded. "Yes, we are *all* here for a purpose. You have the sound of surviving in you. Please don't let the bullet holes in my story steal your hope." I touched Chuck's leg. "So, who wrote on your cast?"

"All the actors from the movie and the extras from Texarkana. I'm never gonna throw this cast away."

"That's great. You should save it. You're going to change lives. You're here for a purpose, too. You have that gift. You sparkle with hope." I smiled. "And your pa's a smart man. Watch his ways. Walk in them."

"I know he is. I'm gonna make him proud." Chuck paused. "Ms. Annie Grace, would you mind taking over for Ms. Clara in Sunday School? We don't have a teacher now that she's gone." He glanced at Pastor Toby.

I almost sneered but held it inside. "So, did he put you up to this?"

"Yes, but it's a good idea. You do like oranges, don't you?"

"I do like oranges, but you'll have to watch out, I tend to spit the seeds out. You don't want to get in the way."

"You spit? Only boys are supposed to spit."

"Well, I do tend to bend rules now and again."

**

The house went quiet right after ten, but sleep for me won't come. I'm doing what any good investigator does, I'm letting the police do their work. I'm retiring. At least for now. I'll write my books and photograph life and see how that goes.

I marched in the darkness toward the police station, carrying the lockbox with all the clues. The full moon held no power over me anymore because I'm a survivor. I'm tired of living as if I'm dead. I'm leaving the box at the station for the authorities to sift through, so they can let Ernie write a story about how this case finally gets solved. They can gather their clues. And close the case.

I don't need to solve this case myself. I don't need to have a say. I don't need to do one more thing that has anything to do with my past. My past has held me back for too long.

I paused, glancing at the box, whispering to the stars because I'm stumped about the clue involving my daddy. The note about Sidecar Ace is no longer in the box, and I'm struggling with sharing that one piece of information with the police. I'm also struggling with whether he's alive or dead—or hiding in some alley in some town—ready to hurt someone.

I trooped ahead, bowing down to pray as I placed the box at the door of the police station. I'm ready to seek and to serve God in a fresh way—one that would make God proud. I placed the key on top of the box, kicking the metal for taking up so many of my nights.

I circled block after block, thinking on this horrible summer, and I came to the tree of my youth, to the tree I climbed, to the tree where I hid my poems. I shimmied up to the highest branch for one last visit. For tomorrow, I'll ask Lester to cut it down.

I'll talk to the people at church and ask Pastor Toby if we might raise some money to put up a memorial on my grandma's property with the names of those who died and of those who were attacked in 1946.

I imagined a bronze statue, six feet high, of a bronze boy who favored Chuck, with wispy hair, and he would reach for heaven with outstretched hands. He would hold a string of eight stars between his hands, one for Martha, Jack, Reed, Patti, Peyton, BayJo, Victor, and Kacey.

And there would be a triangle of small stars placed over the heart of the boy's chest to remember Clara, Gilbert, and Crush. Oh wait, one more star for River—and it should dance like the sun, on the end of those eight stars. Goodness, I never want to forget the real boy who saved my life in 1976!

Ruff! Ruff! Ruff!

I jumped from limb to limb, to meet River's dog at the base of the tree. "Hey Flashlight! Where have you been?"

She nudged my leg, like a pup in need of a home. I ruffled her ears with both hands. "Yes, you can move in with me.

Now, remember I have a cat. You can't be chasing Hank. Understand?"

Flashlight's eyes glistened with innocence, and somehow, I knew we'd have that talk again—whenever she forgot and chased my kitty.

Crossing my hands over my belly, a small flutter inside my tummy caused me to smile and joy burst like shooting stars from deep within me. The surge of strength returned to my life, something given to me by having a strong husband—even if, for a mere ten years. For you see, I held a new secret, one confirmed by the doctor at my follow up visit right before I left the hospital. I'd asked for a test to see—if my instincts were right.

I whispered to Crush as if he stood next to me. "Honey, I'm pregnant. Can you believe it? We'll finally use the nursery. And our baby will know everything about you! You'll be the best daddy ever! I'll make sure our baby knows this!"

A tear rolled down my cheek. "Oh, and if we have a girl, I'm naming her Clara. If we have a boy, his name will be Taggart Raike Jr. But I'll call him Little Crush. I'm sorry honey, I still don't like your name. What was your mama thinking?"

I took the longest walk to my house—ready for the life ahead—with the hope in knowing God called me to this journey. To win with Him. To rise above. To trust His hand. To find my satisfaction in Him.

I've searched for love in the night and in the day, and often walked alone. But God found me in the boxcar and rode with me. He found me in the trees I climbed, and He sat with me. When I dashed down alleys which stretched for blocks, He went, too. And He wiped my tears as He held my heart.

God has gone with me through my darkest nights. Now, I plan to walk into the light—with Flashlight my dog and with Hank my cat! And with the children I'll teach in Sunday school!

I can't wait to have Precious over for iced tea. And Colleen. And who knows—maybe I'll invite those stuffy ladies from the second pew to supper one night.

Someday I'll tell my baby of the roads I've traveled—or better yet—I'll write my story for my child to read.

This way, my little one can ride the boxcar of life from Texarkana to Millerton, to Jefferson, to Old Washington, to Memphis and back! And I'll teach my little boy or girl to climb trees too! To snap photographs! To read the Bible. To play! To live as if today is a gift! And I'll teach my child to wink just like Crush! Hey, maybe I should name my baby, Winky!

**

Glancing upward, I stretched my neck with a longing to sit on the highest branch—one last time. So I made the final climb, straddling the branch, and savored the moment. "I love it up here. This is like flying away to a land where dreams begin. Where hope dances into my life. Maybe, I'll keep the tree, so it can shade the statue. Grandma Elsie would like that—knowing a piece of her history lives on."

A padding sound stopped me from dreaming, and a man wearing a Fedora and holding a box slithered up next to the tree. I sucked in a mosquito, whispering to the night as I choked. "It can't be—"

Frozen, I peered down and into the eyes—those now gazing up at me. I shouted, "You are a ghost to me. You can't be alive!"

"I'm very much alive. I came for the lockbox. It holds the clues to solving the cold case. And some of them point to me."

I yelled, "You drowned in the Mississippi River. We had a funeral for you. And you have a marker at Rose Hill Cemetery and at Elwood Cemetery in Memphis. You're supposed to be dead! Anyone who gets buried twice, should never come back to life!"

"I came to town when I received the call. The one which told me a lockbox might make its way to you."

"Did you follow me to the police station?" My thoughts raced like a boxcar running off the tracks. I scoffed, "So you are the Phantom Killer?"

"You've decided my fate, so it must be true. I just had to see my daughter—all grown up!"

Shaking my fist above his head, clutching the branch with my other hand, I screamed, "I'm not your daughter!"

"You'll always have my blood—we are kin."

"I may have your name, but I'm not your daughter—not anymore."

Daddy embraced the lockbox. "I'm leaving with this. No one will know who I am—or what I've done."

"I know. And God knows. And you know."

He spun around, his wrinkles like crevices of sadness, and he sighed as if his breath might end. "I don't know if it's better to live with the lost memory of who you wished I'd been. Or die as a murderer."

Sliding down from the tree, I locked eyes with my past. With the eyes of an old man—whose breath wreaked of sin—whose choices destroyed his life and that of innocent people. "Daddy, how could you? How could you?"

He didn't answer and pulled the box closer—marching away—like a snake summoned away to the shadows. Like his destiny of doom awaited him. It's as if his calloused heart was ruined and stained and tainted—like he had scales over his eyes and soul.

I charged him. "Wait? Who called you? You said someone called you."

"No one you know."

"Who would call you? What's going on?"

"If you keep investigating, you'll discover this coverup runs deeper than the clues inside this lockbox. They go deep into the heart of those who protected Doodie—and me."

"Are you serious? Do you think I'm going to believe a word you're telling me? You've never told the truth about anything. Even when you took me from my grandma, you made it sound like a vacation riding in boxcars. But you kidnapped me. You were planning on making some money by selling me. Who sells their own daughter? Who does such a horrible thing?"

"I never sold you. I changed my mind." Daddy's hand went to his hat, and he shifted it sideways. "Don't follow me. I had to see your face. You're beautiful just like your mama."

"Stop it. Don't play with me. I'm not the little girl who once trusted you. You can't con me—anymore."

Daddy wiped his nose. "And you've got your Grandma Elsie's strength. And her excellence!"

I shouted, rising taller, finding a strength I couldn't explain. A strength I knew that could only come from God. "I'm getting the police. They'll stop you! It's time for justice!"

A car approached, its lights blinding me, and my daddy rushed to the passenger side as the vehicle slowed, hopping inside. Daddy didn't look my way—but the driver tossed me a glare—his eyes like charcoal, his gaze indifferent.

The vehicle slowed and spun in a circle at the alley, coming faster, picking up speed, headed my way. I dove behind my tree as the driver pointed a gun at me. But my daddy knocked the man's hand down—as if to protect me.

I whimpered at the *lost love* I had missed because my daddy got lost in crime and murder—in listening like Adam and Eve did to that nasty serpent who whispers lies leading to death and destruction.

Kneeling, I watched as the two argued in the idling car and I tiptoed to the driver's side door. I recognized the man clutching the steering wheel—who wore a badge—who was dressed in a police uniform. It was the officer who couldn't stay awake on my porch!

I sank with a sadness—and sirens and flashing lights replaced my screams. "What? Police cars?"

Wee-woo. Wee-woo. Wee-woo.

The officers circled, coming from all four directions, and they surrounded my daddy and the sleepy officer. I slumped behind the bumper of daddy's get-away car, and Officer Teacup motioned for me to come to his side. I shuffled to him, whispering, "How did you know to come?"

"We received a phone call from Taddy."

I cleared my throat. "He called you?"

Across the street, Taddy peeked from behind the curtain of his apartment window—smiling, as he wiped a tear from his face. I waved to him—and he waved back.

Sighing, I grew tired—as if I might sleep without having a nightmare tonight. Whispering to my tree—to Crush—and to God, I declared, "I've become an investigator and a messenger of hope! And the eyes from my past are in handcuffs!"

Finally, brothers, whatever is true, whatever is
honorable, whatever is just, whatever is pure,
whatever is lovely, whatever is commendable,
if there is any excellence, if there is anything
worthy of praise, think about these things.
What you have learned and received and
heard and seen in me—practice these things,
and the God of peace will be with you.
Philippians 4:8-9 ESV

The Lord is near to the brokenhearted and
saves the crushed in spirit.
Psalm 34:18 ESV

Unshackled Courage

Annie Grace Kree Chronicles Series

1 Untied Shoelace
2 Unknown Soul
3 Rescue of Undaunted Spirit
4 Unwanted Sidekick
5 Unwavering Hope
6 Unshackled Courage

Other Books by Pam Kumpe

See You in the Funny Papers
A Scoop of Inspiration
In the Lick of Time
A Goat with a Tote

Rehab Ministry
Things I Learned in Jail
Things I Learned (Again) in Jail / Christmas 2018

Homeless Ministry
My View from the Bridge
My View from the Street
My View from the Heart / Summer 2019

www.pamkumpe.com